Barefoot at Moonrise

Barefoot Bay Timeless #2

Barefoot Bay Timeless

Barefoot At Moonrise

This novel is a work of fiction. Any references to historical events, real people, or real locales are used fictitiously. Other names, characters, places, and incidents are the product of the author's imagination, and any resemblance to actual events or locales or persons, living or dead, is coincidental.

COVER ART: The Killion Group, Inc. (designer) and
James Franklin (photographer)
INTERIOR FORMATTING: Author E.M.S.
Seashell graphic used with permission under Creative Commons CC0 public domain.

ISBN: 978-0-9970627-3-1

Published in the United States of America.

Critical Reviews of Roxanne St. Claire Novels

"St. Claire, as always, brings a scorching tear-up-the-sheets romance combined with a great story: dealing with real issues starring memorable characters in vivid scenes."

— *Romantic Times Magazine*

"Non-stop action, sweet and sexy romance, lively characters, and a celebration of family and forgiveness."

— *Publishers Weekly*

"Plenty of heat, humor, and heart!"

— *USA Today's Happy Ever After blog*

"It's safe to say I will try any novel with St. Claire's name on it."

— *www.smartbitchestrashybooks.com*

"The writing was perfectly on point as always and the pace of the story was flawless. But be forewarned that you will laugh, cry, and sigh with happiness. I sure did."

— *www.harlequinjunkies.com*

"The Barefoot Bay series is an all-around knockout, soul-satisfying read. Roxanne St. Claire writes with warmth and heart and the community she's built at Barefoot Bay is one I want to visit again and again."

— *Mariah Stewart, New York Times bestselling author*

"This book stayed with me long after I put it down."

— *All About Romance*

Dear Reader,

Welcome back to Barefoot Bay Timeless…celebrating the appeal of a 40-something hero and second chances at love! Like every book set in Barefoot Bay, this novel stands entirely alone, but why stop at one? Barefoot Bay is a whole world of romance, friends and family, and unforgettable stories, divided into bite-size trilogies so you can dive in to the water anytime!

The Barefoot Bay Billionaires
Secrets on the Sand
Scandal on the Sand
Seduction on the Sand

The Barefoot Bay Brides
Barefoot in White
Barefoot in Lace
Barefoot in Pearls

Barefoot Bay Undercover
Barefoot Bound (prequel)
Barefoot With a Bodyguard
Barefoot With a Stranger
Barefoot With a Bad Boy

Barefoot Bay Timeless
Barefoot at Sunset
Barefoot at Moonrise
Barefoot at Midnight

Want to know the day the next Barefoot Bay book is released? Sign up for the newsletter! You'll get brief monthly e-mails about new releases and book sales.

http://www.roxannestclaire.com/newsletter.html

Acknowledgments

I absolutely could not have written this book without the assistance, handholding, and patience of a dear friend and fellow writer, Silver James, retired member of the fire service and law enforcement, who helped vet every reference to the hero's career as a firefighter. Additional research and information came from retired firefighter Kristi Kobrin, who wandered into my yoga practice and kindly answered question after question and even took my phone calls. People who help writers do research are wonderful.

And shout out to the team! Kristi Yanta, the Picky Editor, went above and beyond with this one and I am convinced I cannot write a book without her. Much love to my copy editor Joyce Lamb, proofreader Marlene Engel, super-talented (patient and determined) cover artist Kim Killion, and hugs to James Franklin, a talented photographer who would not quit until we got the right silver fox on the cover. Also gratitude to formatter and all around miracle-worker, Amy Atwell. Behind the scenes, Maria Connor is an author assistant without equal and my Rocki Roadies (Roxanne St. Claire Street Team) bring it for every title. (Want to join the street team? We're on Facebook and have tons of fun.)

Barefoot AT MOONRISE

Dedication

Every Friday morning for the last few years, I've posted a silver fox (the two legged kind) on my Facebook page, and the response from readers made it clear to me that a "mature man" can definitely be hero material. This book is dedicated to the many friends and fans who inspired me to write a series that proves sexy comes in silver and romance can be just as dreamy the second time around.

Chapter One

Ken Cavanaugh charged into burning buildings on a routine basis. He faced life-threatening emergencies, unforeseen crises, and potential disasters almost every day with titanium nerves and steady hands. He led a crew of fearless, tough, muscle-bound mavericks who turned to him for wisdom, guidance, life-or-death decisions, and changes in their shift schedule. And, icing on his résumé cake, Captain Cav was the fan favorite to lead the fire station tours because women and children loved him.

So why the *hell* did his feet feel like he was wearing iron boots? Why did his pulse thump as though he was seconds from stroking out? All he had to do was walk across a banquet hall in the middle of a high school reunion and talk to a woman, but he couldn't bring himself to do it.

Because Bethany Endicott had frozen him out this week no matter how hard he'd tried to thaw her. Of course, he might have had that coming, considering their past.

But twenty-five years had passed since he'd been a grieving, angry eighteen-year-old who wanted to hurt anyone named Endicott…including his girlfriend.

All he really wanted to do was put that dark day—all those dark days, in fact—in the past and clear the air.

He *had* to talk to her before this week went up in smoke and he could do nothing but watch his chance burn to the ground.

For the past week, during the interminable "planning" of this reunion, they had yet to have a substantive conversation. There was plenty of eye contact, all kinds of accidental brushes, and a low-grade simmer that stretched his nerves—and libido—to the limits. He'd caught her gazing at him on more than one occasion, but any time he'd initiated a conversation, she managed to be suddenly pulled away or busy.

Who could blame her? He could rationalize what happened between them all those years ago for the rest of his life, but the fact was he'd said hurtful things, and now he just wanted to apologize.

Wasn't that what high school reunions were for?

Time was running out, though, leaving tonight, the night of the all-class Mimosa High reunion at Barefoot Bay's swanky resort, for Ken to make his move. After this, they'd go back to their regular lives, and another twenty-five years might pass before they saw each other again.

This was his last chance.

"Come on, Cav. Tap that powder keg."

Ken didn't even turn to give Lawson Monroe a dirty look when the man sidled up next to him. Law was a few years older, and they hadn't known each other in high school—though Ken knew of Law's reputation for trouble—but this week the two men had had no choice but to hang out together at the various reunion-planning sessions. In the process, Ken grew to appreciate Law's irreverent sense of humor and signature sarcasm.

He'd let Law and Mark Solomon, who'd rounded out the trio of Y chromosomes on the planning committee, think his interest in Beth Endicott was physical—which wasn't a lie. She still got him fired up with one look. But there was more to his need to get Beth alone. Much more.

"Seriously, Captain Cav, what are you waiting for?" Law needled. "A kick in the ass? A glass of courage? I'm so pleased to provide both." Law offered a glass of beer. "For you, since I don't drink."

Ken took the beer and sipped, letting the man think all Ken wanted to do was hit on a pretty woman. He couldn't tell Law the truth. He could never tell anyone the truth, but that was something he'd accepted years ago.

Looking around, he considered his next opportunity to get Beth alone. There would be desserts and after-dinner drinks back on the beach following this. Could he talk to her there?

"When is this dance contest thing over?" Ken asked, checking out the last couple participating in the Dance of the Decades on a stage at the far end of the banquet room. This pair was decked out in a poodle skirt and rolled-up jeans, celebrating the decade when they graduated from Mimosa High.

"It's over when the thousand-year-old couple keels over," Law said.

Ken smiled, taking in the married seventy-seven-year-olds surrounded by several generations of their family cheering them on. "They met at Mimosa High, class of 1956," he mused. "Married forever."

Law grunted like the very thought pained him. "Damn, that's a long time to ride the same love boat every night."

"How does a guy get so lucky?" Ken asked, his genuine question getting a cynical look from Law. Across the hall, the crowd broke enough for Ken to get a glimpse of the short, flared white skirt that showed off Beth's heart-stopping legs and killer red and white high heels. She loved her high heels and short skirts and wore them just as well now as she had in 1991.

She was watching the show, checking her phone, and occasionally glancing at the exit to the deck behind her.

He had to *move*.

"Are you nuts? Boredom sets in fast," Law said. "I need variety."

"Variety gets boring, too," Ken replied. "I'd rather have something steady."

"Shoot me now," Law moaned. "Two-point-five and a minivan in the driveway is my idea of hell on earth. Anyway, I hate to burst your bubble, but I heard your Beth is the poster girl for I Am Woman, Hear Me Roar."

His Beth. If only. Ken's gaze drifted across the room, catching her checking her cell phone for the sixtieth time that hour. Who the hell was she waiting to hear from?

"Weren't you a freaking Navy first responder before you became a firefighter?" Law demanded. "Failure isn't an option for you life-saving types."

No, failure wasn't an option. Not in his line of work, not in his life. But where Beth was involved? Fail all around, even tonight.

"Pretend the place is on fire and you have to evacuate her to the nearest…bedroom." Law took the beer back. "Don't make me show you how it's done, son."

Ken checked out the couple on the stage, twirling—slowly—for their big ending. Everything in his gut told him Beth would never stay for dessert on the beach. She'd been half checked out all week long, barely showing up for any of the committee crap he'd agreed to do when he saw her name on the list.

Maybe it wasn't a man who had her glued to the phone.

Maybe it was work. Maybe it was...*him*. Ray Endicott. He knew only that she was in some kind of housing and real estate business, so it was more than likely she worked for her father.

An old, familiar metallic taste filled his mouth when he thought of the coldhearted bastard responsible for shattering Ken's world. No conversation with Beth would ever change the truth of that, but *she* wasn't responsible, and he wanted her to know he didn't blame her.

"All right," he said. "I'm going in."

"Get 'er done, Captain."

Ken gave a quick nod and made his way across the room. Being six-two made it easy to see over most heads, but the crowd was thick with huggers and dancers and drinkers. To avoid them, and the possibility that someone would stop him to talk, he swerved toward the perimeter of the room. Staying locked on that golden hair spilling over bare shoulders and a sleek red halter top, he was steady and sure now.

Beth's gaze drifted over the crowd and settled on the spot where Ken had been standing with Law. Blue eyes narrowed, and a slight frown creased her forehead. She angled her head a bit, and her shoulders dropped as if she'd sighed.

As if...she was disappointed that he'd left.

Buoyed by that, he powered forward, slipping between two people with a quick, "'Scuze me."

"Oh no, you don't!" A woman's fingers snagged his elbow and squeezed, jerking him to a stop. "Ken Cavanaugh, if you don't remember me, my heart's going to break into a thousand pieces."

He turned quickly toward a petite woman with frosted-blond curls and glasses, with zero recognition of her face. "I...uh...sorry...I'm—"

"Chrissie Bartlett!" she exclaimed, her voice rising along with her wine glass. "Spanish 1? Freshman year? Señora Norton's class?"

Oh yeah. He remembered the name. Remembered that she hadn't given him the time of day in Spanish class back then. "Hi, Chrissie."

She came a little closer. "You've changed, Kenny."

Kenny. The only person who'd ever gotten away with calling him that was…inching closer to the exit. "It's been a long time," he said, trying to move away. "We've all changed."

"Well, you've improved with age," she added.

Another woman joined them, a three- or four-drink gleam in her eyes. "I don't think we ever talked in high school," she said. "I'm Marta Burns."

Marta Burns? No, they'd never talked, because Ken worked construction jobs after school to help support a struggling family while these two were busy with clubs and crap to pad their college applications.

"I hear you're a firefighter. And the captain, no less." Chrissie added a squeeze to his bicep, blocking Marta from getting any closer. "Impressive."

"Yeah." He glanced back to Beth, catching her making a quick scan of the room as she moved toward the door. Was she looking for him?

"Excuse me, Chrissie, but I—"

"Hey, ladies, why'd you slip away?" Another man approached, much shorter than Ken and with way less hair. He threw a look at Ken, who gladly stepped away to let him flirt with the women. The whole thing took two seconds, long enough for him to lose sight of Beth.

Damn it. He made a few comments, shook a hand, threw out one more excuse, and finally got away, muscling through the rest of the crowd to reach the side exit that led out to a large wooden deck.

But it was empty, with no sign of Beth.

Swallowing a dark curse, he took a few steps toward the railing, and then spotted a pair of red and white high heels tucked by the stairs that led to the sand.

He couldn't help smiling, because, hell, this was better than Cinderella.

All he had to do was follow the footprints in the sand.

Timeless.

Beth gave a wry smile as she thought of the reunion theme that had permeated the entire Mimosa High all-class reunion. Plastered on posters, written on ribbons, and etched into the champagne glasses they got to take home...one word. *Timeless.*

What did that even mean? That the years that had passed didn't matter? That the clock stood still when two people made heart-hammering eye contact? Or that time...had run out.

Because it had, at least where Ken Cavanaugh was concerned.

When he'd walked into the first reunion-planning meeting a week ago, she actually gasped audibly. She had no idea he was on the planning committee, too. Why would he have volunteered for that? Could it have been he saw her name on the committee list? That seemed unlikely, but she couldn't help entertaining the possibility.

She'd tried to forget their ugly breakup when he was a senior and she was a sophomore and treat him like another one of the very few men—three, to be exact—on the reunion-planning committee. Okay, a man who'd aged well. Ridiculously well. Like, whoa, he was hotter now than he was in high school, and he'd been damn nice-looking as a boy.

Until he dumped her on a miserable, rainy afternoon and said hateful, hurtful things about her family. Well, her father. Of course, as an adult, it was easy to understand why. His father had died in his arms, for God's sake, on a job site owned and operated by Endicott Development Corporation. Her last name would be a constant reminder of how much he hated Ray Endicott.

She might have even talked to Ken this week, since he acted warm and friendly, almost as if nothing had happened. But during the course of the first meeting, she could feel her whole being respond to Ken the way she had as a fifteen-year-old girl—with a fiery, undeniable attraction. Then she heard the rumors of what kind of guy he was and what he was looking for in life, and she knew she should keep her distance and protect her heart from falling for a guy who wanted...something she could never give him.

So she purposely had missed a lot of meetings and acted distracted and distant when she had to be around him. That left tonight, the big reunion event at Casa Blanca Resort & Spa, which was far enough along that she could call it a night. When the old couple twirled for the last time, she slipped out, ready to end this week and get back to her normal, if lonely, routine.

Inhaling the salted air, Beth let cool sand sift through her toes as she wandered closer to the water. The sky over Barefoot Bay had turned a magical deep purple around a dramatic full moon rising over the horizon, its silvery path glinting on the water. To her left, a row of yellow tented cabanas lined the beach. These were usually lit by tiny white lights and used for romantic cocktails and private parties of two, but all the guests at the resort were in the ballroom judging the Dance of the Decades contest.

So the secluded shelters were dark and empty.

Beth stepped to the open drapes of the cabana farthest from the resort, squinting inside to spy a chaise lounge the size of a queen-size bed, with half a dozen pillows. She felt a little like Goldilocks, but couldn't resist the inviting resting place, which offered comfort, solitude, and a view of that breathtaking moon overhead casting a silver spell on the waves of Barefoot Bay.

As she exhaled, she tried to rid herself of everything stressful or unsettling, distracting or unbalancing.

Like…Ken Cavanaugh.

Oh, he'd been the talk of plenty of women who'd come early to help plan the reunion. How could he not be? Single, sexy, and silver enough to look like he lived life to the fullest.

She closed her eyes and drifted back years and years.

I could love you, Beth. I could love you forever. But I can never be in the same room as your father and not want to kill him. He's the devil, don't you see? So, this is it.

She'd never forgotten his last words. *This is it.*

This is it? She remembered how much she wanted to scream the question back in his face, but she'd been drenched by a downpour and crushed by his fury. Instead, she'd stared at him, watched him walk away through the rain, while she was left…shattered.

And here they were, twenty-five years later.

Leaning back on the pillows, she crossed her legs, locking her hands behind her head to think about him. His boyishly cute features had morphed into handsome lines, strong bones, and shoulders that never—

"Knock, knock."

She sucked in soft breath and popped up, blinking at the sight of…those very shoulders.

"Ken?" His name came out a little breathless.

"Am I interrupting your escape from a reunion from hell?"

Her heart rate tripled. "Not at all," she said. "I just needed some air."

"Want some company?"

And then it felt like her heart actually stopped for a moment, along with time. Pressing her hand to her chest, she considered all the possible, polite ways to say no.

"Yes." It was all that would come out.

He took a step inside, nearly as tall as the heavy yellow drape that hung over them and all around. Forget the air. The minute he was in the cabana, it all seemed to be gone. Space was tight. And suddenly the tropical air smelled spicy and masculine.

She inched up, but he held out his hand. "Stay there. You look comfortable."

Very slowly, she eased back on the cushions, aware of every cell tingling.

He sat on the edge of the chaise at the bottom, not far from her feet. "I've been wanting a chance to talk to you all week."

She managed a steady breath. "Yeah?"

"So I followed you."

"That's…a little stalkery," she said on a surprisingly nervous laugh.

"Not really." He lightly tapped her toes, the split second of contact searing her skin as effectively as his admission. "I was hoping that you left your shoes and a trail in the sand on purpose."

She hadn't…or maybe she had. Maybe that was her subconscious calling card and invitation to him. Deep in her heart, she wanted this moment more than anything, even though she knew she shouldn't.

"So you tracked me like the Eagle Scout you once were," she said.

He laughed, sounding pleased she remembered. "And now I'm a firefighter, which some might say is the grown-up version of an Eagle Scout."

"You *are* grown up," she said on a soft sigh.

He ruffled his hair. "The white stuff started showing up in my late thirties. I blame the stressful job," he said. "I should probably do something about it."

"Something like change the color? Are you out of your mind? It's…" *Gorgeous. Sexy. Hot as hell.* "Nice," she managed.

He jutted his chin in acknowledgment of the compliment, letting his gaze drift over her like he couldn't control where his eyes wanted to go. "You grew up pretty good, too, Beth."

The way he said it, with a little longing and lust, sent a blast of heat through her. "Oh, I…have hit the big 4-0." She tried to keep it light, but nothing she was feeling was…light. Her limbs were suddenly heavy, and each breath was a battle. Ken had done that to her as a teenager every time he leaned in for a kiss. She could only imagine what he could do to a forty-year-old woman who hadn't had a date in years.

She'd always wanted Ken in the most primal way. At fifteen, it made her uncomfortable and scared and curious…and she'd said no every time their make-out sessions got too heated. But now…kissing him would still make her uncomfortable, but in the best possible way.

He placed his hand on the other side of her crossed ankles and leaned over her. The position was casual, comfortable, and made her whole lower half clutch from the mere proximity of him. "You sure have been tough to nail down this week."

"I've been a little distracted, sorry. I tried to give that planning committee my all, but I had some work stuff I was dealing with." It wasn't a lie, but she certainly hadn't been *swamped* this past week. She realized early on that it would be best if she avoided Ken.

He inched closer and let the hint of a smile pull at his lips. "Is that your excuse for missing the all-important arranging of the floral centerpieces that you so kindly signed us up for?"

She'd signed them up in a moment of weakness and hope, before she'd heard rumors about what he wanted in his life. "I had something…unexpected come up."

"Ah, I see. The house-flipping business?" he prodded.

So he'd been asking about her, too. Or maybe he looked her up before the reunion even started. Or looked up her father, a possibility that made her stomach drop with bad memories.

"Yes," she said vaguely. "That's my business."

"Like those people on HGTV?" he asked.

"Only it takes more than a half hour to renovate a house."

He nodded, both of them falling silent for a second, giving the other one a chance to talk. Finally, he said, "Do you work for, uh, your dad's company?"

Yep. Her father. Ken still hated him and blamed him, of course.

"I don't work for my dad," she said. "I own my own company and run my own business."

She could have sworn his shoulders relaxed a little. They needed to avoid that topic. "So, how's your life, Ken?" she asked. "Are you…married?" She knew he was divorced, but didn't want to make it that obvious she'd talked about him with other people that week.

"Single," he said. "Though I was married for a while. It didn't work out." He put a casual hand on her ankle, then lifted it as if he realized he shouldn't have. "I heard you're divorced, too."

But he didn't seem to mind her knowing that he'd been asking about her. "Yeah, I am. No kids, though."

"No kids for me, either." There was just enough sadness in his voice to tell her that the rumors she'd overheard about Ken wanting a family were probably true. Still, she had to be sure.

"Sounds like you wanted them."

"I do," he said. Present tense, she noted with another painful swallow. "I'd love to have kids," he added, unwittingly hammering the nail into her heart a little harder. "What about you?"

She'd have loved to have kids, too. But that ship had sailed…and sunk. "No, none for me."

He angled over her a little bit. "Really?" he said. "I would have thought you…well. I guess I imagined you'd want to have kids."

She had. Desperately. "Well, I don't, and I'm forty years old."

"So? You could adopt." Damn it, he sounded hopeful. She shifted, then started to push up.

"Don't leave," he said, holding out his hand to stop her. "I've wanted to talk to you all week. It's the whole reason I volunteered for that stupid planning committee."

It was? "Why?"

"I wanted…" He placed his hand on her bare foot. "I have…something important to say to you." He caressed her skin, as if talking involved…touching.

She tried to swallow, but failed. During those few seconds, neither spoke. In only moonlight, she could see his dark eyes and thick lashes, and an unreadable emotion.

She braced herself for the worst. The accusations. The lawsuit that never happened. The blame. The family hate. "Okay," she whispered, ready for whatever may come.

"Okay," he repeated, as if getting his thoughts—and nerve—together. "I know it's twenty-five years late, but, man, I…acted like a complete jerk. I said stuff I shouldn't have. I blamed you for things that weren't your fault. And I…I threw away a damn great girlfriend." His voice cracked a little, and he looked as if he might want to avert his eyes, but refused to. "I want to apologize, Beth. I want to say that…I'm sorry. I'm really sorry."

She let out a long, slow breath she hadn't realized she'd been holding for…well, for two and a half decades.

Her heart folded as she reached over and touched the empty space beside her. "Lie down next to me, Kenny. I'd love to put that dark past behind us."

Chapter Two

It was easy to accept the invitation, sliding up the oversized chaise to get next to her. "Only you," Ken said softly as he dropped his head on one of many pillows, facing her.

"Only me what?"

"Can call me Kenny." He gave in to a smile. "And make me like it."

"It suits you, even with your salt-and-pepper hair and a few laugh lines around your eyes." She reached out and touched his cheek with a featherlight fingertip that nearly shocked him. "At least, I hope those lines are from laughter."

"Mostly. And some stress in life and on the job," he admitted, putting his hand over hers. "I have to tell you, Beth, you've gotten even more beautiful, which is unbelievable, because back then, I thought…" He didn't even know how to put into words how he'd felt. "Well, I thought you hung that thing right there in the sky."

"Aww." She smiled. "That's sweet. Thanks."

He inhaled and let it out with a noisy sigh, letting their clasped hands settle between them. "Thanks for letting me apologize now," he said. "How I acted that day has bothered me for all these years."

She didn't say anything right away, her eyes searching his face in a way that made him wonder if she was gauging whether or not he was telling the truth, or merely studying his face. "You were young, in a lot of pain, and I took the brunt of your grief."

His chest squeezed. "Don't let me off that easy."

"Time heals wounds, Ken," she said. "And something tells me the sting of our breakup didn't last as long as the deep pain from losing your father."

He swallowed, agreeing, of course, with that. "The fact remains that you deserved more than that. I know we were just kids—"

"*I* was a kid," she corrected. "I was fifteen and you were eighteen, a senior about to graduate and go into the Navy, and I was a sophomore who really should have been a freshman."

"Not your fault you were a kindergarten overachiever and they pushed you ahead." Somehow, he'd gotten closer, inches away now, their fingers still threaded, their bodies turned to each other like a force of nature had more control than they did.

"Thanks, Beth."

She gave him a questioning look. "For accepting your apology?" she guessed.

He nodded. "And for being so gracious about it."

She gave his hand a squeeze. "Let's close that chapter in our lives."

He swallowed against a thick throat. "You know what I think about?" he asked. "How much died that day. Not only a father of three, a loving husband, and one of the greatest men who ever lived. My family fractured. My world shifted. And *we* died. You and me."

She didn't answer, holding his gaze.

"I know we were from different social universes and just high school kids who were dating, but, Beth…I think we had a shot," he said.

Before his dad died, he liked to think that it didn't matter that his family was poor and lived in Twin Palms, the poorest part of Mimosa Key. It didn't matter that his dad worked for her dad and that the Endicotts were crazy rich, while his mother was a housekeeper at a motel and took in sewing for extra money. They had a chance.

"And if I'd had a molecule of maturity back then," he continued, "I wouldn't have taken all my anger and hatred and blame out on you, on us."

"I don't want to relive that afternoon," she said, letting go of his hand to put her fingers on his cheek. "It happened. It was ugly."

"Ugly? I called you Satan's daughter."

"Shhh." She stroked his jaw lightly. "Let's not talk about it anymore. We have so many better memories."

"We sure do." Even in the dark of the cabana, he could see her eyes were still as blue as the summer skies over Barefoot Bay, fringed by thick lashes and framed with perfectly arched brows. She had a narrow nose over sweet, bowed lips he'd kissed so many times all those years ago. "God, those were a good six months. I remember the first time I saw you."

"At a job site on a blazing-hot Saturday afternoon in August. I remember how much I wanted to go to the beach that day with my girlfriends, but my dad dragged me on a site run before he'd drop me off."

"Believe me, I didn't want to be working construction on my last summer weekend before senior year." But his family needed money. They always needed money. "I was nailing in a window when someone said, 'The boss is here.' I looked up, and there you were with a pink bikini top under a see-through T-shirt and cutoff shorts." He leaned closer. "And I slammed the shit out of my thumb."

She laughed. "I didn't know that. But I remember you. Sweaty and hot and staring at me until I thought I'd melt right into the poured concrete."

Neither one of them said anything for a moment, both lost in that magical memory.

"One look at you and I knew you were probably too young for me," he finally said.

"One look at you and I knew you were going to be my first boyfriend."

He gave her a smirk. "So I really didn't stand a chance, huh?"

She leaned in, letting her forehead touch his. "Nope."

"That must be why I ignored my dad, then." He shook his head, remembering the lecture he got on the way home. "He was like, 'Son, if you so much as talk to that Endicott girl, you'll be grounded for your whole senior year.'"

She closed her eyes, probably at the mention of his dad.

"It's okay," he said. "I love to talk about him, even to this day. He was a damn good father. I always hoped I'd have a chance to be half the dad he was."

"Oh, Kenny, I'm sorry."

"No, no." He pulled her closer. "Tonight's about me apologizing, not you. And let's leave the families out of it. That's what we did for six long months."

"Not long enough," she said on a sigh. "Well. Long enough to get to second base," she teased.

He laughed softly, knowing exactly what she was referring to. "*That* was a good night."

Her eyes twinkled with the shared secret of a make-out

session out by the goat farm on the east side of Barefoot Bay.

She leaned into him. "You know, that was my first orgasm."

He sucked in a little breath on a laugh. "It was?"

"And it's still one for the books."

"You remember it?" He couldn't believe that.

"I remember...the essence of it," she said, her voice sultry enough to send a solid blast of blood from his brain to parts south. "I remember that sort of heady feeling of danger and excitement and...need."

His mouth went dry. "We were...needy."

At eighteen, he'd been in a perpetual state of hard and desperate, and talking about it now, while inhaling the floral scent that clung to Beth's hair, was enough to make him that way again. He trailed his finger down her bare arm, getting a jolt of satisfaction that he could still give her goose bumps.

"You know, it's a damn shame we never got to have sex," he said.

"Sure was," she said. "I would have loved for you to have been my first, but I was way too young."

"See what I mean, though? If we'd stayed together, we could have waited until I came back after the Navy and..." He dragged that finger back up her arm, settling on the sweet skin of her throat. "We could have lost our virginity together."

"If only we could turn back time."

If only. "We could pretend."

"How?" she barely whispered the word.

"Like this." He lowered his face and placed his mouth on hers. Instantly, years disappeared. Bad memories faded and old feelings rose to the surface. It was old times, back in Barefoot Bay, kissing under a sweet, silent moon.

Ken honestly couldn't remember a kiss that felt better.

There was so much left to say, so many years to cover, but Beth let go and returned the kiss. As soon as he ducked into the cabana, she knew she wouldn't be satisfied until she tasted him, flicked her tongue against his, and whimpered in her throat when he deepened the contact between their mouths.

They'd talk later.

She didn't realize how much she'd been aching for him, but her body responded instantly, and so did his, growing harder each second as his hands—large and oddly still familiar—started roaming her body, making her burn to do the same to him.

She tunneled her fingers into his hair, taking control of his head to angle him where she wanted him. One leg curled around his, locking them closer and letting him press against her stomach. She bowed her back, lifted her chin, and invited his kisses down her throat.

A sudden burst of laughter and conversation echoed over the beach as the sound of many footsteps hit the wide wooden deck well behind them.

"The dance thing must be over," he murmured, still intent on pressing kisses on her throat, one hand slipping around to the side of her breast.

She moaned as he thumbed her nipple. "Think we'll get caught?"

Someone shouted. A group howled in laughter. The strains of a Journey song started filling up the night.

"It's kind of like high school all over again," he said.

She laughed, a memory floating back like the chorus to a song she hadn't heard in years. "Like the time we made out in the janitor's closet and that old guy who was always stuffing tobacco in his mouth yelled at us."

"Yep." He pushed up to get off the chaise. "Hang on, these cabanas close up."

Taking one side of the thick yellow drape, he drew it to the middle, then brought the other one to meet it, securing it with hook enclosures.

He turned to her, and her breath slammed into her chest at the look on his face.

Coming back to the chaise, he leaned on one knee, the cushion dipping with his weight, his eyes searing her. "Bethany," he whispered. "Still one of my all-time-favorite creatures who ever roamed the earth."

That made her smile, and when he climbed back on their little bed, his hand settled on the thigh exposed when her skirt slid up, making her mouth go bone-dry and her lower half pool with desire.

"I really came out here to talk to you," he said, hovering over her.

She slipped her bare feet between his legs. "I really came out here to be alone."

He inched up closer. "So neither one of us is getting what we wanted."

She reached up and closed her hands over his shoulders, pulling him down. "Right now, this is exactly what I want."

"Me, too." He eased himself onto her, making her aware that her heart was pounding so hard it drowned out the music. Her leg wrapped around his again, and she brought him closer.

"I've got a room here tonight, you know," he said, just before kissing her.

"Maybe we'll go there later," she murmured into his neck. "But not yet, not now. Now you should..." She wrapped her arms around him and pulled his hard muscles against her body. "Do this."

"You...want the essence of it again?" he asked as his hands moved to cover her breast.

"I want all of it," she admitted.

He slowed his touch and lifted his head. "You really are forgiving me," he said, in a tone of humor mixed with relief.

She answered by kissing his mouth and jaw, bowing her back again so his hands slid down her waist, over her backside, finding his way to her thighs.

"These legs," he murmured, stroking her skin. "They've set the standard for legs on all women everywhere for the rest of my life."

She laughed, but it turned into a whisper of his name as his fingers slipped deeper between her legs. She caressed his back and dug her fingers into his shoulders, moaning in appreciation as she did her own exploring.

All the while, his hard-on grew against her, and they started a slow, rhythmic rub as their hips rocked against each other.

Some things really never changed.

"We're acting like teenagers," he joked, lifting his head to carefully check her expression. "*Again*."

"I don't feel like a teenager," she said. She ran her hands over his arms, giving his hard, sizable biceps a squeeze. "And neither do you. You feel...amazing. This is amazing."

He kissed her mouth and slipped his hand back under her skirt. "You are amazing, sweet Beth."

"Ken." She clutched his shirt, tugging it higher to get her hands on his skin and muscles. It was Ken, but different. Better. Bigger. Older and so much sexier than her teenage memories.

His hand roamed higher, into her panties, making her gasp when he touched her most tender spot, wet and ready for him. She couldn't breathe. Couldn't think about anything but how intense and insane that felt.

His erection pulsed against her as she dragged her hand down to his waist, lower. With shaking fingers, she tried to unbuckle his belt.

"Help me," she pleaded, hearing the desperation in her voice.

He unbuckled the belt and flipped open the button on his dress pants, too, but she pushed his hand away, a whimper in her throat because she couldn't stand one more second without touching him. Dipping her hand in, she captured him, pulling a low groan from his chest as pleasure swamped them both.

Instantly, he returned his hand to the heat between her legs, each caress and stroke matching the beat of her fingers sliding up and down his shaft. Their breath labored, their moans soft, he slipped a finger inside her, and both of them shuddered as need rocked them.

"Hello, second base," he teased, his voice as sexy as that finger. "Is it as good as the night on the goat farm?"

"Better," she whispered, her trembling hands attempting to slide down his zipper. "Because this time…we don't have to stop."

He groaned, then dragged her panties over her hips, and she eased one leg out so she could spread herself for him.

"Beth, babe. This is crazy."

Utterly insane but too wonderful for words. "And long overdue," she whispered.

He agreed with a moan, rocking against her.

"Inside me, Kenny. Fill me up." She'd unzipped his pants and pushed them over his hips, freeing him.

"Beth…Beth."

Sensing he was stopping things she did not want to stop, she quieted him with a kiss, sucking his tongue into her mouth to show him exactly what she wanted.

"Beth," he insisted, pulling away. "Condom. *Condom.*" It was like he couldn't form a sentence. "I don't have one."

"You don't need it."

He stilled against her. "Gotta have one, honey."

She slowed her touch, realizing she had to explain. Well, maybe not everything. Not now. "I can't get pregnant," she said.

"You're sure?"

"One hundred percent."

"I get tested," he replied. "Every few months. Regulation."

That was enough for her, knowing how lackluster her sex life was. "So our bases are covered," she murmured into the kiss.

"Then let's go to the next one."

Her skirt was around her waist now, her legs open so that their bare bodies were rubbing, the friction almost enough to make her come.

Music screamed from fifty feet away, laughter and conversation faded in the buzz of blood in her head. Sweat trickled on her skin, and every muscle battled for control as she clung to him and let go of common sense.

This was just so damn good…why not?

He eased the tip into her, making her back bow in another invitation. Kissing her, sliding his hand under her top to caress her breast, he penetrated further…deeper…hotter…harder.

Drunk on pleasure, she gave up on coherent thought and moved. In and out, he plunged and thrust, and she met every stroke with matching fury. Every sensation was heightened, the sweet, spicy scent of sex filling the tiny space, the distant noises, the echo of her breathless pleas.

She was finally making love to Ken Cavanaugh under the moon on Barefoot Bay.

Everything was perfect. The pressure of him filling her, the primal rhythm of their bodies, her nails in his back, sweat on his brow, and the sight of Ken in the throes of raw, real passion.

She came first, furious and frantic, and then he lost control with her.

She held her hips high to prevent him from doing anything except let the last ebbs of pleasure rock his body. He spilled and spilled and filled her completely.

So…damn…perfect.

It took five full minutes to get their breath and wits back. Then he snuggled her closer, folding her body into his powerful chest. "So, how do we get up to my room without being seen or stopped?"

"Your room?"

"You're not going home tonight, Beth. You're sleeping in my bed, in my arms, all night."

The order, sexy as it was, made her bristle a little. After finally gaining hard-won independence, she didn't relish being told what to do. Even if it was exactly what she *wanted* to do.

"Beth." He kissed her hair, and the tenderness in the way he said her name erased her initial reaction. "I've waited twenty-five years for this, and it isn't going to be over after we smashed in a cabana on the beach."

She felt the arguments rise and fall. Screw control and independence. She didn't want this night to end any more than he did.

"Okay." Two syllables, barely a breath, laden with surrender and anticipation. "I guess we do have a lot of catching up to do."

Chapter Three

The week had sucked, no doubt about it, but the night was one of the best he could remember. Relieved that Beth had agreed to spend the night, Ken timed their escape perfectly, managed to get her shoes, slip her through a back entrance that only a firefighter would know, and used a secluded stairwell in the back of Casa Blanca's hotel building to sneak her into his room without encountering another person.

The sumptuous surroundings that the resort owner had provided gratis to anyone on the planning committee who wanted to stay the night seemed like overkill this afternoon when he'd checked in. Now?

A damn love nest and he was about to settle down with the most beautiful woman he'd been with in years.

As she looked around and made small talk, Ken poured her a healthy glass of wine and grabbed a cold brew, then guided her onto the king-size bed. There, with the balcony doors wide open and the sound of the surf and tropical air floating over them, they nestled next to each other, still dressed, and finally started to talk.

Really talk.

Not mindless chatter with the sole purpose of giving them

time to recover for round two, and not the kind of "let me impress you with my life" conversations they'd both been having all week.

She asked him about being a firefighter and sipped the wine while he told her snippets of his life at the station. He noticed she skipped over his marriage, but dug back a little further to get him to talk about his years enlisted in the Navy, how drawn he'd been to firefighting and emergency situations even then, and how he'd worked for years on and off a submarine as a Damage Controlman.

"Sounds like a person I could use on the job site," she joked when she heard the title.

He thought about her job again, and even though she'd said she had her own company, it seemed impossible that it didn't have anything to do with her father's business. Endicott Development Corporation had started many years ago, long before Ken had been born, when Beth's father inherited a good twenty percent of the island from her grandfather, one of the Mimosa Key founders. The company was responsible for building up all of Pleasure Pointe and for making Ray Endicott a millionaire many, many times over. And it was at the expense of at least one life, Ken thought bitterly.

If she was tied to that company in any way other than sharing the same name, he had to know. "I know it's your business, but is it, like, a spin-off from what your dad does?"

"Not at all," she assured him. "Most people assume that, and I did work for him for a while, but a few years ago I went fully on my own."

He wanted to believe her, but some part of his brain still wasn't convinced. "Surprising, considering how the name Endicott is synonymous with real estate on Mimosa Key."

She didn't answer right away, eyeing him. "How many times do I have to say it?"

Many. He didn't answer, though, waiting.

"Believe me when I say that my business is completely separate from EDC. I love my dad, but I spent the better part of my life doing exactly what he said to do. And the way he shows love is to control things, so it's best if I'm autonomous from him."

Good, because the farther she was from that guy, the better. "So you really are the poster girl for independence," he said, purposely lightening the exchange. He'd talked about her dad enough tonight, and every time he pushed her on the subject, he could feel her slip away.

"The poster girl for independence? Who called me that?"

"Law Monroe. Some version of that anyway."

"Ahh." She nodded. "The poster boy for sarcasm and wry observations. I noticed you've been hanging around with him this week."

"Hey, there were three guys on the whole planning committee. Mark, Law, and I had to unite."

"The silver fox trio. Did you know that's what Libby Chesterfield and a few others started calling you?"

He choked softly. "And the Mimosa High tradition of stupid nicknames continues even for the gray-haired set."

"You're so defensive about that hair." She laughed and leaned a playful shoulder into his chest, getting closer again. "I shouldn't joke, though. Your job is a lot more stressful than flipping houses."

"I don't know," he replied. "You must have some tense moments when you've invested a ton and don't have an offer in hand."

She smiled up at him. "Nice of you to understand that. It can be a little nerve-racking, but mostly it's fun for me. I just moved into a flip a few weeks ago, and the plans are almost finished. I'll start the demo in the next month or so, and live in dust and hell until it's finished."

He drew back, surprised. "You live alone, on a construction site?"

"Yes, I've done it a few times. I know how to live with a makeshift kitchen, and I never buy a house with fewer than two bathrooms. It's so satisfying when a house is done and I know I did so much of it with my own two hands."

His jaw dropped. "You do the work yourself?"

"I use some subs if I have to, but mostly I do what I can. Especially demo." She grinned. "Demo is my favorite part."

He laughed, a mix of amusement and admiration welling up. "I gotta say…you clobbering the shit out of drywall is pretty hot. But so is calling the shots and not letting Daddy and his millions rule you. I like it. A lot."

"It hasn't been easy," she told him. "But I actually have never enjoyed a better relationship with my dad than we have right now. I have his respect, I think, for the first time in my life."

And there they were, back on Ray Endicott. "How about your stepmother?" he asked. "Is he still married to the same woman?"

"Josie? Oh, yes. And, honestly, she takes good care of him."

That guy? "He needs to be taken care of?"

"Actually, he had some heart issues last year. He had to have a stent put in, and he's been ordered to take it easy. Well, easier. Of course, Josie wants him to retire and travel and rest, but there is the question of what to do with Endicott Development."

How about burn it to the ground? Ken tamped the thought down with a swig of beer.

"My guess is he'll give it to my stepbrother, Landon," she said.

"Oh, your gnarled family tree." He peeled at the beer label, trying to remember the family he'd worked so hard to forget. "Landon is the older one, right? The other one was the pest."

She laughed. "Yes, Landon is older than I am, from Josie's first marriage. The pest is RJ, my little brother."

"But Josie's not his mother, right? Sorry, I don't remember those details." He did remember that Beth's real mom died very young, in childbirth having Beth. It had been a shock to learn that when they'd dated, and not something she talked much about at all.

"RJ is my dad's son from Nadine, the woman he married when I was two," she reminded him. "They divorced when RJ was a baby, and she took off without her son but *with* a pile of alimony, which is RJ's little cross to bear and probably the reason he's a pest."

"Still? He's, what, thirty-six now?"

She rolled her eyes. "Yeah, he's taking his sweet time getting his life together. But he's my baby brother, and I love him and try to understand him. He drives my dad nuts, though."

She took another deep drink of the wine and studied him. "What about your family?" she asked, enough sympathy in her voice for him to know the question made her uncomfortable, too.

"My mom moved to Texas after…" He cleared his throat. "After my dad died. She's still there, living really close to my sister and her husband, a cop in Dallas. And my brother is a painter in LA."

"A painter?"

"Houses. Not canvas. Our collars are still pretty blue in the Cavanaugh clan."

She studied him for a long moment. "That always bothered you, I remember. Your family being from Twin Palms and mine…not."

He snorted at the way she'd handled that. "It doesn't bother me anymore." He had way more important reasons to hate Ray Endicott than the fact that he was wealthy. "I yam what I yam, as the cartoon guy says."

"Captain of the firefighters."

He chuckled. "You make it sound way more impressive than it is. There are three captains, it's not a huge station, and at forty-three, I *should* be a captain. I moved around a lot, and that slowed my career."

Finishing the wine, she dropped her head back on Ken's shoulder, sighing. "Hard to believe how much life has passed since we last saw each other and you said, 'This is it.'"

"This is it? That's what I said?" He had no recollection.

"Those were your final words to me." Her voice cracked a little, and she covered it by reaching over him to place her wine glass on the nightstand next to him. "It was after the big explosion of how much you hated the name Endicott."

He closed his eyes, knowing he still hated the name. Ray Endicott, not Beth.

He put his bottle on the nightstand, too, and turned to readjust them both on the bed, lining them up and wrapping his arms around her. "And here I thought we got past that chapter."

"We did. I'm sorry I brought it up. It's just that I remember those words. Three little words. And yet they stayed with me all those years. This is—"

He silenced her with a kiss, taking the last of those three words in his mouth and replacing it with affection. They kissed long enough for her to melt and him to grow hard again.

"Last time I'm going to say this," he murmured into her mouth. "I'm sorry. I should never have put you, or us, in the middle of something you had no part in."

"Last time I'm going to say this," she replied. "I forgive you."

But as he kissed her and started the slow act of undressing her for the night, the words echoed.

This is it.

This is it.

But this time, twenty-five years later, they meant something completely different. Because, damn it all, there was something about Beth Endicott. This *could* be it.

Holding that thought, he proceeded to show her with everything he had in him.

Beth opened one eye, enough to see the first hint of sunrise spread over a masculine chest as it rose and fell with deep slumber. The morning light even highlighted a strand or two of gray against well-developed muscles and smooth, dark nipples.

No tattoos on his lean, angular torso, though she'd seen one on his back when he had gotten up once to go the bathroom. The sheet was low, over his hips, and tented by a morning erection that made her mouth water.

Ken was an amazing lover.

Under the covers, they were both still naked, the way they'd been since making love, talking for a few more hours and finally crashing. With her head on his shoulder, she closed her eyes and remembered certain moments, like the way he patiently brought her to each orgasm and how tenderly he used his mouth to taste every bit of her.

She honestly couldn't remember a night of sex so… perfect.

Would a man like Ken be satisfied with *just* being lovers? Would he understand that she could never offer him much more, at least not that offspring he wanted? Would he believe her if she told him she clung to her hard-won independence with both hands and all her teeth?

And there was still the matter of her father. Ken's jaw still tensed at the mention of Ray Endicott. She may have forgiven him for the things he said the night they broke up when they were kids, but he'd never forgive her for being the daughter of the man he clearly still blamed for his father's death.

They hadn't gone to court after the accident, though, she recalled. Mrs. Cavanaugh had taken a generous settlement and moved. Ken had graduated and gone to the Navy. And no one in her family ever mentioned the incident again.

Under her head, she felt him stir.

"Hey." She whispered the word, looking up at him.

He smiled, sleep in his midnight eyes, sex in that smile. "Hey back."

"It's morning."

"It is," he confirmed, nestling her even deeper into him. "What are we going to do today?"

Today? This went into today?

"Checkout's at eleven," he said. "So how about brunch? A day at the beach? It's Sunday, and I don't have to be at work until…" He thought for a minute. "Oh, hell, Wednesday at seven a.m. We have three days and nights with nothing but…" He rubbed her stomach and thumbed under her breast. "Us."

"Us?" There wasn't an…*us*.

"You know, me and you and a dog named…Sally. Wait

till you meet my Sally, Beth. She's probably not what you're expecting, but—"

"You want me to meet your dog?"

"She's at the station today. I leave her there when I'm not around, but, yeah..." His voice trailed off as he no doubt felt her tense.

They couldn't go beyond this morning, not one single bit. One apology and a few orgasms—okay, maybe more than a few—didn't change what hung between them.

"I, uh, don't have any clothes except the ones you took off me last night," she said, already rooting around for excuses.

"We can sneak you out, get you home, change, and...play."

She withdrew an inch, and even looking away, she could feel his gaze searching her face, trying to read her thoughts.

"Too fast?" he asked. "Too much? Too soon?"

All of the above. But she didn't really know how to tell him that. "Maybe."

"Look, you know I'm not a beat-around-the-bush kind of guy."

"I do remember that."

"So why would I start now?" He turned her to face him, lining up their naked bodies, nothing but warmth and skin in the bed. "We're good together, Beth."

Every alarm bell in Beth's freedom-loving head started blaring, along with a few others that should ring in his, but he didn't know her personal situation. She'd have to tell him.

"So let's be together," he finished. When she didn't answer, he laughed. "It's English. Means to date, get close, spend my days off hanging out."

It would be nice...until it wasn't. "I don't think so," she said, dragging out each word.

He backed off a little. "Okay, forget the hanging out on my days off. Except for today. Today's not too much to ask, is it?"

Very slowly, she shook her head. "I'm sorry, Ken."

His eyes closed like she'd kicked him. "You don't, by any chance, have a good reason, do you? Because if you don't, I'm going to think something absurd, like that wasn't the best sex in my long-term memory."

"It was," she agreed. "But it was, you know, sex."

He tipped his head with a smile. "There's more where that came from."

And that would be amazing and wonderful, but it would never stop there with them. She'd lose her freedom, and he'd have to give up exactly what he said he wanted from life. And there was the little matter of Ken's thinly covered distaste for her father. In the end, neither one of them would be happy.

She swallowed, really not wanting to have this conversation but knowing she had to. "I can't date you, Ken."

"You can't, or you won't?" he asked.

"I…shouldn't."

"Shouldn't? Why not? Is there something you're not telling me?" A look of horror darkened his face. "Someone you're not telling me about?"

"No, no, absolutely not." She didn't want him to think that, not even for a second. She gathered up the comforter and stood, covering herself completely as she rooted for the right words.

"Then what is it?"

She crushed the comforter in white-knuckled fingers. "I think I misled you."

He exhaled a puff of frustrated air. "Look, I'm not suggesting we get our lives all tangled up, make mutual friends, and move in together." He reached for her, but she inched away, knowing one touch would lead to another, then another, then she'd be back in that bed, postponing the inevitable with more great sex.

"Beth, all I'm asking for is a little time. It would be nice to have dinner, maybe go out on my boat. And…" He added a smile. "I *would* love for you to meet my dog."

She laughed softly. "The dog. That's pretty serious."

As if encouraged by her humor, he leaned closer. "Tell me why not, Beth."

"I have reasons," she finally said. "Very real and unchangeable reasons."

"In other words, don't try to argue you out of them?"

She nodded.

"Okay. Hit me. Reason number one."

The easiest one. The obvious one. Would that be enough? "I like being single. I've never been happier than since my divorce."

"You're not lonely?" he asked.

Only some nights, but he didn't need to have that door opened even a crack. "I told you I like making my own decisions."

"And I told you I like your independent streak."

"It's not a streak, Ken. It's not like some temporary color on my hair that I could change if I want to."

"I have no desire to change that or make decisions for you," he assured her. "Give me a chance to show you that. To show you I'm…different from whoever pushed you around in the past."

She hadn't said much about her ex and, honestly, neither had he. They were divorced, and divorce was never pretty, so she assumed his had been as unpleasant as hers. Their exes had no place in this room or in their bed.

Except, one of them was about to show up.

"What's your other reason?" he asked, as if there were only two.

She looked away and gnawed on her lower lip. "I have…baggage," she finally said.

"Who doesn't? At our age, if we didn't have baggage, we wouldn't have lived. We can unpack it together." He reached to give her a reassuring touch. "Very slowly, piece by piece, with no pressure."

After a moment, she met his gaze, wishing this reason wasn't so *final*. But it was. "I don't know how else to say this, but I can't give you what you want."

"I think you're wrong, and can't possibly know what I want, but couldn't we take some time and find out?"

"I'm not wrong. I can't give you what you want. I can't even try." Her voice cracked, the old pain resurfacing.

"What do you think that is?"

"It's not a matter of what I *think*. It's what you said. You want a family. Kids. I can't do that."

She saw the flicker of a reaction in his eyes, but he stayed quiet, waiting for more, giving her the space she'd need to tell him why, which of course she had to now.

She wet her lips and corralled her thoughts. Time ticked by, and he waited silently, but tense, as if he knew that whatever fire he'd accidentally stoked, one of them was about to get burned with this confession.

"When I was married," she said quietly, "I got pregnant and had a miscarriage. It was fairly late into the pregnancy, about a week after the three-month point, so I'd relaxed and was…" She closed her eyes and remembered the bliss of those days. "So happy."

"Oh, Beth," he breathed her name on a sad sigh, reaching for her. This time, she let him hold her hand.

"It happens, of course, but I took it very hard. Very. And so did Justin, my ex-husband."

"I'm so sorry." He squeezed her hand.

"My doctor at the time told us that my uterus was *incompetent* or *weak*." She spat the words that always tasted horrible to her. "Pregnancy for me would always be…problematic."

"Problematic," he repeated. "Does that mean imposs—"

"I got my tubes tied," she said, cutting him off.

This time there was no flicker in his eyes. They flashed, darkened, and registered a little disappointment.

"Justin talked me into it for my own good," she said quickly. "A year later, he filed for divorce."

"*What*?"

"Now he's remarried and has one kid of his own and two stepchildren."

He looked suitably stunned. "Whoa. That's…harsh."

"Yeah. Harsh." It went way past harsh, but she didn't want to sound bitter. She'd agreed to the plan. At the time, in her grief and fear that it could happen again, a tubal ligation made sense. Until Justin left her and started the family he'd always wanted. That was something she'd never endure again.

"When that divorce was final, I swore my days of doing what other people wanted were over. I do what I want, when I want to, and I don't have to be accountable to anyone or disappoint them when I'm not." For Beth, it was the safest way to live.

He shifted, as if considering all that. "I think you might have making your own decisions mixed up with being alone," he finally said. "I don't think the only way to make decisions yourself is to have no one special in your life."

"Well, it is for me," she said.

"And," he continued, undeterred, "if you or the person you are with wants to have kids, there are plenty of ways other than the usual."

"I know that, but it's not for me, not at this point in my life." She stepped back, dragging the comforter along for coverage and, well, comfort. "I have a ton to do today, so I think the best thing is to let me get out before any of the reunion partiers wake up."

"Seriously?" He choked the word. "So that's it? This is over?"

"Well, we can kiss good-bye and have especially fond memories about that night of the high school reunion." And if it was, then she could escape without even discussing the third reason. The one she couldn't believe he didn't think of first.

"No exchange of phone numbers so I can at least pester you with funny texts and the occasional drunk dial?"

"It's not a good idea." She dropped the bedding and turned to go to the bathroom, getting exactly five steps before he caught up with her.

"Just a damn minute, Bethany." He turned her around, and when she dropped her gaze from the intensity of his, it landed on a fully naked man who stole her balance. "You can't have kids. Fine. But I'm asking for a date, not a family."

"But, Ken, I—"

"And you like your independence, which, as you may or may not recall, I stated was a huge turn-on for me."

Then it was time for him to dismiss reason number three, which he couldn't.

"But my name is still Endicott."

He stared at her, silent, as she expected.

"I might not work for my dad, but I'm always going to be

his daughter." She swallowed against the emotion that swelled her throat. "And while I believe you are truly sorry for the things you said to me twenty-five years ago, you will *always* blame him for your father's death. And if you date me, you'll see him eventually. He's very much part of my life."

He didn't argue. He just bore her through with a long look that made her think it was his own soul he was examining, not hers. Time ticked and the room was silent but for the squawk of a gull on the beach and the soft splash of water on sand.

Finally, he exhaled slowly. "Yes," he whispered. "I do still blame him."

She knew it. "So why are we even having this conversation?" she asked. "Nothing's changed in twenty-five years, Ken. We are crazy about each other. In another world or another time, we'd date and probably struggle with a few things, but fundamentally, we'd be great together." Her voice cracked with a sob, but she didn't care. "But I can't change who I am, and you can't change who you hate."

He opened his mouth to argue, then shut it again. "When you're dressed and ready to go, I'll walk you to your car."

That was when she knew it was truly over and done with between them. Her head knew it was the right thing to do, but she wasn't sure her heart would ever understand.

Chapter Four

That evening, Beth wandered from room to room, trying to visualize the changes she'd make in the mid-century ranch that needed a lot of TLC—and money—but all she was able to see was the look on Ken Cavanaugh's face when they said good-bye.

He had walked her to her car, held her hand in the lobby—which was so *not* deserted, even at that early hour—and kissed her on the mouth in the parking lot.

A long, lazy, wish-for-more kiss that she'd relived a hundred times since then.

"Anybody home?"

Beth turned from the kitchen at the man's voice, startling a little at how much she'd hoped it would be *that* man, but let out a soft sigh when she realized who it was.

The other man who'd ruined her morning. Not that she for one minute blamed her father for the accident that killed Johnny Cavanaugh. A machine malfunctioned and a tragedy ensued. But she saw things differently than Ken.

"Dad?" She couldn't keep the surprise out of her voice. He rarely visited her unannounced, and he hadn't yet been to this new house, since she'd moved in only recently.

Frowning, she wandered to the front to find her father

outside the screen door, examining the handle. "This is locked, but really, Beth, you should close your front door and be more secure. Anyone could slice this screen and walk in on you."

"And give up the breeze? Besides, it's Pleasure Pointe, Dad. We don't have crime here." She unlatched the lock and opened the door to let him in, looking beyond him, expecting to see Josie.

"Are you alone?"

"I am."

She frowned, gesturing for him to enter. "Is something wrong?"

"Does something have to be wrong for me to visit my own daughter?"

Unannounced on a Sunday night without his wife? It was a little odd, to say the least.

He looked even thinner than the last time she'd seen him, Beth noticed, and a little hunched over, definitely wearing every one of his sixty-nine years since his recent stent surgery. Not an old man, by any stretch, but no longer vibrant.

"What a dump," he said, glancing around.

"I know, right?"

He beamed at her. "I'm proud of you for picking a good dump."

Beth laughed, knowing glowing praise from her father when she heard it. "Just how I like 'em, Dad. Comps are high in the neighborhood."

"You're welcome for that," he replied with a wink.

She nodded her appreciation for what he continually did to the value of real estate on Mimosa Key. "And I can redo this place for thirty thousand."

He gave her a look. "Thirty?"

"If I do the work myself," she said.

"You didn't get a contractor yet?"

"I might not need one. I have a plan that I think I can file as an owner operator and not have to pull county permits."

He surveyed the place some more. "Kitchen needs work."

"It does, and I can rip down a kitchen and put up a new one." Mostly. "I can demo a tile floor and lay hardwood. I'll use subs for the hardest parts, but if I do it for thirty thousand, I'll get seventy-five more than I paid."

"But it'll take six months."

Actually, nine or ten, she thought. Each flip was slow, and time was truly money in her business. But it was *her* business, and she loved that.

He turned and grinned at her. "You'll make this place nice, Beth. I know you will."

"Thanks, Dad."

He sat on the edge of a white leather sofa that looked out of place here, but it had staged nicely in the house she'd flipped a few miles from here. Only then did she notice the oversized white envelope that he set next to him. He looked around again, nodding. "Yes, excellent choice for a house flip."

"Thanks," she said, sitting across from him. "If real estate has Ray Endicott's stamp of approval, I'm golden."

"You don't need my stamp of approval, Beth." He leaned forward with a sly smile. "Most of the time, you don't even want it."

"I'm trying to make it on my own," she reminded him. "It's your control I don't like, but I do appreciate your approval."

"You have the instinct," he said. "You have the touch. While I…" He closed his eyes and puffed out a sigh. "Better take up golf. With a cart."

So he was getting more and more serious about this retirement business. "That's not a bad life, you know."

He narrowed his blue eyes behind bifocals. "I love my job and am not ready to give it up. But Jo thinks I'm going to keel over any minute and we'll be sorry if we didn't enjoy our 'golden years' together."

"Maybe she's right," she said. "You know, nobody ever looked up from their deathbed and wished for more time at the office."

"Says my workaholic daughter."

"I'm not a few months from seventy, though," she said, standing. "You want something to drink?"

"I want people to stop talking about me dying," he said gruffly. "And I also want a dry martini with two olives, but I'll take water."

She walked around the awkward wall that separated the kitchen from the living area, already wishing for the open concept she'd mapped out. "No one's talking about you dying, Dad. We're talking about you living life to the fullest in the many years you have left."

She heard him harrumph while she poured ice water and found him up and examining a window when she returned. "Double pane," he says. "You don't have to replace these."

"But I will because the frames are hideous." She handed him the water.

"Then you've changed an egress and you'll have to pull a permit."

"Not if I don't restructure the window." She grinned at him. "I'm not a rookie, Dad."

"No, you're not." He took a sip, then returned to the sofa, putting the glass down. "Which is why…"

When his voice trailed off, she guessed the real reason he was here, and without Josie, too. They'd danced around the possibility of her taking over his business a few times since he had the stent surgery, and she'd tried to make it clear, without hurting his feelings, that she didn't want the job.

Was that what he had in that envelope? A contract? An offer? A press release announcing his plans? "Why what?" she prodded, following him to sit again.

He sighed. "I know you said running EDC is not your thing. But I still think you could make a go of it."

"I thought you were leaning toward giving the business to Landon," she said, hoping that was true. She didn't want to reject the offer out of hand, but she didn't want to completely change the life she'd built on her own, either.

"Landon doesn't see homes," he said. "He sees parcels of land. He doesn't see one big company. He sees divisions that can be sold off for profit so he can pay for Rebecca's champagne taste and college for all their kids. He doesn't see the history of the name Endicott on this island."

His father had been one of the founders, and Ray had built the name to a household level on Mimosa Key. True enough, Landon McDowell had been close to eighteen when his mother married Beth's father, and he'd never changed his name to Endicott and Ray had never "adopted" him.

"Landon sees dollar signs," he said with clear disappointment in his voice.

Landon and Rebecca did live high on the hog, but her stepbrother's business acumen would be a boon to EDC. At least, that's what she'd been telling her father. She didn't want to be CEO of his company—because she knew damn well her father would never really stop making all the important decisions. And the unimportant ones.

"Then write the contract so he can't change things," Beth told him. "Put it in the fine print that he has to carry on your business in one piece and continue the development of this island and property on the mainland with the same respect you've shown the environment and the same dedication to success and quality."

He threw up his hands. "See? You get it, Beth. He doesn't."

"He's very smart and a successful businessman."

"Not that successful," he snorted, pushing to a stand. "And, damn it, he's *not* really my son, and not my firstborn. But Josie, obviously, feels differently."

Beth sipped her water, the habit of not discussing Josie deeply ingrained since she was young. Josie had *always* felt differently about the family. She acted like the laws of primogeniture ruled the Endicott family, and despite the fact that he was a *step*son, Landon McDowell was the oldest and qualified as the firstborn.

Beth had shared a special relationship with her father, fueled by that always-present desire to make him happy and somehow make up for the fact that her birth took the life of a woman he loved.

But as she got older—and after a marriage to another controlling man—she realized she had to make decisions for herself, not her dad. So, she didn't really mind the fact that Landon was "favored" in so many things. It pissed off RJ, though, as he got older and realized the unfairness of his situation.

"I don't suppose you'd consider giving some of your business to your other son?" she asked.

Dad huffed out a breath. "The one who wrecked his car and needed money to buy a new one?"

"That was last year, Dad."

"It was the third time, Beth." He shook his head. "RJ has to grow up."

"You need to give him a chance to do that."

"He's not learning on *my* business."

As she suspected, it would always be *his* business. Which was precisely why she didn't want it. She didn't want to be under that thumb. Under *anyone's* thumb.

"You know, this is the kind of thing that tears families apart," she said, standing up to join him and make her point. "I don't want anything to happen to you and Josie."

"Nothing's going to happen with Josie."

"But you know how she is about Landon. She's made you happy for many, many years, Dad, and I am willing to bet everything I have that she'll make you happy for many more. Don't make a decision that could impact your marriage."

He turned to her, his eyes surprisingly misty. "You have a good heart, Beth, you know that? Like Ellie."

The reminder of her mother twisted that good heart and squeezed out that old guilt.

"And a good head for business," he added. "So do me a favor and keep thinking about it, okay?"

"All right. I'll think." She pressed her temples, fighting the headache that always started when she felt like she was disappointing her dad. She had to remember her days of people-pleasing—and Dad-pleasing—were over. "But I'm beat now. I was out late last night."

"I heard."

She drew back at the unmistakable implication in his voice. "You did?"

He slowly walked back to the sofa and picked up the envelope, which she'd forgotten all about. "Some people at brunch today were talking about the Mimosa High reunion last night." He lifted his brows. "Apparently, someone told Josie the sun was up when you were leaving. And not alone."

How could she forget how small a town this was? What if

he'd heard exactly who it was who'd escorted her on that walk of shame? Would he remember Ken? Of course he would—he'd remember Johnny Cavanaugh, the only employee who'd ever died as a result of an accident while working for EDC.

Dad tipped his head, as though thinking about what he was going to say. "You should be very careful being seen at seven in the morning wearing the same clothes you wore the night before."

And there it was. The *real* reason he'd come over, which had nothing to do with his business or who he'd give it to. To tell her what to do, and what not to do. And, possibly, who with.

"You do realize I'm forty and don't exactly need your permission to stay out all night."

"This isn't about my permission, Beth." He looked down at the envelope. "Do you remember the, uh, incident with John Cavanaugh?"

The question caught her off guard. So he did know who she was with, and immediately took that association back to the…*incident*? Is that how he categorized a death at an EDC job site? "Of course I remember."

"Then you know why I would be concerned about you speaking with his son."

"Not exactly," she said. "You do recall that a long time ago, he was my boyfriend."

"But his father was killed on my site."

She swallowed. "It's history, Dad."

"And I'd like it to stay that way."

What was he implying? "You think he'd dredge that up for some reason?"

"I don't know," he said simply. "I don't know what his ulterior motive is with you."

Irritation rocked her. "His ulterior motive?" It might have been to get her in bed. It might have been to date her, but that…wasn't going to happen. "I don't think he has one," she said. "But it doesn't matter. I'm not going to see him again."

"That's good."

Was it? It sure didn't feel good. It felt sad.

"I don't know the man," Dad continued. "But I do know he's held a grudge against us for a long time, despite the settlement on the case, despite the fact that we had irrefutable proof that all the machinery on site had been inspected within thirty days of the accident."

She shivered at the memory of what happened to Ken's father when a huge generator fell on him and crushed the life out of him. She'd never known the amount of the "settlement"—only that there'd been rumors of "hush money," despite the fact that Ray Endicott was quoted in the press as calling it a "gift" for the grieving family, since there was no proof of negligence on the part of EDC.

"He may still hold that grudge," Dad said.

"And that's why you're here? To warn me off seeing him again? You think he can hurt EDC?"

"No, that's not what I'm saying at all. I'm just saying that there is more to the story, and it's…complicated."

Complicated? Yeah, it usually was when people's lives were ripped apart with grief and death and blame.

Dad held the envelope out. "This is a copy of every pertinent document regarding that case. Some of this is highly confidential."

"Why? Does it implicate EDC?" she asked.

He closed his eyes, clearly not wanting to answer that. "Read it and do with it what you will. Except share it with Ken Cavanaugh. That, you cannot do."

Another stab of fury made her stand even straighter. "You can't come in here and tell me what I can and cannot do, Dad." She tried to keep her voice slow and steady and not let him know the conversation was getting to her.

"You'll understand after you read it."

Except she wasn't going to read it.

He extended the envelope over the coffee table. "Take it, read it, and learn the facts. Then talk to me, please. Please." He stepped closer. "But don't talk to him about any of it."

"Then why are you giving this to me?"

"So you know the whole story, but, be warned, if Ken Cavanaugh talks about the incident, he's breaking a nondisclosure agreement his mother signed on behalf of the whole family."

"A nondisclosure agreement? Why would they need to be silenced?" *Had* they been paid hush money?

"Read the papers, Beth." He dropped the envelope on the table and nodded toward the door. "And let me know if you plan to see him again."

She resisted the urge to remind him of her age and independence again. "You don't have to worry about that," she said. "We have no intention of ever seeing each other again."

"Because of…" He gestured toward the envelope. "That?"

Why lie? "Among other things."

He gave her a hug. "That's probably a smart decision, Bethany."

Nothing felt smart about it right now.

When Dad left, she picked up the envelope and flipped it over, tempted to open it and read. But to what end? She wasn't going to see Ken again.

Tossing it onto a pile of work papers that needed to be

stored, she headed to the master bath and forced herself to think of how she'd renovate this little room…all by herself.

Which was how she'd set her life up to be lived, right?

The feeling of loneliness never really left and, in fact, seemed to morph into something completely different over the next month or so. Exhaustion. No matter how much sleep Beth got, she wanted more, and this morning had been particularly awful because she'd started emptying the kitchen in preparation for the demolition and had forgotten to turn on the mini-fridge. The milk had soured overnight, and pouring it into her coffee had made her wretch.

Not tomorrow, she vowed. She needed coffee, so on the way home from a meeting with a designer on the mainland, Beth pulled into the convenience store that sat at the heart of Mimosa Key.

Inside, the bell rang, like a reminder to Beth that she should have gone to Publix in Naples instead. Charity Grambling, the weathered, ancient owner, sat on her perch behind the counter with all the authority of a federal judge, specs lowered, *National Enquirer* opened, opinion at the ready.

"Hi, Charity."

"We have concealer for those circles under your eyes down in cosmetics."

She almost laughed, but nodded her thanks instead. "Just milk today. Vitamin D ought to do the trick."

"It'll take more than that. The house-flipping business keeping you awake at night?" Charity asked, closing her reading material as if her new customer was so much more interesting than the lives of the Kardashians.

"Nope, it's all going fine." She didn't have the energy to argue with the old windbag tonight.

"Too bad. I was hoping we could get those handsome Property Brothers down here to help you."

"Yeah, that's..." She paused as she was about to turn down the last aisle, the milk she had her eye on suddenly swaying in the cooler. She put her hand to her temple, but the wave of dizziness increased rather than went away.

"Anything's better than that redneck Chip on *Fixer Upper*!" Charity's voice floated through the store, but Beth barely heard it because her ears were ringing.

What was wrong with her?

A virus? An allergic reaction to Charity's opinions?

She took a deep breath and waited for the dizziness to pass, but it was compounded by a sudden bout of nausea. Her stomach rolled. Her head felt light. Her tongue thickened and, holy God in heaven, she was going to throw up.

Right in the middle of the Super Min.

"Charity…I…" She reached for the nearest display, her hand smashing on candies and gum.

"What's the matter?"

She tried to answer but couldn't. She heard Charity's footsteps and tried to look over, but bile rose in her stomach and she fought to keep from heaving.

"There's the bathroom." Charity shoved her toward a ladies' room she honestly hadn't even known was back there, forcing Beth through the door.

Inside, she stumbled to the first stall, barely making it in time.

After she threw up, she managed to straighten and lean against the stall wall. When did she pick up this bug?

She wet a towel and pressed it to her cheeks, stealing a

look at her pale face and dark circles. Maybe she should buy that concealer, after all.

A few minutes later, she came out, the bout of sickness finally gone. “Thank you,” she said to Charity, who waited right outside the door, the closest thing to concern Beth had ever seen in the old woman’s eyes.

“Don’t forget your milk,” Charity said.

The thought of milk turned her stomach. “I don’t really want any now.”

“Then how about you buy this?” She stuffed a small box into Beth’s hand as the bell rang and another customer walked in. Charity pivoted and marched back to the cash register as Beth looked down at the box.

Suddenly, she remembered the last time she was dizzy and had thrown up.

Chapter Five

"This is going to be cold, Mrs. Endicott."

Beth braced herself. "It's Miss or, I guess, Ms. Ms. Endicott. I mean, not that it matters, but it's…not Mrs. Just…Beth. Okay?"

"Okay." The sweet technician named Shelley smiled and held the tube of gel a little higher. "You've been shaking since we walked in here, Beth. Relax."

Beth stared at her. Relax? Was she out of her mind? "I can't," Beth admitted. "Truth be told, I've been shaking for two weeks, since I first…suspected. I mean, this was *not supposed to happen*."

Shelley smiled like she'd heard that line before. "Sometimes the best things in life are surprises."

Well, this would be the world's biggest surprise. "I don't know if it's on my chart, but I had my tubes tied."

"Oh." Her eyes widened. "Certainly unexpected, then."

That was one way of putting it. "I kept ignoring every sign," she admitted. "I was late. A little dizzy." She cringed when Shelley smeared the gel over her stomach, which was still completely flat. "I was exhausted," she continued.

"What finally clued you in?" the other woman asked as she settled on a stool and reached for the ultrasound wand.

"I started counting days…in disbelief. Then I took the test. Well, tests."

Shelley laughed. "Everyone thinks the first one's wrong."

"I had my tubes tied," she repeated with emphasis.

"Pregnancy is possible after a tubal ligation," she said. "I had another one in here a few weeks ago. Rare, but not unheard of."

"Was her baby…okay?" Beth asked, the question looming over everything.

She didn't answer, her focus on her monitor. "Oh, I see something."

"You do?" Her voice cracked. "Is it…in the right place?"

She looked from the screen to Beth. "It's—"

A tap on the door stopped her. "It's Dr. Moore," a woman's voice called from outside. "May I come in, Shelley?"

"Yes, Doctor," the technician answered.

The door inched open, and the kind, bright blue eyes of Beth's ob-gyn met hers. "I didn't want to wait for the report," Dr. Moore said with a reassuring smile.

Beth looked at the technician expectantly, holding her breath, her heart pounding so hard she was surprised the ultrasound didn't pick up the thumping.

The doubt, the despair, the days of disbelief had dragged on while she waited to reach the seven-week point to determine if this baby was ectopic or not, since that was the risk with post-tubal pregnancies.

"The baby is right where it's supposed to be." Shelley sounded positively triumphant, and Beth made a little mew sound in response.

"I see that," Dr. Moore said, taking a few steps closer and adding a tender touch to Beth's shoulder. "Your worst worry can now be put to rest. Like I told you when you first came in here, not all post-tubal pregnancies are ectopic, but it is our biggest concern."

"And what about my…uterus?"

Dr. Moore lifted the chart from the side of the table and looked at it again. "I wasn't your doctor when you had your miscarriage, Beth, so I can't really concur or argue his diagnosis of an incompetent uterus. But I will say I've seen far less competent ones deliver many healthy babies."

Beth sighed with relief.

"Not that you shouldn't be extremely careful," Dr. Moore added. "I don't want you lifting anything weighing over fifteen pounds or doing any strenuous activity. Normal activity is fine. You can walk, do yoga, ride a bike, have sex, or even lightly jog. But no heavy lifting. And I want to hear from you immediately if you notice any spotting."

Thank God she hadn't started demo on the house. But now she'd have to hire help, and she'd have to…tell Ken.

Oh yes, she'd have to do *that* today. She'd already put it off too long. "Okay."

"You look a little horrified. Were you planning on moving a piano or something?" Dr. Moore asked.

That might be easier than what she'd have to do this afternoon.

"I do a lot of physical work when I remodel homes," Beth said. "But as luck would have it, I've been waiting for final designs on my current flip. I haven't so much as lifted a screwdriver. It's been incredibly frustrating."

"And a blessing." Dr. Moore replaced the chart. "I want to see you again in two weeks, and we'll get a nice heartbeat to put your mind at ease." She smiled. "Congratulations, young lady."

"Young? I don't know about that. I'll be forty-one by the time this baby is born."

"Haven't you heard? Forty-one is the new twenty-five in my world." Dr. Moore's brows lifted as she handed the chart to Shelley. "Can you return this to the front for me?"

Shelley nodded, slipping off her gloves to take the chart. The door clicked shut, and Beth's heart rate ratcheted up when she looked at Dr. Moore's serious expression.

"I don't know if you're going through this alone, Beth, but I know of some fantastic support groups who love to help others enjoy and relish the experience of having a baby without a partner."

"Thank you, Dr. Moore." She sighed and smiled. "Now that I know it's not ectopic, I'm going to be telling the baby's father today."

"Good. I hope he's there for you."

She had a feeling he would be, but, honestly, Beth had no idea how Ken would take the news. Only that she had to deliver it and couldn't wait one more day now that she knew this was a viable pregnancy.

Only, the last one was viable, too.

"You still look terrified."

"My history," Beth said softly. "The miscarriage, the tubal, and I told you my own mother died giving birth to me."

"History does not need to repeat itself," Dr. Moore assured her. "I'll see you in two weeks and every month after that until you are holding a beautiful baby in your arms."

With one more comforting pat to Beth's shoulder, she stepped outside and closed the door, leaving Beth alone with the indistinguishable image on the monitor.

She stared at it, squinting, trying to see something other than a blob of black and white and gray. Right there, that…was her baby.

"Hi, cupcake," she whispered.

And then she let herself do what she had refused to do for two weeks, three days, and six hours.

She cried tears of pure joy.

"Captain Cav."

Ken looked up from the training manual he was studying in his office. On the floor, sideways with her little legs crossed and suspended in the air over her huge belly, Sally merely opened her brown eyes, showing the same distaste for the interruption that Ken felt. "Jenkins, was I not clear?"

"Totally, Captain. You're preparing a training class, and the only interruption should come from the dispatcher with an alarm or me with another cup of coffee, less milk this time."

"Much less. Nice to know you're listening." He stared at the young lieutenant, raising his eyebrows expectantly. "I don't hear the alarm or see any coffee."

"I forgot the coffee, and my guess is you want this interruption—"

"I don't want *any* interruption." He picked up a pen and looked back at the manual.

"—'cause we're all kind of hoping this puts an end to your dry spell."

"My..." Slowly, he set the pen back down and stared at the other man. "What the hell makes you think I'm having a dry spell?"

"Your mood, which is bordering on foul and sliding right into beastly. Has been for weeks. Maybe months. There's already a pool on how long it's been since you got laid."

Seven weeks was how freaking long. "Is that why you came in here, Jenkins? To drag me into Pookie's latest betting cesspool?"

"No, sir. That's a private pool. She suggested we keep it under the table."

Oh, for shit's sake, did everything have to be a wager around here? He had work to do. "Then what's the interruption?"

"Her name is..." Jenkins looked down at a card in his hand. "Bethany Endicott."

"What?" Ken blinked at the man, feeling a twist in his gut that probably showed on his face. After damn near two months of radio silence, she shows up at the fire station?

"Well, the card says Bethany—"

"I heard you." He practically knocked over his chair standing up, making Jenkins raise his brows. "What the hell is she doing here?" he mumbled.

"Well, right now, Irish is showing her around the bay."

He didn't even want to think about that conversation. He turned away and scanned his desk, looking for something, like...composure.

Beth was *here*?

"All right, all right," he said, as much to himself as to Jenkins. "I'll see her." He absently reached for his collar, the sudden thought that she'd seen him naked but never in uniform throwing him a little off-balance.

"I knew you would," Jenkins said, leaning against the doorjamb, his knowing smirk firmly in place. "She's hot."

"Shut up."

He straightened at the command. "You want me to bring her back, Captain?"

"So you can tell her about my *dry spell*?"

Jenkins grinned. "Ten bucks says Irish did that already."

"Shit." Ken took another breath. "I'll get her as soon as I…" *Collect myself.* "Just give me a minute."

Jenkins got the message and left, closing the door behind him.

Alone but still visible to anyone passing by through the glass wall that enclosed his office, Ken turned to slowly close the manual on his desk and let the fact that Beth was here hit him fully in the heart.

He took a breath, letting the emotions he'd felt for the woman over the past weeks surface. Longing, frustration, anger, and an epic set of blue balls had all devolved into a low-grade level of pissed off at life in general. Also known as the dry spell the entire station was wagering on.

And now? He felt nothing except…some unwanted hope that hung around long after he willed it away. *Damn it.*

Why was she here? Nothing had changed in seven weeks, unless you count how many times he took cold showers and barked at his team.

In all probability, she had some house-flipping favor she needed, or wanted to bring some friend's kid to the firehouse on a field trip. There were a million reasons why she would be here, and all he had to do was find out what it was without letting her get back under his skin like a splinter.

He looked at the ground, meeting Sally's curious gaze. "We can do this, right, Sal?"

She dropped her head back to the floor with a heavy dog sigh, like she had no faith in him at all where Beth Endicott was concerned.

"Thanks for the vote of confidence, kid."

He marched out of his office, strode through the station, and kept his focus ahead. He barely noticed the tangy garlic wafting from Mike Verona's kitchen. He ignored an incoming F-bomb from a raucous game of Call of Duty in the day room. He walked into this particular fire the way he would any other, with caution and trust for his instincts.

Then his instincts saw a flash of golden hair, and he knew nothing could be trusted.

She was flanked by two men, with Billy "Irish" Hanrahan showing off the ladder truck like she was a six-year-old boy who dreamed about outrigger hydraulics.

"Oh, Captain." Irish stepped away from Beth at the sight of him. "There you are."

The men all backed off, giving Ken a clear shot of Beth and making it impossible for him to keep from sucking in a breath. Damn it all to hell and back, she was as gorgeous as he remembered. Silky hair the color of that cream-heavy coffee he'd just had fell over a black top tucked into white slacks that hung like they were made for her body. She looked professional—so she mustn't be doing her demolition work today.

Unless her target was his heart.

"Hi," she offered up a shaky smile.

He dug for that pissed-off feeling that had been his constant companion, but his expression betrayed him with a smile.

"Beth," he said. "This is a surprise."

She gave a nervous laugh. "Yeah, I guess it is."

All of the men and women in the bay stopped what they were doing to observe the exchange.

Ken shot Hanrahan a warning look. "That rig clean yet, Irish?"

"Not quite, Captain."

"Then get to work." He put a light hand on Beth's shoulder. Possessive, yeah. But she didn't shake him off, so he left it there for the sheer pleasure of being connected to her. "Want me to show you around?"

"No, I don't need a tour." She looked up at him. "I need to talk to you."

In his peripheral vision, he saw everyone in the bay taking them in, their heads turning from side to side like it was a tennis match all set up for the entertainment of Station 16.

"Sure. We can go in my office." He guided her away and shot a look at Irish, Jenkins, and the two men behind them. "Get to work, people."

"You, too, Captain."

He could hear them laughing as he guided her around the corner, wishing like hell they were anywhere but at the station. He gestured toward his office. "It has a door, but I'll warn you, the glass wall means we might have an audience."

She took a slow breath. "I'm sorry to burst in on you at work. I'm sure you're busy, but…" She wet her lips as if her mouth were as dry as the desert. "I need to talk to you."

So she'd said. "It's fine. But it is a fire station, and I'm on duty. We could get called out at any minute."

She nodded. "I'll be brief."

He led her into his office, and instantly, Sally hauled herself up for a sniff.

"Well, you get to meet my dog after all," he said, kicking himself for being happy about that.

"Oh, look at her." She bent over to greet the dog with an outstretched hand. "She's a…Yorkie?"

"Maybe. She's definitely a terrier of some sort, bred with…a cow."

She laughed as Sally trotted her wide ass on three-inch legs and looked right up into Beth's eyes. "She doesn't look like a Sally."

"She was left here at the station, and the only command she obeyed was 'lay down,' so the guys started calling her

Lay Down Sally." He crouched down to pet her and whisper an introduction. "Beth, this is my girl, Sally. Sal, this is..." *Not my girl.* "Beth."

Sally sniffed and tipped her head from side to side in a shameless beg for a neck scratch, which she received. He watched, vaguely aware of how the sight of Beth being tender with Sally kind of made his heart come undone.

Damn it, Sal. She's not ours to care about.

"Have a seat." He came around the desk because there was only one extra chair in his office and, from across his desk, he took a good look at her.

She wore more makeup today than he remembered, but then, they'd last seen each other after a long night of hot sex.

He pushed the thought far away, and fast. Too much of that and she'd know he'd had a dry spell for sure. "So, what's up?" he asked, momentarily proud of how chill he sounded. Like they were old acquaintances with a casual relationship and not the reason he'd had way too many sleepless nights.

"I have something to tell you." She looked down and plucked at an imaginary thread on her slacks. "It's not...easy."

He leaned closer, trying to read her expression and brace for whatever it was. "Okay."

"Okay," she echoed, and for the first time, it dawned on him that she was way more nervous than he was. A thousand times more.

And under blush-pink cheeks, her skin looked pale. Below her eyes, she hadn't quite concealed dark shadows. Her cheeks looked hollow, and even her shoulders seemed narrower than he remembered.

Suddenly, his sleepless nights were forgotten as he leaned closer. "Are you all right, Beth?"

"I'm..." She inhaled and exhaled slowly. "I really don't know how else to say this, so I just will."

He had a flash of insight. This was about his dad. She'd come to tell him something had been hidden or lied about, that her family had—

"I'm pregnant."

His whole body went numb. "Excuse me?"

She nodded. "Yeah. I said the same thing when I saw the test."

"But I thought you said—"

"I did, and it was the truth. I had a tubal ligation three years ago. What's happened is rare." She puffed out a breath. "But not impossible."

"You're...*pregnant*." The word lodged in his throat, and all he could do was stare at her as his chest squeezed so hard it was like a vise grip stealing all his oxygen. His head grew light. His ears rang like a five-alarm fire as the words banged against his brain.

"I'm told the odds were one in a thousand," she said.

One in a thousand? "Well, we beat those odds," he said with a masculine stab of pride he couldn't deny.

She narrowed her eyes at him. "Don't get all male smug about your power swimmers. This is real, Ken."

"It sure as hell is." He closed his eyes, letting this new reality roll over him. "I can't believe it."

"Listen to me." She held out her hand as if she wanted to touch him, but then withdrew it before she actually made contact. "I thought you might feel that way."

What way? He didn't know how he felt right now.

"I'm not upset," she said quickly. "Well, I was a little thrown when I had a dizzy spell in the middle of the Super Min."

"Were you okay? Did you faint? Did you get hurt?" Hell,

that was one rescue call he'd have gone on in a heartbeat.

"Only by the look of judgment on Charity Grambling's face when I almost puked in the aisle."

He puffed some air in a dry laugh, thinking of the old busybody.

"Anyway, I took a bunch of home pregnancy tests." She bit her lip and raised an eyebrow. "Seven of them."

"All positive?"

She nodded. "Then I went to the doctor. In fact, I just came from there and—"

"You went to the doctor already? Without me?" He realized that was kind of a dumb question, but what the hell. He was in shock.

"I had to see my doctor and make sure everything is okay because, as I told you, I had my tubes tied, and that can increase the chances of something going wrong."

"Going…wrong?" His gut squeezed. "What do you mean, going wrong?"

"An ectopic pregnancy, which has an increased chance of happening after a tubal, or a miscarriage, of which I've had both. But I had an ultrasound this morning—"

"You had an *ultrasound*?" He could barely croak out the words.

"Yes," she said, her tone reminding him whose body this baby was in. "There was a distinct possibility that it wasn't a viable pregnancy, so I wanted to be sure it was first. Otherwise, what use would it have been to tell you?"

What use? He couldn't even begin to answer that, so he swallowed the question. She was here now and only seven weeks pregnant. "What did the ultrasound show?" he asked. Good God, did she know the baby's gender already?

"It showed that the pregnancy is not ectopic. I'm going back in two weeks."

"I'll go with you."

"I'm not asking for that," she said quickly. "In fact, you don't have to do anything at all. I can completely—"

"Beth, stop." He scooted closer. "Not do anything? Who the hell do you think I am?"

"I know who you are, but do you fully understand who this child is?"

"Other than mine?" he demanded.

"This child is and will always be Ray Endicott's grandchild."

He stared at her, refusing to let that change anything. "And *my* child," he said.

She exhaled and inched back. "Whatever you want is fine. You can have a role in this child's life, of course. And you can give money if it makes you feel better, though I don't need it. Or you can let me walk out of here and forget this ever happened, or you can sign some legal document—I don't care."

"But I do." He finally ground the truth out. "I care like…like…" He shook his head, words eluding him. "Like nothing I've ever cared about in my whole life."

"But this is—"

The screech of a callout alert blasted from the loudspeaker, making her gasp and jump.

"Station one-six, engine five-five, possible house fire—"

He didn't even blink, vaulting up from his desk. "That's me."

"Ken." She looked up, dismay on her face.

"We're not done here." He never even turned to look at her expression, hustling into the station, the callout still screaming instructions he had to process.

Not news about a baby.

Not the fact that his life just changed forever.

Not her list of possible options for how involved he could be in the life of his child.

Not anything but that dispatcher's voice telling him what he needed to know to do his job. Possible house fire meant both the ladder and the pumper. Chief was gone by now, and the rescue crew would come along.

A BFD that had men and women propelled into the action of gearing up to do battle with a blaze…seconds after he was delivered a mind-blowing, life-changing, heart-wrecking sucker punch.

In the bay, he went through the motions of stepping into his bunker pants and boots and moving more from muscle memory than any real thought. In less than ten seconds, he was dressed and hoisted himself into the rig where his bunker coat, helmet, and SCBA gear waited.

Behind him, the crew slid into place, with Hanrahan at the wheel. Ken reached for the radio mic to report their movement. For a second, nothing came out of his mouth. Nothing registered except the impossible reality of…

A *baby*. His baby. His and Beth's.

"Captain, why are you smiling?"

"Love this job, Irish," he said, right before he pressed the talk button. "I freaking love this job."

Chapter Six

Beth's ears were still ringing long after the deafening loudspeaker went quiet and the two engines screamed out of the garage. Now there was only silence.

Even Sally had followed her master out, leaving Beth alone.

The low-grade hum of life was suddenly gone, with only the aroma of something Italian in the air. She sat stone still, staring at the empty chair where, less than two minutes ago, she'd delivered life-altering news to a man who…

I care like nothing I've ever cared about in my whole life.

She dropped back, letting that reaction sink in. Well, what had she expected? A man who'd say, *Not my problem, babe*? Of course not.

Even though she'd spent only one short night with him and six months over two dozen years ago, she knew that honor and integrity ran through every vein in Ken Cavanaugh's body.

Those qualities were sure on display here. She closed her eyes and conjured up the man who'd stolen her breath when he'd come around the corner and walked toward her like he wanted to claim her.

His uniform was so…oh hell. Call it a cliché because it

was, but that uniform was hot. Who knew a blue shirt could look so good with that salt-and-pepper hair and suntanned skin? And all those bars and insignias on his collar and muscles in his shoulders could make her as dizzy as the day she'd nearly keeled over in the Super Min.

When that alarm rang, he shot up like a soldier, marched off to his war, didn't even hesitate to go running into a burning house or face down whatever life-threatening crisis that box was screaming about.

A possible house fire. The announcement blaring through the loudspeakers still reverberated through Beth's bones.

Ken hadn't even flinched.

She closed her eyes as the ringing stopped in her ears and she could think again. She'd done so well compartmentalizing Ken after she'd last seen him. Except for a few long and achy nights when she gave in and remembered every sizzling detail of making love to him, she'd succeeded in not falling into the hole of longing.

And then, two weeks ago, when her life tilted sideways and she found out she was pregnant, her thoughts about Ken changed completely. All that mattered was her baby…and the fact that it was his baby, too. She'd known how he'd react: possessive, happy, maybe a little proud. And of course he'd want—

"Hello?"

Beth whipped around as an older woman in a stiff blue shirt not unlike the one Ken wore stepped into the doorway of the office.

"Oh, sorry," Beth said, pushing up. "I guess I should leave." Or should she? Did Ken's warning of *we're not done here* mean the conversation would continue between fire calls? She had no idea. "I was talking to—"

"Captain Cav, I know. Every person in the station

knows." The woman added an easy smile that crinkled a soft sixtysomething face. "Now you can tell me everything so when they get back, I can curry favors for a week by doling out the truth, or what I want them to think is the truth." She came into the office, extending her hand. "I'm Pookie McPherson, assistant to the chief."

Beth shook her hand. "Pookie?"

"Don't be fooled by the cute name or my thinning hair. I'm tougher than all of these studs put together, and they know it or they wouldn't cry on my ample bosom regularly." She patted that bosom, her hand landing over the fire station insignia sewn into a blue chambray shirt. "So, who are you?" she asked.

"Oh, I'm sorry." Telling a man he was about to be a father had thrown basic manners out the window. "Bethany Endicott."

"Oh, I know that. I mean who are you as it relates to Captain Cavanaugh?"

She let out a soft laugh at this new level of bluntness. "I'm an…acquaintance."

"Ahh." She nodded and reached into the pocket of her khaki pants, pulling out a folded piece of paper and flipping it open. "How long have you been seeing him?" she asked.

"Oh, I'm not…" Good God. "No. We knew each other in high school. What is that?" Beth asked, gesturing to the paper.

"A betting pool. High school, huh? So you hooked up with him at that reunion he was at a few weeks ago?"

Forget blunt. This was an interrogation. "We reacquainted ourselves there, if you must know."

"Oh, I must." She snapped the paper open and did another once-over. "He's my favorite, that's why."

"I see."

"I mean, I love them all, even some of the rookies who have the common sense of a doughnut. But Captain Cav? He's...special." There was a subtle warning in her voice, as if Beth didn't know that.

But she unequivocally did. "He is."

"I don't just mean TD and H, which is kind of the norm for the men around here."

TD and...? Oh. Tall, dark, and handsome.

"They all look damn good without their shirts on," Pookie continued. "Don't think because I don't have a single drop of estrogen left in me that I don't look, 'cause, honey, I do. Captain Cav's particularly nice shirtless. Even better than some of the young ones, you know?"

"I know."

She inched closer. "You do, do you?" Pookie gave a little smirk of victory and fluttered the paper. "So his dry spell is over? Can I put good money on it and win?"

Beth laughed again, more from disbelief than anything. "Is the Spanish Inquisition also the norm around here?"

"When one of my boys is involved, yes."

"Ken is hardly a boy."

"As you apparently well know." She waved a hand, as if pushing away whatever Beth would come back with, not that there was anything.

Beth glanced at her handbag, longing for escape, but Ken's parting shot still echoed in her head.

"How long do you think he'll be?" she asked.

"Could be a while at this one."

"Is it really a house fire?"

Pookie shrugged. "Caller smelled smoke but didn't see flames. Could be a fire, could be a faulty wire in the AC unit, could be a false alarm, could be a raging inferno and somebody doesn't come back."

Beth gasped. "Really?"

The other woman fired a *get real* look at her, then narrowed her gray eyes. "Firefighting is dangerous. Are you aware of that? Do you want to be involved with someone who risks his or her life to save others? Because being a firefighter's spouse is no easy job."

Her jaw dropped. "I'm not going to marry him."

"Really?" She seemed unfazed. "Because after one look at you, I not only put twenty bucks on the end of the dry spell, I also started a new pool. My money is on the 'serious relationship with possible name change involved' block."

Beth blinked at her. "Name change?"

"Oh, you're one of those who has to keep her name, huh? Fine. But the square still works. There are four to bet on." She held up her fingers and started counting. "One-night stand, short-term fling, casual dating that ends in six months, and serious-slash-possible wife." She looked Beth up and down two times quickly. "You're nobody's one-night stand."

Beth lifted a brow. "You might have bet wrong on that, Pookie." Turning, she lifted her bag from the chair and slipped it on her shoulder. "But thanks for the vote of confidence."

She smiled and stepped to the side. "I didn't mean to scare you off, Miss Endicott."

"I'm not scared." She gave the woman a smile. "But I hope you didn't put a lot of money on your bet."

"Ten bucks. Always ten. And I never lose the relationship pools. Never." She leaned a little closer. "Of course, don't ask me about the Super Bowl. I get annihilated every year. Now, Moonshine, he put twenty bucks on short-term fling."

"Moonshine?"

"Dalton Conway. He's from Kentucky. Good firefighter but not a great judge of character. Because Captain Cav wouldn't have brought a fling into his office. Not when Sally's here. That Cara or Carrie creature who kept hunting him down? Would not let her near Sally. That's how I knew about you."

He *had* made a big deal out of her meeting his dog. "No offense, Pookie, but you really don't know…about me." *Like the fact that I'm carrying Captain Cav's baby.* Wonder if anyone had bet on that. Talk about a long shot on the odds.

"If you say so. But I will." Pookie put a friendly arm on Beth's back and led her out. "That's kind of what I do."

As they turned the corner into the now empty garage, Sally lumbered over to Beth, nuzzling her leg.

"Told ya," Pookie said.

"Would you let Captain Cavanaugh know that he can call me? Here's my card."

Pookie took the card and examined it carefully, no doubt off to run a Google search. "I will. I'm sure we'll see you again soon. Bye!" Pookie pivoted and went back into the station, leaving Beth to look down to meet big brown affectionate eyes in a cute face with a barrel of a belly.

"Lay down, Sally." She reached down and rubbed the dog's head and started walking away, but Sally stayed right next to her until the edge of the firehouse property. Then she lowered her girth to the ground and watched Beth leave.

The shift was freaking interminable, with two more callouts, that training session he hadn't been fully prepared to teach, and constant interruptions that made Ken want to punch someone. He needed time to think, and got very little of it, clocking out at seven the next morning, desperate to see

Beth. He'd showered and changed at the station, handed Sally off to the next crew, and didn't even bother going home.

He'd used the only free time he had to call in a favor to a friend in dispatch down in Collier County. His buddy had access to every record in the county, including the addresses that had recently closed and changed ownership.

It hadn't been difficult to find her address. Sure, he had a cell phone number on a business card, but he'd rather show up and talk in person. A few weeks ago, he'd have considered that stalking and killed the idea before it fully formed. But the baby changed the game, and he wasn't going to quietly step away or give her money or sign some stupid document. This was his *kid*, damn it.

He drove through the residential neighborhood, recognizing the signs of money coming in, signs that could actually be seen all over this island, mostly thanks to the resort in Barefoot Bay. Some of these houses, circa 1970 and 1980, were already repainted, remodeled, and redone. Cracked concrete driveways had been paved with upscale bricks and cheap shingle roofs changed out to statement-making barrel tile. Weed-thick lawns were manicured and trimmed with regal queen palms.

Beth was in the right business at the right time, that was for sure.

As he approached the house, the first thing he saw was a large green Dumpster in the driveway, and his heart rate kicked up. She wouldn't demo a house pregnant, would she?

Oh hell, who was he kidding? Miss Independent might do anything.

He parked his truck on the street and climbed out, peering at the house his dispatcher had sent him to. One story, maybe twenty-five hundred square feet tops, plain as dirt.

As he got closer, he heard music coming through the screen door. Not any old music—this sounded like a full fifty-piece orchestra hitting the crescendo of something screechy and classical.

Who listened to stuff like that?

He checked the notes on this phone again, making sure he had the right address. Yep. This was 185 Mangrove Trail, recently purchased by Bethany Eleanor Endicott.

That was his girl. Well, not technically. Not…yet.

He reached the front door, making a face as the music reverberated, lifting his hand to knock but stopping himself at the sight of Beth. She stood in profile in the dining room, staring at something ahead, but hidden behind a wall, one hand on her stomach. She wore a simple white T-shirt tied in a knot at her waist, showing a good two inches of skin above extremely short jean cutoffs and legs that went on for days.

Everything in him stirred, like any time he looked at her.

She was talking—well, her mouth was moving—the music was so loud he couldn't hear anything.

He tapped on the door, but she didn't hear him, tipping her head and continuing her mouth-moving. She pointed at something in what he assumed was the kitchen and noticed a sledgehammer leaning against the wall.

Suddenly, the music stopped, allowing him to hear her.

"We could certainly put the sink there, cupcake."

Cupcake? Who the hell was she talking to?

"But that would depend on the cabinet guys—" She turned, as if she sensed someone at the door, shading her eyes to see what he imagined was his silhouette with the morning sun backlighting him. "Oh, thank God, you're here."

"Didn't think you'd be so happy to see me."

She stopped dead in her tracks. "Ken?"

"You were expecting someone else?"

Her shoulders sank as she took a few steps to the door. "The world's most unreliable subcontractor."

"Who likes Mozart?"

"It was Bach, but no, that's for…" She opened the screen door to let him in, and he could see some color rise to her cheeks. "For the baby," she murmured. "It's supposed to build brain cells or something."

An unfamiliar feeling washed over him, so new he couldn't even name it. A sense of…anticipation? Joy? Pride? A sudden urge to call something *cupcake*?

Her eyes narrowed in distrust. "Wait, what are you doing here? How did you find my house?"

"Firefighter connections."

Still looking at him, she tucked her fingers into the pockets of her denim shorts. "You could have called."

"I wanted to see you."

She inhaled slowly and nodded. "Okay…well, here I am. And here's my house. It's kitchen demo day."

He narrowed his eyes in warning, and they dropped to her stomach. "Please tell me you are *not*—"

"I am *not*," she assured him. "But it's killing me to wait for the sub who is."

He glanced around, seeing an incredible amount of orderliness for a house about to be wrecked. In the corner of the dining room there was a makeshift kitchen with a hot plate, a dorm-size fridge with plastic gallons of water on top, and a few dishes on a single plastic rack. Clearly labeled boxes lined a wall. On a drape-covered dining table a selection of tools was spread neatly, like a chef might line up knives before preparing a big meal.

"There's a method to your madness, I see."

"Of course there is. The water's off in the whole house—for now, anyway—all the circuits to the kitchen are off at the breaker box, everything is emptied and prepped, and the base screws and upper fasteners are out. I've done everything I can except what I normally do."

"Demolish."

"The best part, but I have to be safe."

"Good…" He almost said *girl* but thought better of it. "Call," he finished.

She shook her head slowly. "It pains me, especially because the doctor said normal physical activity is fine."

"Lifting a sledgehammer is not normal physical activity."

"No, I realize that. But…" She peered beyond him to the open door. "The sub was supposed to be here over an hour ago and I'm getting impatient."

"Then it's a good thing I'm here." He stepped deeper into the house, surveying the space.

"Oh, you don't have to—"

"Can it." He flicked at the sleeves of his T-shirt, already dressed for work. "Which cabinet is first?"

"Ken."

"What?"

"You didn't come over here to demo a kitchen. We need to finish our conversation."

"We can finish it while we work. And by work, I mean you tell me what to do while you sit there and not play that god-awful music. Oh, and tell me you have a working coffeepot, because I got off a twenty-four-hour shift less than an hour ago and didn't catch more than three hours' sleep."

Because someone came into the station yesterday and told me she was pregnant.

"I...I can't..."

"*You* can't do the demo, the sub is a no-show, and I'm here to help. Coffee?"

She walked toward the dining area. "Just what I need—another man to tell me what to do," she said under her breath, lifting a coffeemaker from the floor to place it on the table.

"Maybe you didn't hear me. I said, *you* tell *me* what to do and I do it."

She bent down to plug in the coffeemaker, her ponytail falling in a way that covered her expression. "Okay. Sorry. I'm frustrated."

"And pregnant."

She looked up, a few strands of hair escaping the elastic and falling over her eye. "Which doesn't change anything except my ability to pry cabinets off the wall."

"Doesn't it change your mood?"

She shrugged. "I don't know yet. I've been in a perpetual bad mood since I called this sub yesterday. I knew it was a mistake, but everyone else is booked for months."

"Well, I'm here." He grabbed a breaker bar from the table and a pair of clear goggles and headed into the galley kitchen. "These cabinets and the wall behind?"

"Yes, but not the wall yet." She pointed at the first cabinet. "Start with that bank, beginning at the farthest to the left. Be sure to check for screws and cut carefully through any caulking."

He glanced at her. "You saving the cabinets for the garage?"

"No, they're trash."

"You're not donating them or planning to do anything with them?"

"Look at them."

They were yellow and hideous, but he had to be sure. "If you're sure…"

"Yes." She crossed her arms and came closer to the kitchen. "They're going in the Dumpster in the driveway. Why?"

"Back up, buttercup." He slid the goggles over his eyes, threw the breaker bar on the counter, and grabbed the sledgehammer with one hand. He checked to make sure she was standing back, hoisted the hammer, and thwacked the crap out of the top cabinet, knocking down three-quarters of it in one swoop. "I'm a fan of the full bore and blast technique."

He turned to grin at her, only to find blue eyes locked on him. "I'm not."

"Why? You want these down and want to finish today, right? I can—"

"Do it my way. Which is careful, clean, methodical, and thorough."

"Why?"

"Because that's how I do everything."

"You're a control freak."

She lifted a brow. "A pregnant one, so don't cross me."

He laughed at the warning. "Okay, if there's a good reason to go all methodical, I will. But why spend two or three days doing what I can have done by tonight by going full bore?"

"Full bore." She turned to the coffeepot to hide the fact that she was smiling. "Who says that?"

"Your new sub, who is free, by the way. And showed up when you needed him. And…" He took the cup she offered. "Is eternally grateful for the caffeine."

She closed her eyes and sighed in surrender. "Fine. Do it your way."

"Step back."

After gulping the coffee, he turned and lifted the sledgehammer, giving the cheap fiberboard one more solid hit. The impact jolted his arms with satisfaction. He finished it off with two more slams.

"This is fun." He looked over his shoulder to find her sitting in a dining room chair, staring at him with no expression, as if she wasn't sure yet if she'd made the right decision letting him work.

"I guess it depends on your perspective," she said.

Already feeling the first trickle of sweat, he reached over his head and ripped off his T-shirt, tossing it to the ground. "I'll be done fast, I promise."

"Oh no, please, take your time," she said. "Don't rush the *full bore*."

He smiled and creamed the next cabinet with all he had. "So I heard you talked to Pookie," he said.

"Interesting woman."

He laughed before the next swing. "Oh, you know the type. A compulsive gambler with a heart of gold."

"That's a type?"

He smashed some wood, splintering it into fifty pieces. "It is in the firefighting world." Before he took the next swing, he turned, a little surprised to see her blank expression had shifted to something more…interested. And not in Pookie. "You should have stuck around the station and met more of my team. Great men and women."

"I'm sure they are, but I wasn't sure what to do," she said, a rich honesty in the reply. "And that feeling continues right now, right here."

He threw a lazy smile over his shoulder. "We'll figure it out."

"Will we?"

"Soon as I get rid of this bank of cabinets." He thwacked another cabinet and turned again to find her chin resting on her hand, her gaze locked on him, the sweetest hint of a smile. "You just enjoy the view."

"Believe me, I am."

And that made him want to work harder, which, he suspected, she knew.

Chapter Seven

Okay, this wasn't her demo style, but two hours later, Beth forgot to be bothered by that. For one thing, all the uppers were out. For another, the stupid subcontractor never showed up or answered his cell phone. She'd have lost the entire day if Ken hadn't come.

Except for a few jokes and conversation about the project, they didn't talk about anything too serious. He demolished and, good Lord, she watched. And *watched.* Muscles bunched and relaxed. Sweat trickled down a tanned, ripped back and over a simple mariner's star tattoo on his shoulder blade. Worn and faded jeans hung low on his narrow hips, revealing even more muscles and a vague tan line that made her mouth go bone-dry.

Full bore wasn't so bad.

"You have to be hungry," she said when he stopped to power down another half gallon of water.

He put the bottle down and wiped his mouth with the back of his hand, his dark eyes intense on her. "Ravenous."

"Me, too," she said. Starved and itchy and a little too sweaty for a woman who wasn't doing anything physical except eating him up with her eyes. "I was going to have a salad, but…" She let her gaze fall over his torso, which was wet from sweat, with a dark line of hair that ran down to…there. "That wouldn't be enough for you."

"We can go grab a bite. I could use a quick break." He snagged a towel she'd given him and wiped his forehead. "Is the outside water on a different valve? I need to hose off."

"Actually, it's turned off, too."

He glanced outside. "Pool looks good. Can I take a two-minute dip to cool off?"

"Of course."

"Perfect." He flicked the button to his jeans, taking a step toward the door.

"Oh," she said. "You mean…"

He glanced over his shoulder. "It's not like you haven't seen it."

And not like she didn't want to see more.

"You're welcome to join me." One brow lifted in invitation.

"I…uh…" Good Lord, why couldn't she string together a simple response? One that sounded like *no*.

One side of his mouth lifted, and his eyes twinkled as if he knew exactly why she was suddenly tongue-tied. The look finally shook her from her stupor.

"No, thanks," she said with what felt like remarkable calm. "If you want to float around for a while, I'll run out and get sandwiches."

"No, I want to go with you." He unzipped his fly, and she sucked in a breath.

"Oh. Um, okay. Then I…guess I'll get…" *Cooled off.* "My purse."

She headed to the other side of the house, barely in her bedroom when she heard the splash as a six-foot-something man made of solid muscle cannonballed like an eighth-grade boy into the water.

Picking up her purse, she looked in the mirror over the

dresser, noticing bright eyes and pink cheeks. She looked healthy. Happy. Horny.

She hadn't felt any of those things in weeks—well, she'd been horny enough for those few weeks after the reunion and all she could think about was sex with Ken. Since then, she'd felt tired, scared, nervous, tired, excited, worried, and, well, tired. But now? She felt like she could strip down and dive into that pool and—

"Hello? Is anyone home?"

She blinked at her reflection. "Josie?" she whispered. Her stepmother was here...*now*?

Glancing out the sliders from her room to the pool, she could see the water move and the shadow of a body deep under. She had time to get rid of Josie, but not much.

Hustling down the hall, she reached the front door just as Josie stepped inside.

"You should lock your door, Beth."

"So I've been told." Beth blocked Josie's entrance and possible view, adding a quick hug so she didn't seem rude. "Hi, Josie." She got a whiff of cloying designer perfume and a quick squeeze in return.

But then Josie backed away as if too much contact might mess up her jet-black bob or pink age-appropriate tennis outfit. She was only a year younger than Beth's dad, but she'd had plenty of work done and had exercised her whole life, so Josie oozed vitality and strength.

And today, curiosity.

"Oh, you started already." She inched to the side, her attention on the bit of debris left from the last two cabinets that Ken had yet to carry out to the Dumpster. Shards of wood and tools littered the floor.

"A little on the kitchen," she said. "It's kind of messy, Josie, so I'd steer clear."

"Oh, nonsense. Your father told me about the house, and I was driving by and decided it's long past time that I see it. Can I look around?"

No. "Actually, I'm super busy. How about another time?"

"You can take a break." She muscled a little closer, finally eyeing Beth. "You don't look like you've been working. Are you finally using a subcontractor for this man's work you love to do?"

She bristled at her choice of words. And the fact that the *man* was naked in the pool. "Actually, I am, but…" She blocked her again. "I'm not ready for anyone to see the house yet."

Josie lifted both carefully dyed brows, but not too far, thanks to Botox. "Really? I thought you loved to show off the befores of your house flips." She nudged Beth to the side. "Let me look at the kitchen. Surely you're taking down this heinous wall."

"I am, but really, this isn't a good time." Plus, she'd been here for more than two months, and Josie had shown zero interest in the place. There had to be more—

Beth heard a soft splash from the pool and covered it with a noisy cough. "Oh, it's dusty in here, Josie. Not good for your allergies." Beth put a firm hand on her stepmother's shoulder. "We can do this another time."

She didn't budge. "I'm worried about your father, Beth."

At the tone, Beth lightened her touch. "What's wrong with him?"

"He's so tired all the time. And short of breath."

Beth slowly dropped her hand, a tendril of worry wrapping around her chest. "What does the doctor say?"

"Oh, you know…meds, rest, tests, and that he should retire." Josie took her arm. "He listens to you. If you persuade him to give up work and the reins to Landon, he will."

And that was the real reason for this poorly timed visit.

Another splash. *Damn it.* "Josie, I—"

"I need your help, Beth," she said. "For the man we both love. Convince him to turn his work over to Landon."

The problem was, she wasn't completely convinced Landon was the best person for that job. Ever since she'd found out she was pregnant, Beth had been replaying her conversation with her father and…well, things were different now. Security for the future was as important as control and independence.

The baby had changed everything.

"I'm talking to Dad about all the options," she said, purposely vague.

But the vagueness wasn't lost on her shrewd stepmother. Josie leaned in, her eyes narrowing. "You want the business."

"I…I don't…I haven't really—"

Josie swept her hand, silencing Beth. "And of course he'll hand it to you as a way to honor the great and glorious Ellie Endicott."

The subtle dig and the undercurrent of Josie's insecurity over a woman long dead irked. "What does she have to do with this?"

"Oh, Beth." Josie sighed and crossed her arms like Beth was painfully naïve and she loathed having to explain something so obvious. "Everything, at some level, has to do with your mother."

"That's not true," Beth shot back. "Dad's been married to you three times as long as he was married to her, and he's been incredibly happy."

"But she permeates the—"

"Hey, Beth? There are no towels out here."

Beth closed her eyes at the sound of Ken's voice, right on

the other side of the wall. She'd actually forgotten about him for a moment, and that had been a mistake.

"And I'm buck naked, babe."

Now he calls her babe.

Heat crawled up Beth's chest and into her cheeks as Josie's eyes bugged.

"Stay back there, then," Beth said over her shoulder. "Because I have company."

"Oh." Ken gave an awkward laugh.

"Hello, there," Josie called, a little peeved at the interruption, but Beth could see the curiosity in her expression. "Who are you?"

"Ken Cavanaugh." He stuck his soaking-wet head out from behind the wall. "And who are—oh."

For a split second, the two of them stared at each other, then Josie's jaw dropped. "What are you—"

Beth inched her back. "I'll get you a towel, Ken. Josie, you need to leave now."

She blinked at Beth. "What is he doing here? Besides the obvious."

"Demoing the kitchen."

"Naked?"

"I took a quick swim to cool off," he said, obviously hearing every word they said.

Beth pivoted and headed toward the hall bathroom, embarrassment and fury pounding in her brain as she listened for another exchange between them. But it was dead silent out there.

Snapping a bath towel off the rack, she marched back, passed Josie, and turned the corner into the kitchen where Ken was, indeed, buck naked and dripping water off his…oh wow. *Not fair.*

"Sorry," he whispered.

"Not as sorry as I am."

He barely got the towel around his waist when Josie joined them. "I guess I'm interrupting something."

"Demo," they both said in perfect unison, making her look from one to the other.

Josie's eyes dropped and rose and dropped and rose again. Not that Beth didn't understand, but—

"You've grown up, Mr. Cavanaugh."

He nodded. "That happens to people."

"So you're helping Beth with the house?" Josie asked, plenty of skepticism in the question.

"Well, I didn't want Beth to do the demo herself," Ken said.

Oh God. She flashed him a warning look that she was absolutely certain Josie saw.

"She always does," Josie said. "She's such a modern woman, our Beth."

"But now she's a—"

"Desperate woman," Beth interjected. "I'm desperate to get this renovation done as quickly as possible. You"—she pointed to Ken—"please get dressed and back to work. *Please.*"

He must have heard the plea in her voice. He gave a nod, and stepped away, scooping his jeans from the floor. "Nice to see you, Mrs. Endicott."

She gave him one more slow once-over, and Beth took a steadying breath. "As you can see, Josie, I'm busy."

"Busy skinny-dipping with the help."

Which would be how this little incident would be reported to Dad. Whom Beth had told she'd never see Ken Cavanaugh again. For a moment, she considered asking Josie not to tell him, but they told each other everything. In fact, Beth was sure Josie knew about the conversation she'd had with her dad almost two months ago.

"I'd appreciate it if you'd let me get back to work," Beth said.

"Work?" She gave a dry laugh.

"Josie, please."

Josie walked toward the front door, throwing a glance at the hall where Ken had disappeared. "You're playing with fire," she warned under her breath.

"Good thing he's a firefighter, then," Beth replied.

Josie shot her a look and stepped outside, saying good-bye with a single nod.

"That was awkward," Ken said, emerging from the bathroom, dressed, after Josie had left.

"Beyond." She sighed and picked up her handbag from the table. "I think we've lost enough time. If you'd be nice enough to keep working, I'll bring you a sandwich."

"*Oookay*." He dragged the word out, coming closer. "Are you mad at me?"

"No, I'm mad at…" Life. Josie. Her stomach for being so empty and her hormones for being so weird. "This situation."

"The situation is cool, Beth. I don't mind doing the work. I don't even mind you not letting me get lunch with you." He reached out and brushed her cheek, the gesture meant to be conciliatory, but it inexplicably irked her, too. "You're wound so tight today."

She stomped out Josie's warning. *Playing with fire.* How? Ken Cavanaugh had no ulterior motive. He wouldn't be here if she wasn't pregnant, and she wouldn't be pregnant if she hadn't fallen in bed with him and scoffed at the idea of a condom.

She puffed out a breath. "I'm just on edge."

"You feel like you're losing control."

How did he know that? Because she didn't even know

what was bothering her. "I'm really hungry, and my stepmother makes me a little crazy."

"What did she want, anyway?"

"To manipulate me. That's her superpower."

"Then don't let her." He came closer, smelling sweet now, with a hint of chlorine clinging to him. "Let's make you feel better. You get us food, and by the time you come back, that whole ugly Formica counter will be gone."

"It is ugly." She gave him a shaky smile. "You're a good…tradesman."

"Except for when I'm naked."

Especially when he was naked. "Yeah. Don't do that anymore. Talk about ugly."

He just laughed as she left, and she knew damn well he would do it again, every time he got the chance.

And that *would* make her feel better.

A man could starve to death waiting for lunch.

During the hour and a half he was left alone, Ken snagged an apple and some disgustingly thick Greek yogurt from the fridge, powered down another water, and got to work dismantling the countertops.

It was a decent way to work off some frustrations.

Basically, he'd come over to talk, and they'd danced around the elephant in the room while he demolished a kitchen, went skinny-dipping, and had a face-to-face with Josie Endicott, who might not be the enemy, but was married to the devil.

The devil who was going to be Ken's child's grandfather. He stuck his hand in his hair and dragged it back. How was that going to work, anyway? How was any of this going to work?

Yes, they had the rest of her pregnancy to figure this whole thing out, but he wanted a sense of where this was going and how it would get there. What would he tell his friends and family? It was obvious she hadn't told hers, based on her look of sheer terror when she'd thought he was going to announce her pregnancy to her stepmother.

He yanked at a section of counter, tearing it away from the wall with a noisy crunch, holding it in a firm grip to walk it out to the Dumpster. As he reached the door, Beth appeared and opened it for him.

"Oh, awesome, you got that out. Now you can have lunch."

"Ball buster," he mumbled as he passed her holding the countertop overhead, aware of her gaze on his chest. She'd spent a good portion of the morning with her eyes in the same place, he noticed.

Once he was back in the house, he grabbed the T-shirt he'd long ago discarded and pulled it on as she set up sandwiches and drinks for them in the living room.

"*Now* he dresses," she said as he came into the room.

"Sorry to disappoint."

"You heard me talking to my stepmother. You could have stayed quietly in the kitchen until she left."

What was he? A dirty little secret? "You want to hide me, Beth?"

She sat in a chair with a sigh, shaking her head. "No. Have a seat."

"Not on your white leather sofa in filthy jeans." He dropped to the floor and picked up the sub sandwich. "Thanks."

"No mayo," she said. When he looked up at her, she

smiled. "Funny how little things stay with you. I remembered you hate it."

He waited until his heart readjusted a little, starting to get used to the whiplash inflicted on that organ around her.

"Hey, c'mere." He patted the floor next to him. "Let's make it a living room picnic."

She hesitated for a moment, then slid out of the chair and sat next to him, taking her own sandwich from the wrapping paper. "Oh, Ken," she said. "What a mess this is."

He saw the comment as a slightly open door and plowed right through it. "I don't see it that way at all," he said before taking a bite. "It's unconventional and unexpected and un…" *Wanted*? He couldn't bring himself to say that.

"Uncharted territory," she finished for him. "For both of us."

They ate in silence for a moment, and after she wiped her mouth and sipped some water, she leveled her gaze at him.

"I'm not sorry," she said. "I'm scared and uncertain, but I'm not sorry, even though it was never supposed to happen."

"I'm not sorry, either. In fact, I'm kind of…" He gave her a half smile. "Impressed with us."

"Impressed?"

"Well, it's supposed to be so impossible."

"So, what? Now your nickname at the station will be Super Sperm?"

He choked on a bite of food. "Please, don't give them any ideas."

"Oh, I'm sure there will be a pool to bet on delivery date, gender, name, and weight."

Oh man. How long until that pool was started? Not very. And damn, he'd want to be a proud papa like all the guys were, but…would she ever let him be?

"Of course," he said. "There's a pool for every baby. It's tradition. And the father gets to set the menu for his first shift after the baby's born."

A silly tradition, he thought, but one he wanted to enjoy.

He washed down the next bite with a swig of sweet tea, the much-needed food finally giving him enough stamina to have the conversation he'd come here to have. "All right, let's talk about our baby."

She stiffened. "*My* baby."

And just like that, they'd gotten to the heart of the problem. He didn't shoot back a correction, wanting to avoid hot spots. Instead, he asked, "You don't want to share *your* baby?"

"I intend to share her with everyone."

"*Her*? You know what it is already?"

"No, but I have a feeling." She patted her stomach.

"That's right. You'd never call a boy 'cupcake'."

She smiled as if she might, if she felt like it.

"Look, I'm his…or her…father, and I am going to raise this baby with you. So, you better get used to the idea."

Silent for a moment, she put her sandwich down, barely eaten. "I don't really see how it can be done."

"What? Two parents raising their child? It's kind of 'done' every day."

"Of course I understand you wanting to know your child and…and having a role in her—or his—life."

A role? "I'm this child's *father*." How many times did he have to remind her?

She sighed. "I know, and I respect that, believe me. You are the first and only person I've told. But…" She clasped her hands, pressing so tightly her knuckles whitened. "But I don't want anyone making decisions I'd rather make myself. It's compromising, and I don't want to do that. It's letting someone else call my shots." He could hear her voice tighten on every word. "It's everything I've worked to change in my life, and now you automatically get the privilege of doing all that, too. I want this baby to be mine."

"This baby *is* yours. And mine. That is a fact of life, Beth."

She looked at him. "It's important that she knows I'm one hundred and fifty percent there for her."

"Why wouldn't he?" He said the gender to tease and lighten the mood, but he could see that wasn't happening. So he leaned a little closer and lowered his voice. "I think there's a reason God gives you two parents."

"Two parents who love each other, like yours did," she replied. "Two parents who are of one mind and soul. But two people who barely know each other and, for painful, historical reasons, can't exactly blend seamlessly? That's going to be hard for a child. There's nothing worse than being born into a broken home."

He took a breath and finished closing the gap of space between them, close enough to let their shoulders touch, although somehow he managed to resist the temptation.

"We're not broken, Beth," he whispered.

She stared at him. "But we're not—"

He reached out and put a light finger on her lips. "Shhh. We can do this. We can become of one mind and soul and…what was the other thing? Oh, blend seamlessly, which sounds kind of fun. In fact, I think it's how we ended up at this point."

She eyed him, silent.

"Your overwhelming excitement for my idea is flattering." He smiled and nudged her shoulder with his. "C'mon. Tell me what you're thinking."

"I'm thinking that it sounds good on paper." She slowly shook her head. "In execution? It won't work."

"There's the attitude."

She tried to say something but didn't seem to be able to make a word form. Instead, she eased away, lifting the sandwich and putting it back down again. She started to push up to a stand, but he clasped her arm.

"Don't leave. Talk to me about this."

"I hear my phone buzzing."

He heard it then and let go. She got up and walked to the dining table, fishing her phone out of her handbag to answer it.

"Hello?"

He finished his sandwich while she listened to her caller.

"But I don't understand," she finally said. "I didn't cancel today."

She listened for a minute, trying to say something, but whoever was on the line kept cutting her off. Then she sucked in a breath. "What? Why?"

Her eyes squinted as she listened to the caller, she came back to the living room and dropped onto the leather sofa, clearly not happy with what she was hearing. He watched her face, trying to imagine what news she was getting, but mostly got a little lost in the pretty angles of her cheeks and the softness of her lips.

So soft. How was he possibly going to get through this day without kissing her?

"But why didn't you know that when you took the job in the first place?" Her voice rose in frustration. "The whole kitchen and both bathrooms?"

He could hear a man's voice coming through, but couldn't make out the words. But he certainly got the gist of the conversation. She was not a happy house-flipper right now.

"I don't understand where this is coming from, Dave. Okay, okay…" She squeezed her eyes shut in surrender.

"Yeah, I guess I will. Thanks. Bye." She tapped the screen and dropped the phone on her lap.

"Bad news?" he guessed.

"The worst. I hired a contractor, which isn't something I normally do at this stage, but I knew I needed subcontractors to do the labor. Good subs are always tied to one contractor, and this guy was the only one who'd take the job at the last minute. But he just backed out of the job because, after looking at his schedule, he couldn't fit this one in after all." She dropped her head back with a grunt. "What a mess."

"Wait, did that contractor hire the tradesman who didn't show today?"

She lifted her head and looked at him. "He said he had a message this morning canceling that sub. He thought it was me, but I didn't call him. It's all BS. He got a bigger job, and now I'm out of luck. *Damn* it." She reached for her water, but he pointed at the uneaten sandwich.

"But you do need food. Eat your lunch."

"I'm not hungry anymore."

"Baby needs food."

She glared at him.

"Or not." Because giving orders to a woman who lived for independence was one thing. A *pregnant* woman who lived for independence? Death by dirty looks.

"What am I going to do, Ken?"

"Do you have to have a contractor?"

"I can't find the subs to do the work on the bathrooms and kitchens without one, and all the good, reliable ones are booked through next fall. By then I'll be…" Her eyes widened. "Very fat."

"You'll be so pretty." Aaaand she sliced him again with a vile look. So, no orders and no compliments. "Or not."

"Sorry," she said with a laugh.

"S'okay. You're stressed about this."

"Incredibly. The baby's due December twentieth. I have to be in another house by then, with this one sold and money in the bank. Without a contractor and subs lined up? I could wait months to get anything done."

There was the slightest note of panic in her voice, and without really thinking, he said, "*We* can get it done."

"We?"

"If I'm your sub, you don't need a contractor."

"But…can you do it?"

"Go look at the kitchen and tell me I can't. I've worked construction on and off for years." He folded up the paper that had held his sandwich, purposely making it neat as a pin to impress her. "I have plenty of days off, including four in a row every so often and twenty-four-hour days in between. With your direction, we can renovate this house before the baby comes."

"Ken, I can't—"

He shot up on his knees in front of her. "Stop saying you can't. You can't get pregnant. We did. You can't share the baby. We are. You can't finish the house. We will."

"We…" She whispered the word. "It's not the *can't*. It's the *we*."

"You hate that word."

"It's not my favorite."

He leaned against her legs. "Then I'm gonna make it your favorite word. Just like I'm gonna make this your favorite house. And I'm gonna make me your—"

"Shhh." This time, she put her finger on his lips. "Don't push your luck."

He kissed the sweet, soft skin and smiled at her. There was no luck involved. Only timing, and now, if he renovated this house with her, he'd have all the time he needed.

Chapter Eight

Beth pulled the plug on work around dinnertime, and without an invitation to stay or go out to eat, Ken finally left her house with the kitchen well past halfway demolished. She'd promised not to lift a thing, and he'd promised to be back on Thursday morning, his next day off. That, and the four days he had free from Saturday through Tuesday, would give them a huge jump on the work and hopefully make her feel better.

It hurt to see her tense and stressed out at a time when she should be happiest.

But with a plan to help her in place, he felt like he'd made progress, but he desperately needed a shower and bed. When his cell phone rang as he drove out of her neighborhood, he almost didn't answer, but then saw it was Law Monroe.

The high school reunion had sparked a friendship, which Ken enjoyed because it was damn nice to hang out with guys who weren't firefighters for a change. He and Law and Mark Solomon had been the only men on the planning committee, and that had given them a chance to get to know and like each other.

He took the call. "Hey, what's up, Law?"

"You're off tonight, right? Mark's in town for a few days,

and I'm off tonight, too. I thought we could grab dinner together at the Toasted Pelican in half an hour. Can you come over to Mimosa Key?"

He closed his eyes, the need for sleep strong after a twenty-four-hour shift and taking a kitchen apart. "I'm on Mimosa Key, but dead on my feet."

"You gotta eat, man. Burger and a brew. Hour, tops."

"Why the Toasted Pelican, Chef?" Ken preferred to use Law's official title than the unofficial nickname he'd carried for years—Lawless. Though, to be fair, he'd earned them both. "You hate shitty food, and you don't drink, so it can't be for their cinder-block burgers and flat beer."

"I'm still trying to figure out who owns it—or at least who's running it—so I can buy that dump and use my incredible talent as a chef to turn it into the gastro pub this island needs. If I need to suffer a bad burger, I will. Come on, Mark's only here for a couple of days."

"Here to see Emma, I assume, not us."

"Yeah, but she's got a work thing at the resort," Law said. "So Mark's ours for a while."

Mark and Emma had met two months ago at Casa Blanca Resort & Spa, and following a highly unorthodox courtship that included convincing everyone involved with the reunion that they were engaged. But they'd fallen hard and for real.

Maybe Mark could give him some tips, Ken thought. "I'll be there in ten minutes."

He turned toward town at the four-way intersection and found a parking spot in front of the watering hole that had to have been part of Mimosa Key longer than any other business. The TP hadn't been updated in decades, despite the fact that it allegedly was under new ownership since the guy who'd been behind the bar for Ken's entire life had died many months ago.

And Law was right. With the money coming onto the island faster than ever before, the upscale concept Law had in mind for the local landmark—especially with his considerable culinary skills—would be a boon to the little town.

But now, the Toasted Pelican was a bust. Inside, the bar was mostly empty and the dinner tables not even half full.

"Hey, Cav!" Law was in a booth in the back of the bar, holding up a bottle of O'Doul's in invitation. He flashed Ken his easy smile and ran a hand through the hair he'd recently cut short.

Ken wandered over and slid in, giving his friend's hand a shake.

"Man, you do look dead." Law's dark green gaze moved up and down over Ken. "And filthy."

"I was house renovating, so I do look the part."

Law made a face. "Get a brew, then. And make it stronger than my usual."

His usual was always a non-alc beer. Law didn't talk much about the fact that he didn't touch booze, but he made no bones about the love-hate relationship with the stuff, and that he'd been stone cold sober for ten years.

Ken looked around and immediately caught sight of Mark Solomon walking into the bar area. At forty-eight, Mark was the oldest of their trio. A professional adventurer who'd made a killing when he sold his Internet company, Mark strode toward them with an air of authority and confidence. But there was something different about the widower Ken had met when the three of them realized they were the only Y chromosomes on the planning committee. Something…lighter.

Emma had made him whole and happy, Ken thought with a surprising twist of envy.

Mark approached the table, greeting the men with a smile

and handshake. "Reunion-planning committee 2.0," he joked, sliding in next to Law.

"You can have my left nut before you get me to sign up for that again," Law said.

"Keep your nuts away from me," Mark told him. "Anyway, we're off the hook. The annual reunion now falls under the responsibility of the vice president of marketing for Casa Blanca Resort & Spa, who, as you know, is my fiancée. She can handpick her own team next year, and I have a lot of influence over her. We won't be on next year's committee." He added a smile. "Although that extra week at the resort sure worked out well for me."

"So it's all final and official now?" Ken asked. "Emma's taking the job in marketing for the resort, and you're both moving down here?"

"And getting married on the beach at Barefoot Bay," Mark added with a very satisfied smile. "We've already met with the wedding planners and, get this, one of them is the daughter of Donny Zatarain."

"The lead singer of Z-Train?" Law asked, clearly impressed. "Is he going to play the wedding?"

"No, but even better, she thinks she can get Eddie James and The Lost Boys. Emma's favorite 80's band."

"They're still alive?" Ken asked.

Mark cut him with a look. "Eddie James is a year older than I am, young man. They're thinking about a reunion and might do this favor as a test run. And I will get my wife to be her dream band." He slipped into a smile. "I want to make that woman happy."

"Damn," Ken said, unable to keep a note of longing from his voice.

"Damn," Law echoed, only his sounded like Mark just got a death sentence.

Mark laughed at the two reactions. "You're right," he said to Ken. "Law, you're pathetic."

"All right, all right. You're happy." Law signaled the waitress, a twentysomething surfer blonde who was already on her way over. "Let's celebrate."

"What'll it be, gentlemen?"

Law leaned toward her, no doubt about to deliver a one-liner about a real man. "How do you like working here…" His gaze dropped. "Shelby?"

She gave him a dubious look. "Uh, s'okay."

"You like the management?"

She nodded slowly, not at all sure how to take the unexpected interrogation.

"Who are they?" Law asked, diving right in for the kill.

"I…I don't know. Some corporation."

"You don't know the name?"

"No."

"Ever notice what it says on your paycheck?" he asked.

She looked at the other two men. "Are you guys like secret shoppers or something? They told us someone might be coming in to check on our work, and you three sure aren't locals."

"Who are 'they'?" Law demanded again. "What are they checking on?"

"Why does it matter to you?" she asked.

"I knew the former owner pretty well," Law said, as if that explained the questioning. Then, as if he realized he'd derailed the ordering process, he gestured to the others. "Sorry. Order."

She hesitated a second, looking around the table again. "I still think y'all are the secret shoppers."

When she left, Law shook his head. "I don't get how someone can take over a place and make their identity a freaking state secret."

"You still haven't figured out who it is?" Mark asked. "I thought you had the name of a company."

"I do," he said. "But it's a dead end. There's no website, no phone number, only a PO box in Miami and the staff gets contacted by some guy named Sam."

"Maybe the place isn't for sale," Ken suggested.

"Maybe they don't have any right to own it." Law looked around, his expression a little sour as he offered no explanation for the cryptic comment.

Ken turned to Mark. "So have you and Emma decided where you're going to live?"

"Short term, we're staying in a bungalow up near the resort that is reserved for staff, but we're definitely buying a house." He shook his head. "After thirteen years of being alone and traveling every continent on this earth with nothing more than a one-bedroom in New York to crash in, I never thought I'd be saying those words again."

"I'm happy for you, man," Ken said. "Emma's an awesome woman. And if you're looking for a house, maybe I can interest you in a fixer-upper on Mimosa Key that I spent the day demolishing. Move-in ready by fall, I guarantee it."

"We don't want to wait that long, but what are you doing demolishing a fixer-upper?" Mark asked.

"Yeah," Law chimed in. "You're supposed to be saving houses from burning to the ground, not tearing them apart."

"It's Beth Endicott's."

"Really?" Mark's brows shot up. "Wasn't she the one who froze you out at the reunion?"

"Yeah, I thought she didn't want to see you," Law said. "That's what you told me, what, a couple of months ago?"

Ken hadn't told them all that had happened at the

reunion, only that he and Beth talked and that Beth ultimately said no go to seeing him again.

"Word is she's a loner," Law added. "Runs her own business, takes no shit from nobody."

"She may run her own business and like to control her life, but..." She was pregnant with his baby. "Things have changed."

"How so?" Mark asked.

"She...came and found me at the station."

"Nice and easy," Law said. "I love when they don't make you work so hard."

Ken shook his head, not answering as the waitress delivered their beers.

"I asked our night manager if he knew anything about the new owners," the young woman said to Law. "And I found something out for you."

Law sat up straighter. "Excellent. I hope there's a name and phone number involved." At her surprised look, he added, "Not yours, honey. The owners."

She shrugged. "No such luck. But I can tell you they have something to do with the beach."

Law frowned. "What does that mean?"

"I don't know, but they are some kind of company that sells seashells. Or maybe gas, like the Super Min sells. That's a Shell station, right?"

All three men stared at her.

"Shell Oil owns this bar?" Law asked, confused. "Or a seashell company?"

"I don't know," she said. "He just told me it's a shell company."

"Ohhh," the guys said in unison, understanding what she didn't. The company was dormant, inactive, or set up as a tax shelter.

Law thanked her, and when she was gone, he grinned. "Long on looks, short on brains. That's all they hire at this place." He took the cold beer and sipped, closing his eyes. "Sometimes I wish this shit were real. Now get back to Beth, Captain Cav. What changed?"

Ken studied his own beer, deciding what to tell them. He knew he could trust his friends, but was it his secret to share?

It was his baby.

But her secret.

"Everything changed," he answered, purposely vague.

Mark laughed. "Man, I know how that can happen. What are you going to do?"

"Well, I know what I want to do, and I know what she wants to do, but they aren't necessarily the same thing." He took a swig of his beer while the other two waited, withholding their comments. "I want to make it work and…" *Raise the kid together and…* "Ride off into the sunset."

"You poor, deluded man," Law said.

"I like that plan," Mark replied.

Ken laughed, reminded of his conversation with Beth about having two parents. "This is why you need two friends instead of one."

"What does she want to do?" Mark asked.

"She's cautious. She's been burned and has a history. Doesn't want to necessarily have a, you know, traditional life."

"Who does?" Law asked.

"Not everyone hates the idea," Ken said. Although that small group might include the mother of his child.

"Okay, I'm outnumbered in this crowd, but…" Law's attention shifted toward the bar. "Hey, isn't that Chesty Chesterfield? I'd know those knockers anywhere."

Ken turned to look at the woman leaning against the bar, deep in conversation with the bartender.

"Please tell me you don't call Libby that to her face anymore," Ken said.

"Not often? She earned that name with that rack, but shit." Law locked on the woman across the bar. "When I look at that face, the only thing that comes to mind is angel. Damn, she's hot."

"I misjudged her at the reunion," Mark said.

"I misjudged her in high school," Law shot back, his attention back on their table. "Stood her up and evidently missed out on the best sex of my life. At least that's what she told me. That body, though. I can't believe she's forty-five."

"I heard at the reunion that she's a yoga instructor," Ken said.

Law made a low growl. "I'd like to do the downward doggie style with her."

Ken looked skyward. "It's a miracle you can get a woman to go out with you."

"Are you kidding? Watch this." Law inched to the side to get a better look, then lifted his finger and crooked it in her direction with a wink. "Come to Papa, little kitty," he said under his breath.

Ken didn't insult Libby Chesterfield by turning to see if Law's ridiculous technique worked. "If she comes within five feet of this table after that, I'll buy you dinner."

"Three…two…one." Law lifted his drink an inch and clinked Ken's glass. "Hope you brought your money, son." He broke into a sly smile as Libby sauntered up to the table.

"Holy shit," Ken choked, and Mark hid his surprise by taking a drink.

"Well, look what I've spotted in the wilds of the Toasted Pelican," Libby said, one hand on a hip that she notched to the side with the confidence of a woman who loved every inch of her own body and knew exactly how to work it. “A trio of rare silver foxes known for their smoldering eyes, broad shoulders, and deceptively sweet smiles.” Shiny red lips kicked up as she pointed at Mark. “Mates for life.” Then Ken. “Drawn to danger.” Then Law. “Suffers from inflated self-opinion that experts believe is nature’s way of compensating for its tiny…beak.”

Ken and Mark laughed in unison at the dig. Law’s jaw dropped a little, but nothing came out.

“The male of the species is easily rendered speechless,” she continued, unfazed, “when females don’t immediately melt and mate.”

Laughing so hard he had to wipe his eyes, Mark waved her to the seat next to Ken. “Join us, Libby. Dinner’s on us to make up for the tiny-beaked butthead.”

She folded her arms, which accentuated an abundant cleavage on full display in a white V-neck that didn’t quite meet the top of sleek exercise pants. “No can do, guys. I’m off to do sun salutations and find my inner peace. This”—she ran her hand up and down in front of her generous bosom—“is my temple.”

Law grinned. “When can I worship?”

She angled her head and flattened him with a gaze. “My temple is closed.”

Law, recovered now and undaunted by her teasing, leaned closer. “Then can I ask you a question first?”

“You can ask, but the answer is going to be no. Not tonight, not next weekend, not ever, Lawless Monroe.”

“Honestly, I have a legit question. In all seriousness.”

“I *was* being serious.”

“I saw you talking to the bartender.”

“I said no to him, too, if it’s any consolation.”

"I've been killing myself trying to track down who owns this place now that the previous owner passed away. All I've found so far is some shell company out of Miami. Do you know who it is?"

She studied him for a second, then slowly shook her head. "Beats me."

"But you live around here and know everyone and everything."

She shrugged. "Sorry, can't help you. Gotta go. *Namaste*, gentlemen."

She pivoted and walked off, shiny black hips swaying in perfect time to a long ponytail that swayed like a yellow silk pendulum. Mark and Ken turned back to the table, but Law was still staring.

"Nama-stay a little longer next time," he murmured.

Mark nudged him. "If you're seriously interested, you might try not treating her like your personal plaything."

"Shit," Law mumbled, falling back against the seat. "I swear she knows who owns this place now and isn't saying. Someone knows, damn it." Law combed his hair back with his fingers and looked around for their waitress. "I need food. It cures all."

"Not this food," Ken joked. "It makes things worse."

"Exactly why I need to take over and bring this place into the twenty-first century."

They ordered, relaxed with another beer, and let Mark fill them in on his new life with Emma. A life, Ken had to admit, that sounded damn good to him. A life he couldn't figure out how he could have with Beth. Because even if she had his last name—which was laughable to even think about—that wouldn't change the one she was born with.

Chapter Nine

It was still dark, predawn, when Beth woke on Thursday. She turned and drifted out of a heavy sleep, the same first thought she'd had every morning for nearly three weeks tumbling over.

I'm pregnant.

Her heart kicked with joy. And then she remembered Ken, and her heart kicked again, maybe not with joy but with…

Expectation? Optimism? Just plain old lust?

He'd be here in a few hours, and she wasn't unhappy about that at all. She'd spent the day without him yesterday and had done some shopping and gone over to the mainland to look at fixtures for the bathrooms and kitchen to get some ideas.

Oddly, she was excited to share the concepts with him. It was nice not to have to do a house alone, she admitted in her state of half awake. Turning over, she sighed into her pillow and stretched her leg across the empty expanse of the bed.

It would be nice not to have to do a lot of things alone. Like sleep.

Maybe he was right, she mused. Maybe she was

confusing being alone with having control. Alone wasn't all it was cracked up to be, especially when the alternative was...Ken Cavanaugh.

Her whole body tingled and tightened at the thought.

She'd read that a woman's sex drive can increase in early pregnancy, and that it didn't take much to get...stimulated. She drew in a deep breath and listened to the soft exhale.

He stimulated her, that was for sure.

She threw back the covers and sat up, awake enough to start the day. It was a little past six, so she got up, stopped into the bathroom, and remembered she couldn't brush or flush until she went outside and turned the water back on.

It was a short-term and minor inconvenience of living in a house being renovated, but when the kitchen was in such a state of tear-down, it was stupid to leave the house valve open overnight. Even keeping the sink valves closed, there could be leaks after all that sledgehammer action.

Mmmm. Sledgehammer action. Shirtless sledgehammer action.

Just the thought of seeing more shirtless sledgehammer action today got her rushing down the hall, picking up speed as she rounded the wall, and—

In a flash, she slid across the kitchen floor and landed flat on her butt.

"What the hell?" She gasped as cold water seeped into her sleep pants, the shock of it impossible to process. Was there a flood, a leak, a—

"Oh my God." She pressed her hand against her stomach as the real impact of the fall hit her. The baby.

She froze for a moment, waiting for something...anything...a pain or pang or warning sign. But nothing hurt and or felt different. A flash of déjà vu pressed hard, the memory of the miscarriage from years ago remarkably fresh. That had been morning, too, a cold and damp day that she'd never forget.

She pressed her hand against her wet pants and reminded herself that this was water, not blood, and she had to figure out where it was coming from.

"Okay," she whispered. "Okay. We have a flood." She could deal with anything as long as the baby was okay.

Finding her footing, she pushed up, swearing softly as she realized how soaked she was and how bad this situation could turn out to be.

"I know I turned the water off," she said, moving gingerly while mentally reviewing last night's activities. She'd gone out after her shower and final trip to the bathroom and twisted the water valve completely clockwise. She was certain of that. She'd taken a flashlight and could see her fingers on the handle. She remembered testing it to be sure it was tight and thinking how she'd replace the old-school valve with a modern flip style.

And now she was standing in water. Which, with the number of open outlets, even with the circuit breakers off on this side of the house, was incredibly dangerous.

She needed light. She needed to be dry. She needed…Ken.

That hit her almost as hard as the current disaster. She didn't want to need anyone, but these were extenuating circumstances.

She tiptoed out of the water and back into the hall, getting to dry tiles in a few steps. So the bulk of the damage was in the kitchen and dining room.

She made it back to her room, still too wet to try to find a light. Instead, she got her phone and opened her contacts with a surprisingly steady hand. Ken had given her his cell phone number when he left the other night, thankfully.

He answered on the first ring. "Beth. You okay?"

She wanted to resent the question, but she couldn't. Instead, she let her heart sink into the fact that he cared about her. Well, the baby. He cared about the baby.

"I'm fine, but my kitchen flooded even though I know I turned off the water last night."

"Do not go into a flooded room, Beth." Warmth evaporated as he delivered the order with tense authority. "There are compromised electrical outlets."

"I know. I'm in the back of the house, where it's bone-dry."

"It's best to get out of the house. I can send a local Mimosa Key fire team over."

"No, don't. Just..." She swallowed. Help me. "I'll get out of the house, and you can...help me figure out what to do."

"I'll be there in half an hour," he said, the sound of movement clear through the phone. She could picture him in that blue shirt, vaulting up like an alarm had called him out, and the very thought made her a little weak in the knees.

"Don't you have to stay at the station until seven? What if you get a call?"

"The next crew is already here," he continued. "And I know every cop and state trooper between here and there. I'll be there soon. Get out of the house and stay safe."

She ended the call, stripped out of the wet sleep pants, and changed quickly into yesterday's cutoffs and a clean T-shirt. She had to figure out what happened to the water valve, she thought while brushing her teeth with bottled water.

Wanting to avoid the main part of the house, she headed out the sliders to the pool, phone in hand. She rounded the back of the house and froze, stunned at what she saw.

The old-school valve was not just turned on, it was broken off.

Now she couldn't even turn the water off as it flowed into the house. At least, she couldn't unless she had a wrench and a lot more muscle. Dropping to her knees, she peered at the pipe, spying the round, rusted handle she'd battled with last night lying on the ground.

Had she turned it so hard, she'd broken it and hadn't realized it?

Then why wouldn't the valve stem be set to off? The tiny metal sticking up from the pipe was definitely turned toward the flow position, and it was so old, rusted, and beat-up that even with a wrench, she might not be able to turn it.

Frustration rose through her as she considered going back into the house for a wrench, which was either in the flooded dining room or kitchen. It really wasn't safe until every breaker was off on the panel, and even then…it wasn't only Beth taking that chance anymore.

Every decision she made affected the baby inside her, and stopping further flooding in rooms that were going to be remodeled anyway wouldn't be worth taking a risk.

She called a plumber, left a message. Called a house-flipper friend, left another message. Managed to get in the garage and find some crappy second-rate tools. Then she turned all power off from the outside box, even though she still wasn't going in the house.

Instead, she went to work trying to turn the stem, fighting, sweating, and swearing every time the metal slipped with no change, until she heard a car door. Then another. And another. And men's voices, footsteps, and—

"Beth? Where are you?"

"In the back," she called, pushing back from the fruitless task.

Ken came around the back…followed by another man. And another. And another. And—

"A few friends wanted to help," he said, taking in her wide-eyed expression.

She wasn't sure whether to thank him or…stare. She recognized a few of them from the day at the fire station, but not all of them.

Immediately, Ken was on the ground next to her. "You okay?" he asked, his voice soft and concerned, his eyes so direct she felt like melting.

"I am now," she said, earning a hint of a satisfied smile. "I fell," she admitted, and not just because she should tell him everything that might impact the baby, but because she wanted to.

His expression registered a flash of fear, but it was gone so fast she wasn't sure she saw it. "Are you injured?"

Now he sounded like a medic and firefighter. "No, I honestly don't think so. I slipped in the water, but I didn't notice anything hurting or feeling different. Still, I promise I'll call my doctor as soon as her office opens and tell her what happened."

He looked hard at her, then nodded. "I trust you."

She sighed a word of thanks and jutted her chin toward the water valve.

"The handle broke off," she told Ken. "It was closed and not broken last night, I'm sure of it."

"Moonshine," he called to one of his men. "Get me a wrench."

"Is the house open?" he asked.

She closed her eyes. "You guys are going to go in there and take over everything, right?"

"Yep."

"And I'm going to let you."

"Yep." He touched her nose in a gesture that from anyone else would have been condescending, but from Ken it was sweet and somehow supportive. "Let me help you, Bethany."

She didn't even think about arguing. "The sliders into my bedroom are open to the patio. That's the only way in and out without my key. I turned the breakers off."

He turned to the two men behind him. "Jimbo, Irish, head in, check everything, and assess the damage."

Smiling at her, a young man handed the tool to Ken, who went to work, still firing orders. In ten seconds, he twisted the valve stem, and the water stopped with a clunk to the pipes.

He shot her a satisfied look.

"The power of good tools," she said under her breath. Of course, big muscles helped, too.

"Who you calling a tool?" he teased with a wink.

When she smiled, he leaned closer to study her. "Are you sure you're okay? No pain? No bleeding?"

"None at all," she promised him. "I'm fine. We're…fine."

The shadow of a smile crossed over his face again. "We. Your favorite word."

Right at that moment, with him helping her…it wasn't a bad word at all. She returned the smile. "I hope we can dry out this house and fast."

He gave her shoulder a squeeze. "You've got my team, and they're the best in the business. Relax." He took another look at the valve. "So, vandalism?"

She shook her head, not quite ready to buy that theory in this neighborhood, but gave him a smile. "But thanks for not assuming I'm an idiot."

He drew back. "Who would assume that?"

"Well, I was the last person to touch that valve last night."

"You think you were the last person to touch the valve last night." He inched her to the side, tossed another order at one of his men, then headed to the patio where the other two had opened the sliders. "Stay here."

Two other firefighters, in the same Navy T-shirt and camo fatigues as Ken, came around the corner, carrying a bright red gas-powered water pump between them.

He'd brought the damn cavalry!

"Miz Endicott," one said, nodding. "I'm Jenkins. Remember me?"

"And I'm Mike, aka the chef." He grinned. "Can we get past you and start drying things up, then?"

"Of course, thank you."

If she hadn't been pregnant, she could have done all this. She could have rented a pump and checked all the circuits and closed up the outlets. She could have dried out the house and fixed the valve—eventually—and handled her problem on her own.

But this way was so much…nicer. Big, strong, handsome helpful men who jumped when Captain Cav issued an order.

Two hours later, the house was secure, most of the water was out of the kitchen and dining room, and a water damage and remediation team was on the way to set up industrial fans to dry out the walls and floors so mold wouldn't grow.

Oh, and Beth had five new firefighter friends, plus a crush on their captain the size of a small house.

Ken walked into the living room after sending his team

off, hearing Beth's voice from the back of the house. He figured she was on the phone and hoped like hell it wasn't a friend she planned to stay with since she couldn't live here, for a couple of days at least. The whole morning he'd been planning how he'd persuade her to stay at his place.

But something told him Miss Independence wasn't going to jump all over that idea—or him.

He surveyed the house again, which was clean but still damp. Even with the remediation crew coming and the fans they would set up to dehumidify, it would be a day or two until the house was truly habitable. And it was Florida; the likelihood of mold growing was almost a guarantee. The fans would be screaming like jet engines, and no one in their right mind would sleep here.

Not when she could sleep with him. Which was wishful thinking, but the idea had planted and taken root. Now he had to see if he could sell her on it.

He turned as Beth came down the hall, a phone to her ear.

"All right, thanks. I'll swing by and pick up the keys when I have a chance." She walked into the living room, sliding her phone into her back pocket, an overstuffed tote bag on her shoulder.

His heart sank. "Where are you going?"

"My dad has a house on the market a few blocks from here. It's empty, but I have an air mattress in the garage, so I'm going to move in there until I can come back."

"Don't do that." He came a little closer, wishing he had finesse in these kinds of situations, but he'd always be blunt. "Stay with me."

Her eyes widened a little. "That's…"

"So much easier and smart. No air mattress." He reached out and touched her chin, lifting it a little. "I have a second bedroom."

Not that he wanted her in it, but he had to go slow or she'd run like a scared rabbit.

"Do you think that's smart?"

"Genius, actually."

"Seriously, Ken, we'll…" She fought a smile. "You know we will."

He definitely hoped they would. But he reminded himself that wasn't supposed to be the selling point. "You'll be so much more comfortable in my house than some empty place with an air mattress. Plus, I have Sally."

"Well, yeah. Sally's a bonus."

He could feel the seismic shift as she started to warm to the idea. "And a boat," he added. "We can take a sunset cruise."

"All that and my problem-solving firefighter." She sighed.

"Beth, I don't mean to step in and solve your problems," he said, reaching to take her hand. "Helping someone isn't taking control, and letting someone make your life comfortable isn't waving a white flag over your independence."

"I know. You're right. I'll stay there. For a day or two, no more."

He squeezed her hand. "Good call."

"But…" She looked around. "I still don't understand how this happened. I know the valve was secure when I went to bed. And now I'm going to lose so much time." Absently, she touched her stomach. "I have a lot of work to do."

He looked outside as an engine revved on the street. "Your water guys are here. I'll wait while you set them up and—"

"No, you go and get some rest. Leave me your address, and I'll come later. I still have some things to do here and some business in town."

"That sounds like a plan." Not really thinking, he leaned forward and planted a kiss on her forehead.

"What was that for?" she asked.

"Uh…good-bye?"

She smiled up at him. "You know I could have done all of this myself. It would have taken longer and cost me more, but I could have. So, thank you very much."

"You're welcome," he said, sliding an arm around her. "And as you know, I think all that DIY stuff is hot. But thanks for humoring me and letting me show off all my boys and our skills."

"They are nice…skills."

He laughed and reluctantly released her to go outside, exhaustion pressing as he zeroed in on a bright yellow Corvette that had pulled up. Definitely not the mold remediation team.

Ken walked toward the man who climbed out, sizing him up, guessing him to be mid-thirties, with the perfect amount of calculated scruff and a decent build.

"Who are you?" the man asked.

"I take it you're not here for the leak."

The other man looked Ken up and down, mostly up, since Ken had him by a good two inches. Ken had long ago abandoned his blues and wore a filthy undershirt and wet jeans that had been crawling in dirt and floodwater.

"Which sub are you?" the guy asked.

"All of them," Ken replied. "How about you?"

"I'm the special one."

Ken's fist tightened, but he stayed cool. "Can I help you with something?"

The guy inched back. "I'm here for Beth."

Who was this guy?

"RJ?" Beth's voice came from behind the screen door just as she pushed it open. "What are you doing here?"

RJ. Her half brother.

"Meeting your new boyfriend."

She popped out the door, frowning at both of them. "He's not my boyfriend. And, actually, you already know him. RJ, this is Ken Cavanaugh. Ken, my brother RJ Endicott."

"Really." RJ looked surprised, then extended his hand.

"RJ. It's been a while."

"Twenty-some years," RJ said. "I think I was twelve when…you two dated." RJ shook his hand, still eyeing Ken.

Beth immediately came closer. "What's up, RJ? Do you need something?"

"Rumor has it you've had a flood."

"Rumor?" she choked. "Nobody knows that."

"I happened to be with Bob Kinsley's administrative assistant when you called this morning. He had his phone forwarded to her." He gave a fake angry look. "Thanks for the interruption, sis."

She rolled her eyes. "Yes, I did call him since he's flipping a house one street over and I thought he might be close by."

"How bad is it damaged?" RJ asked.

She shrugged. "Some, but I can handle it."

"So, what, you went to bed and didn't turn off the water?" He threw a look at Ken. "I guess you were distracted."

Ken opened his mouth, but Beth was too fast, placing a quieting hand on Ken's arm but a warning look for her brother. "Sounds like Bob Kinsley's admin pushed you out of the wrong side of the bed. I don't need your help, but thanks."

He laughed. "But I'm right. You forgot to shut off the water. Rookie mistake."

"She did not forget to shut off the water," Ken said, the need to defend her strong. "Someone broke the valve. On purpose."

RJ blinked. “Damn. Place is going to hell in a handbasket.” He gave a look past Beth. “Um, are you too busy to talk? In private.”

After a moment, she nodded, her expression softening. “Come on in, RJ. Ken was just leaving.”

“I’ll see you soon, Beth.” He made sure it wasn’t a question, and he hoped to hell her little brother didn’t try to talk her out of staying with him.

Chapter Ten

After checking out the damage, RJ dropped onto her white leather sofa with none of the concern that Ken had shown for dirtying it. She prepared for some comment about Ken Cavanaugh, but RJ looked too wrapped up in his own thoughts to pursue it.

"What's up, RJ?" she asked.

He let out one long exhale. "I need money."

"Shocker."

"No, Beth, I don't mean money like a loan. I mean money like a…purpose. A job. A career."

"Don't tell me, my little brother is growing up." She stood in front of the chair, not willing to commit to the long conversation that sitting would imply.

He didn't laugh at her joke. If anything, the anguish on RJ's sharp features deepened. "Your little brother is about to become a father."

She fell into the chair with a thud. "What?"

Grim-faced, he nodded.

"Bob Kinsley's admin?" God, she hoped it was the woman he was in bed with that morning, although with RJ, one never knew for sure.

"Of course. Her name's Selina Montgomery."

"I can't believe it." She fell back, barely aware she put a hand on her own stomach. "Are you…do you…what are you going to do?"

He looked at her, his blue eyes so much like their dad's and her own, but full of pain. He didn't answer right away, making her realize she was literally holding her breath as she absorbed the fact they were in the same situation.

"Oh, we're getting married. I love the shit out of that girl."

Or not. "Oh, RJ. That's awesome!" She practically jumped out of her chair to join him on the sofa and hug him.

But he didn't return the embrace. "I'm not worthy of her, Beth."

"Of course you are! And you're the father of her baby." The minute the words were out, they hit her hard. Why would she think Ken's role in their baby's life would be diminished? She certainly didn't want that for her brother.

The sudden insight made her burn with shame.

"But I'm such a loser."

"You are not!"

He leaned back and gave her a *get real* look. "I've essentially lived off Dad's money when I don't have a steady job, which is never."

"You did that real estate stuff in LA," she said encouragingly. "You sold a thirty-thousand-square-foot office building in Van Nuys. Not many people can say that."

"One deal and then I came home with my tail between my legs because LA commercial real estate is a shark tank and I was chum."

That was true. "But you've been talking to that recruiter, and she thought there might be something for you over on the mainland, right?"

He puffed out a breath and shook his head. "Fell through.

Face it, Beth. I suck. I take after my mother, whose entire existence has been built on taking things from other people—like Dad's money."

Her heart cracked when he said it, mostly because the truth couldn't be denied. Nadine had married Beth's father when he was at his most vulnerable, just a year and a half widowed with a baby daughter. And at twenty-two, she'd secured her future with a baby of her own almost immediately after she got the Endicott last name.

When that marriage had inevitably broken up, she hadn't even wanted her young son. She'd taken the cash, which had to have hurt RJ in indescribable ways. And Beth always thought it explained a lot of his problems, and gave RJ a pass on some of his poorer life decisions.

But this? This wasn't really a decision, as she well knew.

"Well, now you have a chance to be a different kind of parent," Beth said, pressing his arm. "And you'll find the right career. I know you will."

"You'd think there'd be something for me at EDC."

She couldn't argue that. "Dad offered you a job in the commercial department."

"A very low-level job," he said bitterly.

"You could work your way up."

"Landon won't have to work his way up," he shot back. "He's going to walk into the CEO's office."

Maybe, maybe not. "He has business experience," she said.

"And Josie," RJ added.

"Even if Landon is CEO, maybe he'll give you a job," Beth said. She would, if she took that role, which would be another reason for her to seriously consider Dad's offer.

"Landon give me a job?" RJ snorted. "Maybe goats will fly to the moon."

She tried to laugh, but Landon treated RJ like the black sheep so many families had, especially when they had three different mothers. But RJ had always held a place in Beth's heart, no more than right now.

She gave him another hug, fighting the overwhelming urge to confess that she was going to be a parent, too. But something kept her quiet. It was still a secret she shared with Ken, and now…now something felt different.

Maybe it was seeing how much this affected her brother. Ken must be feeling the same things, and she'd been so busy clinging to control that she hadn't given him this same consideration.

"So tell me about this Selina Montgomery. Will I like her?"

"I think you'll love her," he said. "I sure do."

A pang of envy twisted her heart as she leaned in closer. "How do you know? Are you sure it's not the fact that you're having a baby together that you love?"

"I loved her before she got pregnant," he said.

As it should be. "What's she like?"

"Awesome. Smart, funny, and so chill. She's going to be a great mom."

"Oh, RJ." She put her head on his shoulder and blinked against the sting of tears. "You're going to be a great dad."

"If I get my shit together."

"You will. When's the wedding?" she asked.

"I'd like to wait until I have a real job," he replied. "I know that sounds stupidly old school, but I have to provide for her. Baby's due November twenty-second."

A month before hers. "So she's eleven weeks along?"

He threw her a look of surprise. "Good math, Beth. Yeah. She'll be twelve weeks on Tuesday. And we want to start telling people, but, man, I wanted to ask her to marry me first."

"I know you'll figure something out, and I'll have my eyes and ears open," she assured him. "I'm going to need help on this place, but I know that's not the kind of work you want."

"You're right. I want a long-term, secure job. I'll help you if you need it, but it looks like I might have to take on the firefighter for that job." He gave her a quizzical look. "Talk about a blast from the past, huh? Kenny Cavanaugh."

She smiled at the name she'd used when they were dating in high school. "Yeah."

"You mooned over that guy."

"I recall you *actually* mooned him when he showed up to take me out once."

RJ cracked up. "From the top of the steps. Man, that was epic. Josie just about plotzed."

They shared a long look and a wistful smile. "Good times, RJ. Except I really wanted to kill you."

"Many times, I imagine. So, what's going on with him? I recall that relationship went down in flames, if you'll excuse the bad pun. Was he here when the flood happened *overnight*?"

"No. I was alone, but…"

"But what?" he asked.

"But…" She heard the door of a truck and knew the water remediation guys had arrived. "I'm probably going to be staying with him for a few days while this place dries up."

He lifted a brow. "Want some brotherly advice?"

"If you tell me he's just seeing me to drum up some kind of retribution against Dad for what happened to his father, I'll slap you. Because he is not, believe me."

"That's not the advice I was going to give. I'm no expert on that history and don't even care about it. I do have good advice for you, though."

"What?"

He leaned close to whisper, "Use protection."

Too late.

Seeing his Cape Coral home through Beth's eyes, Ken felt an unexpected mix of pride and scrutiny. The three-bedroom house certainly wasn't grand and likely wasn't decorated to her renovation-worthy standards, but at her slight gasp when she walked into the living room and looked out to the wide canal and dock at the edge of his property, he knew he had her approval.

"My personal playground," he said with a laugh, knowing what his weathered dock—home to a sixteen-foot outboard, a Jet Ski, a few kayaks, some paddleboards, and a whole mess of fishing gear—must look like to her.

"Heavenly," she said, surprising him as she walked through the living room and went straight to the sliders to look past the patio and tiny pool to the gem of a backyard. "It's straight out of the Keys."

"That's what I always think."

"I'm turned around." She pointed down the straight canal that ended at his house, connecting in a T to another waterway. "East or west?"

"That's east and will take you right to the Caloosahatchee River."

She turned, surprised. "You can get to Mimosa Key by boat?"

"Easily. It's a nice two-hour ride if you have the time to go that way."

"Fun." Her eyes lit up.

"We'll take the Boston Whaler tonight on that sunset cruise I promised."

"I'd love that." She finally tore her gaze from the water view and glanced around at his humble bachelor pad. "This is really nice, Ken. How long have you lived here?"

"Five years. I moved in right after…" His divorce. "When I was single again."

She eyed him with the curiosity of a woman who couldn't hide her interest in his ex, then suddenly shook her head as if talking herself out of it. "Would you mind showing me around and letting me"—she gestured toward herself—"wash off the flood?"

As much as he wanted to steer her right to his bedroom in the back of the house, he took her to the one he'd set up as a guest room, which also had a small bathroom with a shower.

"Thanks," she said, tossing her bag on the double bed. "I have some calls to return, too, so I might be a while."

Of course she wanted time alone, and a chance to get used to the place. "Sure. I'm going to shower, too, and run over to the station and pick up Sally. You can just chill and get comfortable. Are you hungry? I can make lunch when I get back."

She sighed. "I'm *always* hungry," she admitted.

"Then you're at the right place, because I love to eat. And cook. Is there anything you can't have?" His gaze dropped automatically to her stomach.

"I'm trying to eat healthy. No alcohol, obviously."

"Anything you crave?"

She narrowed her eyes at him, and he could have sworn he saw a little spark in them, and a hint of color rose to her cheeks. "Not yet, but I'll let you know when you have to make a run for pickles and ice cream."

He smiled and took a step closer, his whole body

humming with a sense of anticipation and optimism. He had so much hope that this could work out really, really well. "It's going to be okay, Beth," he said, working to temper that enthusiasm, because he knew it scared the daylights out of her.

"Oh, I know. The house will dry."

He just stared at her. "I don't mean the house."

"I know. But I can't be sure anything is going to be okay until it is." She touched her stomach. "When I fell this morning, it scared me."

It scared him, too. "What did the doctor say?"

"Nothing to worry about. I should let her know if there's any pain, and I promise there hasn't been so much as a twinge. I hate feeling fragile." She brushed her hair back like she could push the admission away. "Pregnancy doesn't make a woman breakable, but after last time and knowing that my tubes being tied puts my baby at some risk, I'm skittish."

Her baby. He decided not to correct her. "You should be skittish, and careful. That's why I want you here."

She backed out away a few inches, silent.

"Which doesn't mean I'm going to watch you like some kind of science experiment that could go awry at any second," he added.

"I appreciate that, and that you care."

"I do."

"Because there's a baby," she said. "You care about me because there's a baby involved."

It was like she was trying to convince herself of that. "You don't know that."

"But I do. I was thinking about it driving over here. It's all very romantic, and the betting at the station is cute, but let's be real here." She angled her head and gave him a look that said she most certainly did know that. "We had a *one-night stand*."

"It was your call to end it at one night," he replied softly.

"It was good sex and…fun," she finished.

"It was great sex, and we blew past fun in the first five minutes."

"And then the impossible happened."

"Clearly, nothing is impossible with…" Damn it, he almost said *love*. "Us."

"I'm just not ready to make this out as the greatest romance of all time."

He honestly didn't think he was doing that, but why did it bother her so much? "Because you won't ever feel that way about me?" he asked.

She smiled. "Blunt, as usual."

"Why dance around it? I want to know."

She turned away, deliberately setting her attention to opening the tote bag. "Let me shower."

He didn't budge. "Beth."

"I'm sweaty and—"

"Answer me."

She thought for a minute, quiet. Then, "This"—she gestured from her to him and back—"is built on a faulty premise. You can't get serious about someone because there's a baby. Like I said, you don't care about me, you care about the baby inside of me."

"I care about both." Why did she stomp all over his optimism? Didn't she need a dose of that as much as he did? Frustration zinged up his spine.

"But what if something happened to the baby?" she asked. "Then what?"

He opened his mouth, but nothing came out. Because nothing was going to happen to that baby. But if it did, then what?

"Exactly," she said. With a solid hand on his chest, she moved him away. "I need some time and space."

He stood firm for a moment, then backed away. "Take all the time and space you need." Because when she didn't want them anymore, he'd be waiting.

Chapter Eleven

Beth fell in love with the dock the minute she set foot on the first plank. It was wide and worn, bathed in sunshine, and clearly the center of Ken's otherwise ordinary home. He'd spent money and time down here, and the minute she slid into an oversize Adirondack chair that looked out over the water, she wanted to stay right where she was.

And she had stayed all afternoon since they had lunch. Ken had puttered around with his boat, let her try her hand at fishing, and all the while, Sally slept by her side in the sunshine, utterly relaxed.

And Beth felt just about the same way, watching a few boats pass, catching glimpses of a dolphin leaping out of the water and the ripple of a giant manatee cruising by. The air was clean with a gentle brine on the breeze, the only sound the splash of a pelican hitting the water and the clanging of a sail mast a few docks away.

She thought about RJ, but didn't share his news with Ken, since it wasn't hers to share, and the fact that they *weren't* talking about babies and futures was kind of lovely right at that moment.

By late afternoon, the sun had dipped behind the house,

leaving the sky a hundred shades of peach and pink and the water an inviting silvery blue as Ken cranked the lift to lower the boat into the water for their cruise.

Then Beth's utterly Zen moment was ruined by the buzz of her cell phone on the table next to her.

Out here, work and phones seemed all wrong. And this text in particular jarred her as she read the request from Dad to attend an "important meeting about the future" at his office tomorrow.

"Oh boy," she murmured.

"What is it?" Ken asked.

"My dad has issued an official summons."

The boat hit the water with a soft splash. "About what?"

"I have no idea."

"It's probably because Josie told him I was at your house the other day," he said calmly.

"Most likely," she said, putting the phone back on the table to take a sip of lemon water. "And he might be calling me in to issue another warning."

He froze in the act of wrapping a tie around one of the dock posts. "What do you mean 'another warning'?" His voice was wary. "About what?"

"You," she said simply. "We were seen leaving the resort together the morning after the reunion, and that got reported to my father and stepmother."

He snorted. "Welcome to Mimosa Key."

"He came over that night and brought up, you know…what happened with your dad."

"You mean my dad's death." His voice grew tight. "No euphemisms. We know what happened. So what did he say?"

"Just that I should…" She turned and squinted into the setting sun. Maybe talking about babies and the future would be easier that way. "Be careful with you."

He stood straight and glared down at her. "What the hell does he think I'm going to do? Hurt you because he hurt me?"

"He was being a father, Ken. My father, in particular, who likes to control things." She looked up at him. "And by things, I mean me. There's a reason I cling to independence, you know."

He huffed out a breath. "Well, you can tell him you're fine. I won't hurt you, and I won't dredge up the past. Was that all?"

"He, uh, gave me some paperwork. About…the accident." Which, up to this moment, she'd forgotten she had.

"Paperwork."

"I didn't open the envelope. I wasn't interested. I stuck it with some old business files. Look, I accepted your apology for how and why you broke up with me all those years ago, and I don't see any reason to dwell on it now." Obviously, a time would come when Ken and her father would come face-to-face again, brought together by the baby growing inside her.

When that time came, she'd deal with it.

"Maybe you should read those papers," he said.

"Why?"

"You'll see that your father had every base covered. He proved the straps holding the generator had been inspected. We had no grounds for legal retribution, then or now. If he's worried about that, he can relax." He finally met her gaze. "My opinion, however, will never change. I was standing there, Beth. I saw the strap break. I saw it happen."

His voice cracked just enough that her heart did the same thing. "Ken, I'm sorry."

She saw him visibly shake it off, returning his attention to the boat. "So what are you going to tell him?"

"I don't know. I guess I'll see what he says. I'm definitely not ready to share the baby news. I'm not out of my first trimester yet and haven't heard a heartbeat. I have to be sure this pregnancy is viable. I have to be."

He stepped onto the boat, making the vessel rock. "I'll go with you to the meeting if you want."

Her jaw loosened. "Ken. I know you…no. You can't do that. You can't go to EDC offices. I would never put you through that."

"I'm going to have to see him sometime," he said. "When the baby's born, birthday parties, family…things."

How was that all going to work? She put her hand on her stomach, no answers in sight. Except that whatever happened and however it worked, it had to be good for the baby.

"Well, let's wait on that. His message had a distinctly businesslike tone. He may want to talk about something other than us…or you. In fact, that's far more likely, knowing my dad. He'll slip the insidious instructions on how I should live my life in after he asks my opinion on something or tries to convince me to take over the business again."

His head snapped up. "You wouldn't."

His sharp tone and the dangerous look in his eyes surprised her. "I…wasn't planning to." But she bristled at his reaction. "But if I wanted to, I would."

"Beth, I have my limits."

"What the hell does that mean?"

He threw a tool on the deck with a thud. "It means you can't run the company that…you can't run that company."

Was he serious? "You can't tell me not to do that."

"Do you want to?" It sounded as if even asking the question scared him, as if he couldn't handle the answer.

"I haven't wanted to because I happen to love what I do for a living." She looked down and tugged at a loose thread on her cutoffs. "But things have changed."

"No shit."

She looked hard at him. "I have to consider this child's security," she said. "EDC is a good, healthy business that guarantees a substantial and steady income."

She could see his shoulders tense and his jaw tighten. "I have a steady income," he said. "Maybe it's not as great as the owner of a big development corporation, but I can provide for our child."

"But…I…" She exhaled. "I can't depend on that."

"Why the hell not?"

"Because this isn't a normal relationship, Ken. There are no guarantees. There's no way to know what could happen in the future. I have to be sure my child has everything she needs."

He cringed, more likely at the sentiment than the gender, angrily scooping up the tools he'd been using.

"So you think a firefighter can't provide for a child in the manner you're used to?"

"I haven't thought about it," she said, hoping the honesty in that came through. "I'm still figuring out how we might make this work, not our finances. But, yes, I've thought about my future now that I'm not alone."

He moved a seat cushion on the boat and lifted the bench below it to store the tools. "Because I can and I will take care of our child."

"I think it makes sense to consider all my options."

"Running EDC is not one of them."

Resentment punched her hard enough to make her stand. "Please don't tell me what to do."

He turned to face her, blinking at her tone. "I just mean—"

She pointed at him. "Don't tell me what to do," she repeated.

For a long moment, they stared each other down, the sun as hot as the silent clash of wills, bearing down on them. Finally, Ken sighed and brushed his hand over his hair. "How about I *suggest* we take a boat ride now?"

Sally pushed up with interest immediately. Her stub of a tail ticktocked rhythmically, and she gave one noisy bark.

"Those are her two favorite words." Ken laughed. "Boat ride."

But Beth stayed right where she was on the dock, frozen after the conversation.

Ken held out his hand to help her on board the boat. "Come on. It'll lower your blood pressure."

"You know…" She turned, fighting the urge to take a stand by saying no, making him go alone, and punishing him for saying the very things he knew would raise that blood pressure.

Things that made her face the fact that this baby tied them together in a way that he actually *did* have a right to hold an opinion about how she lived her life.

He still hadn't lowered his hand. "Man, you're thinking hard."

She sighed and closed her fingers around his. "I thought I had it all figured out, this life of mine. And now…everything's changed."

He guided her onto the boat deck, holding her hand as she got her footing. "That's how life is," he said, turning from her to grab Sally by the belly and hoist her girth onto the boat with a grunt. He placed her on the deck easily, bending over to scratch her head. "There you go, Chunky Monkey."

Beth watched the exchange, aware of the soft sigh she let out, making Ken look up at her.

"What is it?" he asked.

"You're going to be a good father."

He straightened, smiling. "I'm going to be exactly like my dad, the best father in the world."

Her heart hitched again, and a surprising sting burned behind her eyes. "Oh, Kenny."

"Only you," he joked softly, taking a step closer, making the boat rock. He reached over to touch her face, to graze his knuckles along her jaw, silent. "Can get away with that nickname."

"What are we going to do?" she whispered.

"We're going to talk things through and get to know everything about each other. And we're going to make joint decisions when they affect our child. We're going to work on your house together, keep you safe and healthy, and then we're going to have a baby."

She waited for another stab of resentment, ready to react at his list of things *they* were going to do. Except, there was no resentment. Because he was right.

She closed her hand over his, turning to press a kiss on his palm. "I'm sorry I jumped down your throat," she said.

"I'm sorry I tried to run your life."

She smiled up at him. "You make everything sound easy, you know that?"

"What do I keep telling you? Nothing is impossible. That's going to be our motto, baby. Nothing is impossible."

He stepped closer, lowered his head, and kissed her. The boat rocked again, but Beth held on, stayed steady, and kissed him right back. The kiss felt solid and sure, despite the way the world and water swayed under her feet. His lips were warm, his hands strong, and at that moment, Beth started to believe that maybe nothing *was* impossible.

Chapter Twelve

Beth woke to an empty house, sensing even before she was fully awake that Ken and Sally had left already. She turned in the double bed, waiting for her first morning thought.

I'm pregnant.

And another thought, which made her smile. Nothing is impossible.

What do you know? They had a motto.

The sunset cruise had been a visual overload of the beauty of southwest Florida on a warm May night. By mutual agreement, they avoided land-mine subjects and talked very little, the sound of the engine and the rock of the waves lulling their problems away for a few hours.

It had been dark by the time they got back, and she could tell Ken was exhausted, and facing a twenty-four-hour shift that started—she glanced at the clock at her bedside—half an hour ago. She'd slept in the guest room, and she appreciated that he didn't even suggest otherwise. And now he'd be gone until this time tomorrow, which gave Beth a full day of the time and space she swore she craved.

But, damn it, she missed him already.

And based on the sweet note he left next to the

coffeemaker, with a K-Cup of decaf coffee and a clean mug waiting for her, he'd miss her, too, and promised to call or text. Holding the note, her gaze drifted out to the blue morning water, taking in the sunrise that seemed to hold more promise and hope than anything she'd ever seen.

Could it be that easy? Could they start a life together…backward?

She touched her belly and whispered their motto, saying a silent prayer that he was right. She was nearly eight weeks now. Four more and she'd be home free.

Although, she'd been almost fourteen weeks the last time.

She closed her eyes and tried to push the memory away, not wanting to think about the stab of pain, the blood, the broken sensation of utter loss…and the decision that had followed.

She put her hand on the counter, bracing herself as the unwanted memories flooded back, frightening her with the possibility that history—and her stupid incompetent uterus—could repeat itself.

And every minute that passed with Ken Cavanaugh, that possible loss would hurt even more. She really enjoyed being with him, but she knew that the only reason she was in this house was because of the baby inside of her.

What would happen after this child was born?

What would happen if it wasn't?

On a sigh, she shook off the what-ifs, took a shower, and forced herself to think about the day ahead, which would include the meeting at EDC. Would Landon be there? Would Josie? She suddenly realized she had zilch in her tote bag that was suitable to wear for a meeting at the corporate offices.

So, on her way to her father's office, Beth took a detour to check on her house and change.

Inside, the rooms were cool and as noisy as an airfield,

with the seven industrial fans the water damage guys had left running in the dining room and kitchen. Everything appeared to be dry, but wrecked.

The kitchen, in particular, hung in that horrendous state of half demo, most of the cabinets gone and the holes under missing countertops gaping and dark.

All she wanted to do was finish and sell.

Yet, here she was, dressing for a serious meeting that might mean taking over a serious company and running some serious business. And she'd told Ken the truth about it last night: As much as she wanted that kind of stability and security for her child's future, running a multimillion-dollar, many-faceted business didn't hold as much appeal as ripping a house down to its studs and starting over. She even liked buying and selling property. But the heavy business end? The big developments, the financial wrangling, any non-residential real estate was not her cup of tea at all.

She walked down the hall to her bedroom, frowning at the sight of the open door. She never closed the door normally, but the water damage guys had recommended she close every door inside the house to facilitate the drying out, so she'd shut the door to the second bedroom and the office and the hall bathroom.

And her room.

But it was open, and the other doors were closed.

She had been the last person to leave the house yesterday; she was certain. Or was she certain?

She'd been certain about the water valve, too, so maybe she had pregnancy brain.

Walking slowly and trying to ignore the slight chill that raised the hair on the back of her neck, she stepped into her bedroom and sucked in a breath at the sight of the sheer curtain fluttering.

She rushed to the sliding door and swore softly when she found it unlocked and open an inch. Had she left it that way? It had been a crazy morning with all those firefighters traipsing around. Yes, she could have stupidly left it that way and left her bedroom door open even though she distinctly remembered walking down the hall to close it.

Had she checked the slider then? She pressed her fingers to her temple and cursed softly. The pregnancy hormones were attacking her brain. That was the only explanation.

But if she had closed and locked the slider…then someone had been in this house after she'd left.

Her heart thumped as she turned slowly to examine the room, which looked utterly untouched. No drawers open, the jewelry box on her dresser still closed and, under examination, still holding the few pieces of good jewelry she owned.

Biting her lip with a little trepidation, she whipped open the closet, half expecting to find a dead body in there.

Nothing but her clothes, shoes, and, way up on the top shelf, her storage boxes. But… "Wait a second."

She flipped on the light and stared at the shelf that held three clear plastic bins of important papers she didn't want to keep in storage somewhere.

Something was different.

They were stacked…in the wrong order.

She peered at the bins, a crystal-clear memory of the last time she'd had them down. A month ago, maybe, after getting some bank paperwork. But she'd glanced at them a hundred times and could have sworn—would have sworn—they were in a different order.

She distinctly remembered bringing the storage bins down, because the step stool had been wobbly and she almost fell getting them, but she wasn't sure which bin held work stuff and which held personal.

Would someone actually break into her house and rifle through her papers and photos and…what else was in there? Closing documents on this house, a divorce decree, and….she gasped softly.

The paperwork on John Cavanaugh's fatal accident on EDC property.

Her heart flipped. Would someone be looking for that? Why? Who?

Who would even know it was there? Her heart turned over again, but this time, it fell into her stomach with a thud.

Ken. He knew she had the paperwork. She'd told him about it yesterday, and he….

"No, he didn't," she said out loud, trying desperately to talk her brain out of the direction it was going.

But who else could it be? Who else knew exactly how to get in and out of this house? The firefighters who had been here? Could they have moved the bins?

No, they hadn't been in her closet. But Ken? She hated that the thought even planted itself in her head.

She marched to the garage, got the step stool, and brought it back to the closet, carefully climbing up. She held on to the clothes and, this time, to be safe, brought one bin down at a time. Only one was particularly heavy, but she very gingerly leaned it against her clothes and had them all on her bedroom floor in less than a minute.

All the while, she was thinking about that white envelope her dad had given her. If it was unsealed, or missing, then she had a problem. A big, fat problem.

With shaky hands, she snapped off the plastic lid and right on top was the envelope, as she'd put it in this bin nearly two months ago.

A punch of relief hit her. At least no one had taken it. But had they opened it? Read it? She remembered the seal; she'd run her fingers along the flap before she'd tossed the packet aside to be filed.

Very slowly, she lifted the envelope, which wasn't that thick. Please be sealed, she thought. Please be sealed.

It was taped closed.

"What?" She stared at the tape, shaking her head. Had it been taped before? Or had it been sealed? She squeezed her eyes shut, trying to remember. Once again, pregnancy could be blamed for her less-than-stellar memory.

Turning, she gazed at her desk in the corner, seeing her tape dispenser right where it always was.

But she could have sworn…

No, she couldn't swear to anything. It was lunacy to think someone broke in here, opened this envelope, and read its contents—because it was just about the same weight as when her dad gave it to her, so nothing was taken. She hoped. She wondered.

She let out a noisy breath, rocking back on her heels. This was crazy. She could have easily put those bins back up there in the wrong order.

The envelope was still here, and it had probably always been taped, and she didn't have a big, fat problem.

Except, the first person she'd mentally accused was the one person she needed to trust most in the world.

So maybe she did have a big, fat problem after all.

By ten o'clock, it was clear that today would be merciless. Two callouts already and he was down a man until eleven a.m. Ken barely had time to suck down some coffee and review a report log in between a kitchen fire and an old man with chest pains.

He'd sat down to concentrate when Pookie waltzed in and gave a treat to Sally.

"Is that all you wanted?" he asked. "Does Chief Banfield need something?"

"Chief Banfield needs a vacation." She dropped into the guest chair uninvited. "And he could probably use a little smashup from Mrs. Banfield, if you catch my drift."

Ken looked up at her. "Your drift is so highly unprofessional, it hurts."

"Pah!" She flicked her hand at him. "Speaking of smashups…" She lifted a graying brow. "How's Beth?" she asked in a singsong voice.

"You know, I really think you're a thirteen-year-old boy trapped in a middle-aged woman's body."

"Oh, honey, I'm past the middle and into the final quarter. So, why should I bother with professionalism? You don't look happy enough to have gotten laid last night, but I could be wrong."

"You could be."

She crossed her arms and stared at him. "Soooo?" She drew the question out. "How serious is it?"

"I'm not helping you win that bet."

She leaned forward. "Hon, you know you're my favorite."

"Moonshine said you told him the same thing."

"He's too much of a redneck for me, to be honest, though he's sweet and single. When you're no longer single, he'll be my favorite."

He had to laugh and abandon any hope of finishing the email he was trying to write. "You'll give up any chance of our finally being together, then?"

"Reluctantly. Plus, there is Fred, my sadly still alive husband." She cracked a ravaged knuckle that looked like it had been on the receiving end of that action for many years. "But you could be my third, if we knock him off."

"I'll put it on my to-do list." He narrowed his eyes. "Which is long. If you're done flirting with me and prying into my personal life, Pooks, I need to get back to work."

"Almost done. I have one more question—"

The alarm screamed, silencing her.

"Station one-six, engine five-five, squad two, respond to an accident with injury. In the intersection of Colonial Boulevard and Fowler Street. Map number 18-41. Time out, ten-o-six."

"I'm going." He was up in a flash and around his desk, his ears tuned for any more information from dispatch.

"Bystander reports victim is female, conscious, still in vehicle, and pregnant."

He stumbled as the word hit, and swore under his breath.

Aware that Pookie stayed by his side, he bounded to join his crew as they turned the corner to meet at the rig.

"What was your question?" he asked before Pookie slipped away to the chief's office.

"Never mind. You just answered it."

He forgot about the conversation before he had his gear scooped up and thrown into the rig. They'd need to dress for an extraction, but dispatch hadn't said it would be anything but an MVA with injury.

They'd beat the ambulance by at least three minutes, which could mean life or death for the victim…or the unborn child.

The rig blew out, full siren, before he even had his seat belt on.

His whole being hummed. It always did on every call, but

the words victim is pregnant sucker-punched his chest like they never had before. He shook it off and grabbed the radio mic to deliver a departure time and get more information from dispatch.

"Victim is conscious and speaking," the dispatcher said. "There's a state trooper on the scene who reports that the victim is still in the vehicle, airbag damage."

To her baby. He squeezed his eyes shut, only able to see Beth behind the wheel of her Ford Explorer. No, he couldn't go there. He, along with two of the men in this rig, were EMT2 certified. He had to think about this woman and this baby, not his woman and his baby.

Irish took a wide turn fast, shaving precious seconds off their arrival time, as the radio crackled with more information.

"Trooper reports that the vehicle was hit on the driver's side, traveling south on Fowler." He processed that, pictured the intersection. "Two cars involved, second driver and passenger not injured."

Just the pregnant woman.

"Victim is hemorrhaging… Lee Memorial ER has been alerted."

About fifty feet ahead, he saw a bottleneck, with someone in a red van refusing to move to let a compact car get out of their way. The screaming siren apparently meant nothing to that jerk.

"Come on, come on." Ken tensed and growled out the words under his breath as their speed slowed and Irish navigated around a bus that had pulled over. "Get the fuck out of the way, asshole."

Irish threw him a look. "I got this, Captain."

Damn it, he never showed emotion on the job. Never. It wasn't even in his DNA.

But now that that DNA had created another human being? He felt…different.

Irish blew past the van, whipped onto Colonial, and had them on the scene in seconds. Ken snapped on latex gloves and leaped out of the cab, two men close behind, already knowing he was going in as the lead medic until the EMTs arrived.

He approached the vehicle, which was totaled, as the state trooper stepped aside to let Ken reach the victim.

He took a deep breath and looked at the bloodless, wrecked face of a woman he already knew was losing her baby.

If only he could save that baby…if only nothing really *was* impossible. But he knew better. Every single day in this job, he knew better.

Chapter Thirteen

The mood in the Endicott Development offices was tense. Beth didn't get the usual bright smile from Jenny at the front desk, and no happy music played from her desktop speakers. In the back offices, most of the doors were closed, including her father's.

Beth checked her watch, confirmed that she was on time, and turned the corner toward the conference room, nearly slamming into her stepbrother, Landon.

"Whoa there, sis," he joked as they narrowly avoided a collision. "Are you that anxious to get to the meeting?"

"You're here for the same meeting?" she asked. Then it couldn't be about Ken or a twenty-five-year-old accident, she realized with a surprising amount of relief.

She greeted him with a quick hug, seeing a spark of humor in his hazel eyes and…something else. A pull and a tug. Maybe a few hair plugs in his thinning, but still dark, hair. Always striving, that was Landon.

"Looks that way," Landon said.

"Anyone else?" she said.

He shrugged. "Not sure. He's behind closed doors, and everyone seems to be breathing doom and gloom around here."

"I noticed that," she said, following when he gestured toward the still-empty conference room where she and Landon would no doubt engage in the only kind of conversation they ever had: small talk.

"So how are you?" she asked, already digging for something in common to talk about.

"Busy." He was always busy. Landon ran a small investment firm over in Naples. He had four kids and was a soccer coach, Cub Scout den leader, and first in line for every recital. He collected old cars, golfed regularly, traveled extensively, and showered his wife, Rebecca, with nice jewelry and newly renovated rooms in their giant house on the mainland.

All in all, he had an ideal life and, honestly, Beth wasn't entirely sure why he'd want to take over Endicott Development, but he'd made plenty of noise about it.

"How's Rebecca doing?" Beth asked as she slid into a chair along the side of a long, mahogany table and he headed to the coffee bar in the back of the room.

"Oh, you know Rebecca."

Actually, she didn't. Like Landon, Rebecca was always a little distant and cool, like a woman wrapped in cellophane who you could see but not touch. "Busy with the kids?"

"Always," he agreed. "She said she was going to call you, actually, because she wants to completely redo our master bathroom and thought you might have some ideas."

The suggestion surprised her, but she liked being able to help family. "Of course, but I'm swamped with my own renovation nightmare right now."

"I heard." He turned from the coffeepot and placed a cup in front of her. "Black, right?"

"Actually, I'm off coffee at the moment."

He lifted a brow, but the exchange was interrupted by the

slam of a door. “Jennifer!” Josie’s voice echoed in the hallway. “Someone call 911! Ray is having a heart attack!”

Landon and Beth exchanged a quick look before they both shot out of their seats and darted into the hall.

“You call 911, and you will lose your job!” Dad hollered over the commotion of several people running in the same direction. “I am not having a heart attack.”

Landon and Beth reached Dad’s office at the same time, but Landon pushed in first. “What’s going on?” he demanded.

“Your father is having a heart attack.”

“I am not...” Dad ground out a few more words Beth couldn’t understand, but the anger underneath them nearly made her stumble.

“Dad, are you okay?”

He was standing behind his desk, the same crisp, white, long-sleeve button-down he wore to work every day. This one looked a little too large on him now, and he flicked at the collar as though he expected it to be tighter.

“I’m fine,” he shot back, but his attention was on Josie. “And I’ll have you remember that.”

She bristled, smoothing her hair. “I don’t like the way you look, Ray,” she said. “You’re pale and you were clutching your chest.”

“I was not clutching my chest, and if shoving me in the hospital again is your way of controlling this situation, it won’t work.”

“I’m only trying to help,” she said softly, her voice cracking. Immediately, Landon was next to her, putting a comforting arm around his mother’s shoulders.

“Should I call 911?” Jenny asked tentatively from the door. Behind her, three more EDC employees watched with concern.

"Absolutely not," Dad said. "Josie is overreacting, and we just need to be left alone."

Two of them backed away, but his admin stayed and gave a questioning look to Josie, as if waiting for the real order.

"Not yet," Josie said.

"How about a glass of water?" Beth suggested to Jenny, getting a nod from the other woman before leaving and taking the others with her. Wordlessly, Beth closed the door and turned to the scene. "What's going on?" she asked.

"My wife is trying to stop me from sharing my retirement decision, and when I scratched my chest, coughed, and inhaled a little too deeply, she was ready to schedule open-heart surgery."

Josie sniffed at that, crossing her arms. "I'm not trying to stop anything. You know I want you to retire. Believe it or not, I love you, Ray, so sue me if I'm overreacting. You were very pale for a moment."

"Dad, seriously, don't play it tough if you don't feel well," Beth said, coming closer to his desk. "How about you call the cardiologist to be on the safe side?"

He closed his eyes. "I have an appointment in three days. Beth, Landon, can you sit down? I've reached a decision."

"One I think has true merit," Josie added.

Beth took one of the guest chairs in front of his desk, and Landon sat next to his mother on the sofa. Finally, Dad dropped back into his plush leather chair and took a slow breath.

"I've decided to give you each part of the company to run."

Beth's jaw actually fell open. "You've decided?" An age-old resentment prickled, making her sit up straighter. "Without discussing the details first?"

"This is the best way to go for the future of EDC," Dad continued, as if she hadn't spoken.

When would he stop trying to run her life? She was forty years old. She opened her mouth to argue, but Landon interrupted her.

"How are you dividing it?" he asked, as if the whole thing were a done deal.

"Business and financial holdings to you. Real estate and development to Beth." Dad turned back to her. "It's not the whole company, Beth, which I know seemed daunting to you."

Not exactly what she'd said, but she let it go and tried to process what was unfolding.

He went on, "Real estate and development is the part of the business you do so well. I think it's a good compromise."

She geared up to argue, then something silenced her. She didn't have only herself to think of. What he was asking was a lot of work for a single mother. But it was also a lot of security for a child.

Beth shifted in her seat, still silent.

"How will that work, exactly?" Landon asked. "The two parts of the business are so interconnected."

"That's what I want you two to figure out," Dad said. "I want you to pound out a strategic plan and explain exactly how you'd handle your end of the business and present it to me in two weeks."

Beth inched back. "Dad, I need to think about whether or not I even want to do this." Like it or not, she needed to talk to Ken.

He gave her a hard look. "Beth, do you want a multimillion-dollar company to run, with the income that goes along with it, or do you want to flip houses for sixty grand every six or nine months?"

Two months ago, she'd have stood up, smiled politely, and left. She wanted to control her life, not have him—and by extension, Josie—in charge of her business decisions. But now? An income like he was talking about was important for her child. A family-owned business was child-friendly, too. There were many benefits, even ones Dad didn't know about yet.

"And," Dad leaned forward, looking at Josie, "I'm keeping control of commercial development."

"What?" Landon practically launched off the sofa. "That's not retiring."

"Precisely!" Josie said, slapping her hands on the leather. "But he won't listen to me."

"That way I still get to come into the office a few days a week," Dad said. "And I don't have to look for a room in a nursing home quite yet."

Josie tsked noisily. "I want to travel and enjoy these years, Raymond." Her voice rose with genuine emotion, along with her color, as she leaned forward. "I don't know how much longer I'll have you."

Dad grunted and looked toward the ceiling. "I am so sick of this…this obituary writing."

"Well, I for one hate the idea," Landon said, getting all their attention. "Finance and the business end is part of both commercial development and residential real estate. I'd end up answering to both of you. No, thank you."

Josie gave Dad a giant-eyed *I told you so* look.

"Then Beth can take it all," Dad shot back.

"Whoa, whoa." Beth held up her hands. "I'm not sure I want any of this, Dad, let alone all of it."

"You'll come around," her father said, his cockiness rankling her.

"What about RJ?" she asked pointedly.

"RJ?" Her father shook his head. "He's not in the picture."

"Why not?" she demanded. "He could do commercial development."

Landon snorted. "Beth, come on."

"Yes, Beth, come on," her father agreed.

"He's done commercial work." Her natural tendency to defend her little brother rose, their recent conversation still fresh in her mind. "That Van Nuys deal was awesome."

Dad angled his head at her. "Honey, I flew a crop duster once when I was fifteen, but that doesn't mean I could pilot a 747 over the Atlantic Ocean. RJ doesn't have the skill set we need, and you know it. I'll take care of him financially. RJ and I have a deal, so you don't have to worry about him."

But she did worry about him, and a "deal with Dad" was not what he needed right now. But this wasn't the time to get into that. "Well, I need to think about this and talk to…" She almost said Ken, but her voice trailed off. "Friends," she finished, standing up to end the conversation.

"There's not much to think about, Beth."

"There's plenty for *me* to think about." Landon shot up. "I have a thriving business and a growing family, so there's much for me to consider if I'm going to let my investment firm suffer while I try to cobble together a strategic plan for EDC's financial issues."

Beth tried not to give him a look, but really. Did he have to be such an arrogant ass? And did they both have to be so dismissive of RJ? Her brother had every right to be in on this conversation and decision.

"If you're done, Dad, I need to get back to work."

"Is Ken Cavanaugh still doing your demo?" Josie asked innocently.

Beth closed her eyes. "He's helping me, yes."

"Beth." Her father came around the desk, and she braced herself for another lecture about the problem of seeing Ken

Cavanaugh. Which she would have scoffed at yesterday…but that resealed envelope in her file bin still loomed over her. "Give up the house-flipping business," her father said, surprising her. "You can have so much security and a solid future at the helm of this company."

"A third of this company," Landon corrected.

But she just looked at her father, who didn't even know how weighty that advice really was. "Let me think about it, Dad," she said, leaning in to give him a hug. "And let me know what the cardiologist says, okay?"

"Pfft. Damn doctors."

She gave him a kiss on the cheek and said good-bye to the others, wishing her decision was clear and easy. It was anything but.

Chapter Fourteen

Ken's shift hadn't gotten one bit better. In fact, by the time he pulled into his driveway, he was gripping the steering wheel hard enough to break it.

In the past twenty-four hours, he'd battled a car fire, a kitchen blaze, seen two heart attack victims taken off in ambulances, and barely saved a nineteen-year-old who'd OD'd on painkillers.

And then there was Rhonda Orsini, who'd been doing nothing but driving to work—she was a nurse, he'd learned later—when some moron checked his phone and ran a red light.

Rhonda survived. Her twenty-week-old unborn baby had not.

He dragged a hand over his unshaven face and over his hair, trying to pull out the stress.

He tried to shake off the images of the accident, using years of training to remember what he did and why. He *couldn't* let it get personal. The shift had sucked balls, but it was over now, and ahead of him were four days—and nights—with Beth.

Law had left a message, asking to meet up for lunch over on Sanibel Island to check out another place he was thinking about buying, but Ken hadn't called him back with an answer. Because Ken had a completely different plan for how to spend this day.

No more boat rides and small talk. No more distractions and distance. And no more freaking separate bedrooms.

A quick shudder blasted him at the sight of the morning sun spilling its first light on Beth's Explorer parked in his driveway.

"Look at that, Sal. If that isn't the damn finest thing we've seen in the last day or, hell, year, I don't know what is."

Fat Sally couldn't be bothered to look, as she lay curled on the passenger seat next to him. He pulled into the garage, thinking about Beth asleep in bed.

And how he wanted to just climb in and join her.

His body stirred and tightened with every step. His jaw clenched, he entered the quiet house. He walked through the living room to the guest room. The door was open, but the bed was empty and made.

His room? Doubtful, but maybe. On the other side of the house, he stepped into the master to find it exactly as he'd left it. A fresh wave of frustration rolled through him.

Her car was here, so where was she?

He followed Sally when she barked, shifting his gaze to the dock.

Not as good as finding—and joining—her in bed, but he'd take it. He took a minute to check out the back of her head and her legs outstretched on another chair in front of her, a cup of tea or decaf, he assumed, on the armrest of the Adirondack chair.

Anticipation made his hands itch and his chest swell. And something else tugged at his gut, too. It felt a little like a pang of hunger that suddenly threatened starvation.

He needed her. Not just for sex, but for comfort. Assurance. Grounding.

Life.

And the pregnant, sexy, precious woman who sat on the dock was humming with everything he needed.

Sally made her way to the dock right before Ken did, barking in warning and making Beth startle as if she'd been lost in thought or even asleep.

She turned and slammed him with a smile that reached right down to his gut and twisted it into a knot. "Hey."

When he got to her chair, he couldn't help himself. He bent over and kissed her sweet hair. "Hi, honey, I'm home."

She laughed lightly and flipped her long legs down, freeing up the chair facing her. He sat down and looked at her for a moment, fighting the urge to do more.

Holy, holy shit, Beth Endicott was a beautiful woman. She wore a thin tank top with no bra, making the shadows of her nipples visible. It hung over flannel shorts that barely covered an inch of her thighs. Caramel hair spilled over her bare shoulders, and her eyes were exactly the color of the morning sky, only prettier.

"Morning is your hour, you know that?"

One brow twitched in question.

"You wake up gorgeous," he explained.

She gave in to another sweet smile. "Well, I'd love to return the compliment, but you look like you might collapse any second."

He leaned back and shook his head, running his hands over his whiskers again, regretting that he hadn't taken the time to shower or shave before he left the station. "That was the suckiest shift in ages. I don't think I slept a solid hour. It was nonstop crap out there."

"Did you save lives?" she asked, the slightest tease in her voice.

He closed his eyes. "Not every one."

"Oh." Her smile evaporated as she leaned forward. "I didn't mean to joke."

"S'okay."

"You want to tell me about it?"

He started to say no, but closed his eyes. Because if he looked at her too long, he'd be on his knees, begging to touch and hold her. "Not yet," he finally said, digging for a calm and normal conversation. "How was *your* twenty-four?"

"Good enough."

He eyed her suspiciously. "What did your father want to meet about?"

She swallowed visibly. "His plans for the company."

He leaned back, waiting, aware of a low-grade dread building.

"He wants to divide part of the company between Landon and me. And keep a bit for himself."

Dread was building for a good reason, but he reined in his response and vowed to tread carefully. "Is that what you want?"

"I don't know what I want. And I'm not happy about RJ being squeezed out, because..." She didn't finish the thought, but shook her head. "Because it's not fair to him. I don't know if I want to run even a third of a company that size, but I don't know if I can afford not to."

He studied her for a minute, following the train of thought as it slammed right into his pride. "I told you I do okay."

"This isn't about you," she replied. "Except..." She sighed softly. "I guess I can't make everything about me anymore."

He appreciated the concession and knew how hard it was for her to make. And, God, he was too tired to argue about this now.

His gaze dropped to her cup. "No chance that's coffee?"

"No caffeine for cupcake." She smiled. "I found some lemon herb tea."

Which probably expired three years ago, but he decided not to freak her out. He took a sip anyway, regarding her over the rim. "What do you think you're going to do?" he asked.

"I honestly don't know. If my dad were completely out of the picture, one hundred percent retired, could you handle the mother of your child being the head of a company you blame for your father's death?"

He studied her, first taking a moment to appreciate the straightforward question, then realizing that in some ways he was being stubborn and stupid. But he couldn't change how he felt about Ray and the company that bore his name.

"I don't know if I could handle it…well," he finally said.

"But you could handle it."

"I suppose I'd have to and, to be fair, I don't have a right to tell you where you can work or what you can do for a living. If that were the case, you could tell me to stop being a firefighter because I risk my life every day."

She nodded, as if she'd thought of that, but hadn't said it. His temples throbbed, and every inch of him wanted rest and peace and…her.

"Beth," he said softly. "Trust me when I tell you I had a really shitty shift and don't want to fight about this or even talk about it."

She angled her head, an expression of concern. "What happened?"

He gave a negative head shake. "How'd you sleep?"

"You know, new place. I missed…" She reached down and scratched Sally's head. "The dog."

He nudged her knee with his, the little bit of body contact

already warming his blood. "I missed you, too. A hell of a lot."

She leaned forward and surprised him by touching his knee. "Whatever it was, it was rough on you."

The words, the touch, the sympathy, and wholly unexpected understanding ripped right through him. This was what a man who did what he did needed. This woman, this tenderness.

"Tell me." She leaned back and lifted her bare feet to settle them on his thighs.

He closed his hand over her ankle and stroked her foot. "I don't want to...talk." No, he wanted to touch more. All. Everything. That's what he needed now, not conversation about darkness and death. "I have a better idea. Let's go into the house."

"I like it out here. It might be my new favorite place in the world."

"I have a better new favorite place for you." He slipped to the ground to kneel in front of her. "My bedroom."

She exhaled a soft laugh. "Blunt. You are so damn blunt."

"All right, I'll be subtle. Hey, Beth, why don't you come back to the house, because I'm going to take a shower? Which means I'll be naked. You can join me, and who knows what might happen?"

"That's subtle?"

"Okay, okay." He cleared his throat and leaned closer, letting his finger inch up her calf again, rounding her knee to tickle behind it. "Beth, it's been a tough twenty-four. I could use a...back rub. And a front rub."

"Better, but still not, you know, *seduction*."

"That's what you want? To be seduced?" He pulled her into him, spreading her legs, worming his way closer to her.

Her chest rose and fell as he slid his hands into her hair, then dragged his fingers over her throat, down her breastbone, and to her chest. He thumbed one nipple, the curve against his hand larger than the last time he'd caressed her, reminding him that she was pregnant.

She took a shuddering breath and lifted a little to offer him more of her body.

He leaned in close and let his lips brush hers. "I can't think about anything but you, Beth," he whispered into her mouth. "I want to be inside you again. I want to feel you come in my hands. I want to put my mouth on every inch of your body. I *need* you."

He kissed her and let their tongues touch, her nipple budding hard in his palm.

"Come to bed with me, baby." He kissed her harder, drawing her lower lip with his teeth before he broke the contact and looked into her eyes. "Bring me back from hell, Beth. And I promise you a little bit of heaven."

Very slowly, she pushed him back, her pupils dilated and dark now, telling him he was definitely having an effect. "Now *that* was a seduction."

He stood, letting his hands slide over every inch of her again, then tunnel into her hair as he tilted her face up to his. "If you want me, I'll be in the shower."

He left her on the dock, one hundred percent sure she'd follow. But this was Beth, and he had to let her make that decision herself.

Chapter Fifteen

If you want me. That was sarcasm, right? Because right then, trembling and turned on, Beth didn't think she'd ever wanted anything as much as she wanted Ken Cavanaugh.

She'd never seen him like that, she thought, closing her eyes to remember the bit of…desperation etched on his face and evident in his touch. Like he didn't want to go another minute without sex.

Which was exactly the way she felt.

But was feeling that enough to justify it? This was no commitment-free hookup at a high school reunion. Everything was different now. She was carrying his child. They were connected in a way that terrified her, that felt permanent but still so risky.

If you want me.

Her nipples burned. Her lower half melted. And her hands ached to touch every muscle on his body. *Every* one. That probably counted as "wanting" him.

Still, she stayed glued to the chair, her eyes on the water and the rising sun that turned the sky gold. What was stopping her?

The obvious, of course. What if something happened in the next four weeks—or eight months? Where would that leave a couple—a couple who'd severed their ties twice already because of the clouds that hung over them—if they attempted to build an entire, shaky relationship on a child they both wanted?

Having sex again would really complicate things, wouldn't it?

Or make her insanely happy, satisfied, and blissful. And him.

I need you.

That need had been stamped all over his face and made her ache with the desire to give him the comfort and escape he wanted.

So sex could be satisfying, blissful, comforting, and an escape. What the hell was she waiting for?

She pushed herself up to cross the dock and pad barefoot over the grass to the patio. With each step, her heart rate ratcheted up. The closer she got to the house, the more tense she became.

Inside, she could hear the shower running in the master bedroom, and that sound stole her breath and made her a tiny bit dizzy.

Could she do this?

She visualized the water sluicing over his hard body, wetting every muscle, falling onto the sweet curve of his backside and the mighty erection that no doubt hardened and grew in anticipation.

Could she *not* do this?

A few more steps toward the bedroom and she could practically smell the soap and feel his hands lathering her and taste lemon tea-flavored kisses as he toweled her off and took her to the bed.

And then she imagined the pain of it all if the worst happened.

He stepped out of the bathroom, stealing her breath as he looked exactly like she'd imagined. Naked, primal, ready, and soaked.

"You showered already."

"You took a long time."

Her gaze dropped over every inch of him, and fire licked up her body and down her back, lodging in her lower half, searing and softening everything.

"I can go back in if you want to shower with me."

"I'm…scared, Ken." The admission popped out without her thinking, because who could possibly think when faced with a semihard, naked god whose sizable chest rose and fell with his own strangled breaths?

But there it was—the truth. She was terrified.

He closed the space between them to wrap his arms around her. He pulled her into him, tight enough for her to feel his heart hammering in his chest and his erection like a ridge against her.

All she wanted to do was…*touch*.

"If it makes you feel any better, I'm scared, too," he said into her ear.

She closed her eyes, her body so heavy with need she had to lean against him. He didn't feel scared. He felt hard and ready and perfect. "A little better," she said. "What are you scared of?"

He tipped her face up. "The fact that I haven't even thought about another woman since the night we were together. I've wanted you and only you. I'd be lying if I didn't tell you that scares the crap out of me sometimes."

She searched his face, not answering, but always appreciating his candor.

"You're so worried about me dumping you if something happened to the baby," he said. "Well, guess what? I'm worried about you dumping me. It would *hurt*."

She tried to breathe, but the thought that she had that kind of power over his feelings took her breath away. "Well, once we do this, with a baby involved, then—"

"The baby can't get hurt." He spoke with the authority of someone with medical training. "But if you're worried—"

"No, not about that. My doctor said sex is fine."

"Then what? Why is it different?"

"Because we're connected now. There's a child."

A slow smile spread on his face, lighting his eyes. "I'm still trying to understand why that's a bad thing."

He just didn't get it. "How can you be so optimistic?"

"In my line of work? If I weren't, I'd kill myself."

"Something could happen to the baby," she said. "Not because we had sex, but because I'm still physically vulnerable." And emotionally, but she didn't add that.

"You think I'd disappear if something happened to this baby?" He stroked her back, pulling her closer, pressing kisses into her shoulder and neck.

"I…I don't know. I can't think when you do that," she admitted, purring as he nestled deeper. "It's so hard to say no to you." Her hands moved over him, finding muscles and flesh and hard curves of masculinity on his shoulders and back.

"Then don't." He moved some of her hair away and kissed her ear.

She almost melted as his breath tickled her down to her toes.

He dragged his hands up and down her waist, lifting her tank top slowly, but she inched back, denying him the chance to get it off.

"Wait." There was one more thing she needed to know. Absolutely had to know before she went one little bit further. "I have to ask you a question."

Maybe it was the warning in her voice, but he looked wary already. “Okay.”

“Have you, um, possibly been in my house since I left it?”

He frowned as if the question made no sense. “No. Was I supposed to be? Did you want me to go over and check on it?”

“No, no. I just…wondered if you had.”

“Why?”

“I thought maybe someone had been there while I’ve been gone because something was different than the way I thought I’d left it, but I could be completely wrong. There is such a thing as pregnancy brain, you know.”

He drew back, concern in his eyes. “Could it have been the water remediation team? My guys when they helped with the flood?”

“No, I don’t think they went back there.” She shook her head. “Never mind.”

“Never mind nothing. If someone was in your house and you didn’t know about it, that’s a big deal.”

She quieted him with a touch. “Nothing was stolen, nothing was missing. There were some storage bins in my closet that I file papers in that seemed to be different, and the sliding door was open partway. It was—”

“What’s in the files? Bank statements? Passwords? Your passport? Are you sure nothing was missing?”

She shook her head. “Nothing was missing.”

“Why would you think I would have…” She saw the wheels turning and turning, then click into place as realization registered on his face. An ugly, unwanted realization. “The papers your dad gave you. The stuff about my father’s death. That’s in those files, isn’t it?”

She looked at him without answering. But she didn’t have to.

He breathed out a curse and backed away.

"That's great, Beth," he barked. "You really thought I'd break into your place to get my hands on that? To do what? Blackmail you? Seek damages? Get back at your dad?"

He marched across the room, snagging a pair of boxers from the floor but she caught up to him before he got far. "Ken, don't—"

"I'm right, though, aren't I?"

"Yes, and I was wrong to even think it. Obviously, I imagined the whole thing, I'm sure."

"Then why did you ask me about it?"

"Because…I needed to know."

He closed his eyes, a whirlwind of emotions playing out on his face. "I want this to work so bad," he said, his voice gruff and trapped in his chest. "I thought that we're smart and good enough to do it. But this thing, this memory, this *fact of life* is always going to be between us."

She nodded slowly, vaguely aware that she put her hand on her stomach, that place where their baby grew and formed an incredibly tenuous bond between them.

"I…I'm going to Sanibel today," he said, all that lust channeling into frustration so palpable she could taste it. "I need some time and space. You know what that's like, right?"

All too well. Except, right now, she didn't want time or space without him in it.

But she didn't argue as he walked out of the room and left her standing there, all alone with her doubts and fears and uncertainties. She'd fed off his optimism, drank in his hope, and when it was gone, she felt so empty inside.

Chapter Sixteen

Beth was still trying to make sense of the roller coaster that was her morning while she drove to meet the water damage team at her house. When her cell phone rang, she felt her heart rate kick up with hope, like a car chugging to the top of the track before the next big drop. When she saw RJ's name on the caller ID, she thudded back down again.

On a sigh, she tapped the speaker and opened her mouth to answer, but RJ's voice cut off her greeting.

"Listen, Beth! Listen to this!"

She cocked her head toward the phone, listening to nothing. Well, a faint…swoosh.

And back she went for the next stomach-flipping loop on the roller-coaster ride.

"Did you hear it, Aunt Beth?"

Yeah, she did. She heard pure joy in the voice of a man who hadn't experienced a lot of it in his life. She simply couldn't deny him a second of it no matter how she felt about her current situation. "You have a heartbeat."

"And a gender." His voice cracked a little.

She beamed. "Are you sharing?"

"It's a girl."

"Oh, RJ." Her throat swelled with emotion. "I'm really happy for you. And I assume I get to meet Selina now that I've been called from the doctor's office."

"Yeah, we're going to work something out," he said, clearly distracted. "Give me a few days and we'll get together."

"Sounds good." She wondered if he'd heard anything from Dad or even Landon—though that was unlikely—about the company "split."

"Beth, can you believe it?" he exclaimed. "I'm going to be a father. It's the most amazing thing in the world."

"I know," she said, her own eyes filling at his unbridled joy. "I'm thrilled for you both. Have you told Dad yet?"

"I called the office, but Jennifer said he took a sick day."

"Really?" She thought about Josie's insistence that they call 911 yesterday, which, at the time, seemed a tad overdramatic. But could something be wrong?

"Yeah, he's probably home practicing his putting," RJ said. "I'd bet anything on it. Anyway, I don't have time now. We'll get around to telling him soon enough."

She couldn't blame him for the lack of enthusiasm. Who knew how Dad would react to the news? He'd always been so tough on RJ, so disappointed in him.

"Gotta go," her brother said.

He said good-bye just as Beth crossed the causeway and drove onto Mimosa Key, stopping at the four-way intersection. Impulsively, she swung left and headed toward Pleasure Pointe. It didn't take long to drive to the waterfront home Dad and Josie had built a few years ago. She pulled into the circular drive and immediately spotted Landon's Infiniti SUV parked there as well. Rebecca drove that car, and it came stocked with four kids, which meant Dad couldn't be too sick.

Josie opened the front door and greeted Beth with a tight

smile. "Hello, Beth," she said, standing right in the middle of the doorway, not inviting her in.

"I came to see Dad."

"Maybe another time. He's resting comfortably."

Just then, one of the boys went zooming by, screeching at a high pitch, followed by one of the twins, who screamed, "You're it, Cooper! You're it *now*!"

Beth gave Josie a look. "Not that comfortably."

Josie turned and let out a sigh, then stepped back. "Rebecca and I are up to our eyeballs planning the twins' birthday party here tomorrow."

Beth hadn't been invited. She didn't even know it was Capri and Catalina's birthday. "Oh, well, I want to say hey to Dad. I won't stay long," Beth said, following her stepmother over the creamy marble, past the elegant tufted furniture of the living room to the back of the house where Rebecca sat at an expansive coffee table covered with arts, crafts, and party favors.

"Oh, Beth, hi." She pushed up immediately, coming around the table. "Didn't expect to see you here today." Rebecca was, as always, dressed in country club chic, flawless makeup, shampoo-commercial black hair, and a flash of diamonds that let anyone who saw her know her economic status was in the top one percent.

"I just dropped in to see my dad for a second."

"Yes, but…" Rebecca grasped Beth's arm, eyes wide. "How are you?" There was always a tinge of sympathy in her tone when Rebecca talked to her, as though Beth couldn't actually be happy or fulfilled, not like Rebecca, happily married mother of four, was.

"I'm fine."

"I heard about the flood and the delay in that house you're working on."

"Good news travels fast," she said.

"Was it awful?" she asked, concerned.

"No, it could've been much worse. We'll be back on schedule soon. I heard you're—"

"Look, Mommy! Look!" One of the twins came tottering in on high heels, wearing a heavily bedazzled crown. "I'm the princess!"

"I am Princess Capri!" The other one, a mirror image, barreled in and tried to snag the crown. "Catalina! Stop!" Capri wailed.

The situation went south in seconds.

"I want that crown, Mommy!" Catalina screamed at deafening decibels.

Josie took Beth's hand and pulled her back. "Your father's outside."

"I'm right here!" Dad's voice boomed over the noise from the open French doors, and Beth turned to find him holding a putter, looking one hundred percent healthy. RJ had been dead-on about the putting practice, she mused.

"Dad. I heard you called in sick."

He shot a look over her shoulder at Josie. "My wife *thought* I wasn't feeling well, but as you can see, I'm great." He put a hand on her shoulder and led her out through the pool patio, taking her off to the side of the yard where he'd created a beautifully manicured putting green. "Let's get away from the mayhem."

"Party here tomorrow, I understand."

He blew out a sigh. "They're bringing in some kind of giant bouncy thing and at least twenty-five six-year-olds."

For a moment, she closed her eyes, trying to picture twenty-five six-year-olds in her yard...except she didn't even know where she'd be living when this child had a bouncy-house birthday party.

Yeah. She did need some security. But not on Dad's terms.

"That can't be good for anyone's health," she joked.

He laughed. "Thankfully, I just have to show up and pay the bill. I hope you're here with good news for me."

Maybe. Maybe not. "I really did stop by to make sure you're okay." She followed him to the putting green, inhaling the smell of fresh-cut grass as they walked.

"*Are* you okay?" she asked.

"Oh, I had a little, you know…incident."

She stopped short on the well-trimmed lawn. "What kind of incident?"

"Little dizzy spell, is all."

"Did you talk to the doctor?"

"I told you I'm seeing him soon." He got in front of a ball, lining up a shot. "So have you decided to agree to my plan?"

She crossed her arms and squinted into the afternoon sun. "I have a different plan."

He tapped the ball much too hard, puffing with disgust when it passed the hole. "I like my plan."

"Well, I like mine, and if you don't, my answer to yours is no." She shocked herself a little by the pronouncement, not having even fully articulated it to herself yet. But with the sound of her brother's exuberance still ringing in her ears, she knew what she had to do.

He looked up from his shot, waiting.

"Split the company three ways if you like, but give the commercial development to RJ."

He stared at her.

"He'll work hard, Dad."

He took the next putt then lifted his head and scowled at her. "Are we talking about the same RJ?"

"He wants to be given a chance. Landon is an investment pro. I love residential work, and it feels like something I could handle with a..." She stopped short of the word *baby* spilling out. "With no trouble," she finished. "But I think it's only fair that RJ get a piece of the business, too."

"No."

"Why not?" she demanded.

"Because he's not responsible enough for it," he said. "Because he'll run it into the ground. Because he's thirty-six going on seventeen. And there was the little part about me wanting to stay involved in the company."

Which was exactly what she didn't want. "You're wrong about RJ. I believe in him, Dad. He deserves a shot. He's your son, too."

He shook his head.

"He's not?" she asked with a choke.

"Of course he's my son." He leaned closer to her, glancing toward the house. "But it will put Josie over the edge, honey, to give a third to RJ."

What difference did it make to Josie? "It doesn't matter. He has a right to a piece of the company as much as I do. Or Landon." More, since RJ was blood, but she wouldn't go that route.

"I don't disagree completely," he admitted. "But Jo wants Landon to have it all. This would be a huge compromise. If I bring RJ in, a move I'm not fully certain is a good one, she'll go crazy. What should I do?"

She let out a soft laugh.

"What's funny?" he asked.

"Nothing, and everything. Honestly, I don't think in my entire life I recall you asking me for advice. You like to give advice, not take it."

He managed a smile. "Maybe I *am* sick."

"Nor do I ever recall you letting someone else call the shots, especially with regard to EDC. It's like Josie has some strange power over you."

He shrugged. "I love her," he said simply.

"Love usually makes you tell people what to do, not listen to them."

He sighed, nodding. "Then you'll understand why I say what I'm about to say even if you don't like it."

She stiffened. "Can't wait."

He switched the club to his other hand to lean on it and get a little closer to her. "You're still seeing Ken Cavanaugh, aren't you?"

Seeing? She managed not to snort or touch her stomach in a dead giveaway. "He's helping me with the flip."

Dad sighed. "Have you read those papers I left with you? About the Cavanaugh case?"

"Actually, no. I have no interest in them."

"Grandpa!" The two matching girls came running out, each wearing a glitter crown on platinum tresses. "We're both princesses!"

He dropped the putter and spread his arms to capture both of them. "So you are, and I'm your royal servant."

Suddenly, she wondered…would he love her daughter—or son—like that? Or would he look at her and always be reminded of a mistake he'd made and covered up years ago?

"Dad, listen, I need to—"

"Girls! Girls!" Rebecca marched outside, clapping like a preschool teacher with a rowdy class. "Grandma JoJo has cookies, and you have to leave Grandpa alone. He's not feeling well."

He shot her a harsh look. "I'm fine, Rebecca."

She shook her head. "Josie needs you inside, stat. Time for your meds, Grandpa." She managed to get the putter out of his hand and put it down as she walked back inside, leaving them.

Dad sighed and threw a wry smile to Beth. "See?" he said. "This is the life of an invalid."

"They love you, and you're not an invalid."

He harrumphed. "Feel like an invalid. Now, about those papers I gave you—"

"Wait, Dad. I have to ask you a question about them. Did you tape that envelope closed or was it sealed when you gave it to me?"

He frowned for a second, long enough for Beth's fists to tighten into balls. "So you *did* look at them?"

"Taped or sealed?" she asked.

"I taped it. I never lick envelopes."

She actually exhaled in relief. She had been imagining things.

"Beth, when you read them…" He put his hand on her shoulder. "Don't judge too harshly."

Oh God. *Was* he responsible for John Cavanaugh's death? She inched away from his touch, hating the thought.

"Raymond Endicott!" Josie's voice cut off the discussion, and Beth couldn't have been more grateful.

Chapter Seventeen

Ken powered his little Boston Whaler over crystal blue water to Sanibel, a barrier island not much different from Mimosa Key in size and scope, wishing like hell that Beth was with him instead of Sally. Well, in addition to Sally.

He docked in the public marina and leashed up Sally to come along on the errand, spying Law sitting on a bench near the wharf, barefoot, hat over his eyes, looking sound asleep.

"This is how you check out a possible place to buy?" Ken asked as he approached.

Law tipped the hat but didn't lift his head. "Is that a dog or a hairy beer keg?"

"This is Sally. Don't tease her about her weight. She's sensitive."

He sat all the way forward, then leaned over to greet Sally, who nuzzled and won him over with one look. "But she has a pretty face," Law joked.

"And a nice personality," Ken replied. "Plus, you said she'd be welcome in this place."

"Outside, definitely. It's right there." Law pointed to a stucco building with a yellow awning and a cheesy sign reading Lighthouse Landing. Outside were tables under umbrellas and a few dogs tied up with their lunching owners.

"So this restaurant is for sale?" Ken asked.

"He hasn't officially put it on the market yet, but we talked by phone and he's very close. At least this owner isn't a shell company with no person to talk to."

"It's a lot fancier than the Toasted Pelican," Ken said.

"But it *isn't* the Toasted Pelican," he replied. "It's like getting in bed with the wrong woman and pining for someone else. You ever do that?"

"Not today," he said, giving Sally's leash a tug. Today he didn't get into bed with *any* woman because he let his damn twenty-five year old grudges get in the way.

Law eyed him suspiciously as they walked. "So it's going well with the reunion babe?"

"Her name is Beth," he corrected. "And it's going okay."

They settled at a table under the awning alongside of the restaurant. While Law chatted up a waitress, who promised to bring out the owner, Ken checked his phone. Twice.

"So what does okay mean?" Law asked after she left. "A weekly booty call or a daily plow of the field?"

Ken snorted. "No wonder you're single."

Law shrugged. "So which is it?"

"We're still getting to know each other."

"My least favorite part of the process," Law said with a rueful smile. "Especially when you just really want to fuck and duck, you know?"

"You actually *are* a Neanderthal, aren't you?"

Law grinned as the waitress returned with a Heineken for Ken and the ubiquitous O'Doul's for Law. "Just calling it like I see it. But seriously, how's the chase treating you? You happy? Relaxed? Getting laid?"

"Is none of the above an option?"

Law almost choked on his drink. "You poor bastard."

Ken had to look away, scanning the docks. "I can't say I've ever been in a situation like this."

"Come on, she either wants you or she doesn't. It doesn't have to be complicated. If she does, she'll come around. If she doesn't, pull out your rod, add fresh bait, and stick it in new waters."

Ken laughed lightly. "I can't wait for the day when the right woman comes along and tames you."

He snorted. "Let her try. So why is this one complicated?"

Ken looked down at the beer and considered his response, the need to talk about the baby with someone other than Beth strong. Not that Law could give him advice or that it would be anything he'd actually follow, but he needed to say it out loud. "There's a past."

"Dude, there's always a past. That's what makes people interesting."

"And there's a future," he said before he could stop himself.

"Whoa. You're that serious about her?" Law asked.

"I could be. I want to be. I need to be."

His friend dropped back and snorted. "The only thing you need is a few hours in the sack and a gourmet meal. Good sex and great food cures all, you know."

If only it were that simple. "She's pregnant."

Law choked again, hard this time. Then his face screwed up into an expression of comprehension and disbelief. "Damn. Did you hook up with her at the reunion?"

"I hook up with ladders," he said. "Not women. Not that woman, anyway."

"You did. You totally boned that night." Law inched back, impressed. "I'm taking full credit for that, by the way.

But no raincoat, Cav? Do you go into a burning building with no gear?"

"No." He shifted uncomfortably, not really wanting to share intimate details with his unenlightened friend, but desperately needing to talk to someone. "She had her tubes tied, but apparently, pregnancy can still happen."

"Whoa." He picked up his beer and tapped it against Ken's. "Way to shoot cannonballs, my friend."

He couldn't resist a secret smile.

"So, wow." Law took a drink, nodding as it sank in. "You got some shit going on." He dropped back in his chair and shook his head. "I do not envy you, son."

An older man came up to their table, frowning as he approached. "Mr. Monroe?"

Law sat up and turned. "That's me. Joe Canton?"

They shook hands, and Law introduced him to Ken. Then Joe took an empty seat. "I'm afraid I have bad news," he said straightaway.

Law swore under his breath. "You're not selling?"

"My son wants the place after all," he said.

Law stared at him. "Your son." His voice actually cracked with disappointment.

Ken pulled himself out of his own misery for a moment to think about Law's and appreciate that, for all his joking, this gastro pub was important to him.

"Hey, I'm sorry," the restaurant owner said. "He's not the best restaurant manager in the world, but he's my son. You know what that means."

Law's mighty shoulders dipped a little as if the words pressed down. "More or less," he said vaguely. "I understand, Joe. Your decision's made."

Joe stood and put his hand on Law's shoulder. "Lunch is on me. I'll have them bring out our best burgers."

When he left, Law let out a disgusted sigh. "Of course he gave it to his son, because *that's what people do*."

The words were loaded, but Ken wasn't quite sure what they were loaded with. Bitterness, anger, frustration. "Hey, man," Ken said. "Sorry that didn't work out."

He shrugged and took a swig. "It's for the better," he said. "It's not the place I really want. Not the place I…" His voice trailed off.

"The Pelican?" Ken guessed.

Law just looked beyond him, gazing at the wharf, his eyes dark with the closest thing to sadness Ken had ever seen in them. "That's where I belong," he said softly. "And, damn it, I'm not going to give up that easily. There has to be…" He stopped as if he caught himself.

"Be what?" Ken prodded.

Law waved it off. "Forget my crap, Cav. You got way bigger problems."

"I guess." He angled his phone to check to see if any texts had come through.

"Brother, you have it so bad," Law said. "Why don't you put yourself out of your misery and tell her to marry you?"

"Or I could drag her by the hair to my cave and take what's rightfully mine."

"Ahh, the good old days."

A waitress came over, smiling at Law. "Mr. Canton forgot to ask how you want your burgers done."

Ken leaned forward. "Medium for me. My friend Tarzan wants his raw with a fire."

Law laughed and took a deep drink after she left. "I know exactly what you should do, you know."

"Whatever it is, it's illegal, immoral, or outdated."

"Make her jealous. Start seeing someone else."

Ken looked at him, incredulous. "There isn't anyone else."

"Oof." Law grunted. "My heart aches for you."

"Haven't you ever met anyone you wanted to spend the rest of your life with?" Ken asked. "Haven't you ever met a woman you really couldn't live without?"

"My friend, no such woman exists, and if she did, I'd run so fast you'd call me a cheetah instead of Tarzan." Law pounded his sizable chest lightly. "I like that, by the way."

"It wasn't a compliment."

Law pinned him with a gaze exactly the color of the Heineken bottle Ken was holding. "Look, dude. It's simple, and you know it. Get rid of the thing that's keeping you apart. Say you're sorry if you have to stoop to that level."

"I did already, but it's deeper than that. More complicated. And it isn't going away. If anything, it could get worse if she..." Takes that job or continues to distrust him. "Does something I'm not sure I can handle."

"Color me intrigued, man. What is it?"

Ken literally pressed his lips together, the nondisclosure agreement that had loomed over his life for twenty-five years as clear as the day his mother signed it on behalf of the entire family. He had agreed to be silent so his mother could avoid years of litigation and take the money, the *hush* money, Ray Endicott threw at her.

Law frowned. "Why are you being weird about this?"

"I'm not being weird. I'm just...not at liberty to say."

The waitress arrived with their food, and they didn't speak until she was gone. During the brief time, Ken checked his phone again. The blank screen kicked his gut.

"So what do you want to do?" Law asked.

"Honestly?" Ken lifted his burger, staring at the bun, thinking how to answer that question. "I want to love her, marry her, and spend the rest of my life with her and our child. Simple and, to you, stupid. But that's the truth."

"Not stupid," Law said, surprising Ken with the note of sadness in his voice. "And for a guy like you? Totally doable."

"No, it isn't," he said. "There's an obstacle that will never go away."

"Have you told her that's what you want?"

"Not exactly. Remember, this is the poster girl for self-sufficient women."

"I hate that kind."

"I love that kind," Ken shot back.

Law put his burger down and narrowed his eyes. "Do you or do you not love this woman?"

"I could. I'm close. It's possible."

"Then lay it all out there. Tell her everything. Tell her it's forever. Tell her you'll never be happy without her." He took a bite and grinned over his bun. "Chicks eat that shit up with a spoon."

Some chicks might, Ken thought. But not Beth Endicott.

Long after the last fan was removed from the house, the water remediation guys had been paid, and the house was as back to normal as a semi-construction site could be, Beth's internal war raged.

She had to know the truth.

As much as she didn't want to read those files, she and Ken needed to throw this whole issue on the table and decide if it had the power to keep them apart. And if it didn't, then the past really and truly had to be the past and they could move on.

But she put it off, busying herself by looking at the

kitchen plans, reading email, tidying up where she could, and taking a long bubble bath in the hideous master bath tub, all the while imagining how the pretty room would look when she was done.

Slipping on flannel sleep shorts and a tank top, she ran a brush through her wet hair and stared at her closet, already visualizing walking down to the garage to get the step stool, climbing up to the bins, and digging for that envelope.

She picked up the phone and stared at the blank screen, no longer able to ignore the ache of Ken's silence or the guilt of hers. All day he'd gone without texting or calling, on his day off when they could have spent a lot of time together if she hadn't accused him of breaking and entering.

"I hate this," she mumbled, pushing off the bed. "I hate games. And fights. And days without him."

She was as much to blame as he was.

Giving in, she walked out to the kitchen, through the door to the garage, and snagged the rusty step stool leaning against the wall.

Back in her closet, she opened the squeaky steps and, careful to stay on the right-hand side of the unstable metal, she reached up and grabbed the top bin where she knew she'd put the envelope.

She brought it down to the ground and bent over to lift the lid. On top was the white envelope she'd refused to open. With a sigh, she ripped off the tape and reached in to slide out the documents. The first one was an autopsy report.

She shook her head and refused to look at the sad details.

Under it was a letter from a lawyer representing Mrs. Carole Cavanaugh and the estate of Jonathan B. Cavanaugh informing Endicott Development Corporation of their intention to file suit.

But there was no suit, Beth recalled. Was that because it

was twenty-five years ago and personal injury law suits weren't as common? There was defective machinery, so why wouldn't they have sued?

Next was a letter from EDC to Mrs. Cavanaugh arranging a meeting to discuss details, as well as a copy of an official machinery inspection report.

The report looked legit, with long descriptions of cranes, hooks, and safety latches, and a county inspector's seal in place.

Underneath that was a nondisclosure agreement and some paperwork finalizing the transfer of two million dollars to Carole's account.

No wonder Ken was bitter. Dad had used his considerable cash to ward off a lawsuit that could have cost him much more than two million and probably had preyed on Carole Cavanaugh's fears that she could lose, based on that inspection.

What did Dad want her to see in these files except that truth? She totally sided with Ken on this one. EDC paid his mom hush money to stave off a lawsuit that, frankly, the Cavanaughs might have won.

The whole thing made her feel sick. The truth was she hadn't really believed that until now. She'd given her father the benefit of the doubt, not Ken or his family.

Still holding the paperwork, she walked out of her closet to grab the phone on her bed. The standoff was over. She was calling to—

It rang in her hand, startling her. But instead of the name she hoped to see, it was the very last one she wanted to see right then.

Ray Endicott.

She let it ring and ring, then go to voice mail. She didn't need to hear how she was dredging up ancient history and Ken could have bad intentions.

She tapped the screen, but her finger hit the wrong button, and the voice mail started to play through the speaker.

"Beth, it's Dad."

She was about to delete the voice mail, but something in his tone stopped her.

"I'm sorry we didn't get to finish our conversation today. Honey, I hate that you think I'm trying to run your life."

And everyone else's.

"Please open that envelope and look carefully at the contents."

"I did, Dad," she snapped at the phone.

"I paid a lot of money—"

"No shit."

"—to keep the autopsy out of the hands of the press and John Cavanaugh's children."

The autopsy? She looked at the papers she still held.

"But John's wife had to see it, and when she did, she had to back off her lawsuit. I paid her anyway, because it felt like the right thing to do. But if you pursue a relationship with this man's son, the truth could come out along with the fact that it was John himself who attached the generator to the crane, and then happened to be under it while it was lifted two stories. And that could hurt a lot of people, especially Ken. I won't be able to protect him anymore."

What?

A wave of dizziness threatened. What was he talking about?

Her heart pounding, she tossed the phone on the bed and started to sift through the papers, getting to the autopsy she'd refused to read.

Her eyes skimmed the details of death, her face contorting as she read words that conjured up nothing but sadness. His lungs collapsed under the weight of the generator that fell off a crane and hook, and that was the official cause of death.

He'd suffocated to death.

Why would that "hurt a lot of people, especially Ken"? Ken knew how his father died.

Then she flipped to the second page.

Blood Alcohol Content: .15%

Her legs weakened as she stared at the words, trying to remember what was legal intoxication in Florida. .08 percent. She was sure of it. And this was…way higher than that.

Johnny Cavanaugh had been drunk on the job, and *he'd* been the one to attach the generator to the crane. He caused his own death and Dad knew it. He'd saved the Cavanaugh family from embarrassment and, surely, the loss of a costly lawsuit. And he'd given them two million dollars. The nondisclosure agreement was to protect *them*, not EDC.

She dropped onto the chair, quivering as it all processed.

If Ken knew this, he would know his father was drunk and caused the accident that killed him. And, he'd have to let go of believing that her father was covering up for his company's negligence. He was covering up for John Cavanaugh's negligence caused by being drunk on the job.

The worst barrier to their relationship would be removed, opening up the door to a possible future.

But at what cost? The memory of his father—the father he had high on a pedestal—would be ruined.

The truth would break his heart.

Yet if she didn't tell him, they'd have no chance to be together. "Oh, Ken. What should I do?"

She closed her eyes, vaguely aware of a dog barking in the distance. Her head throbbed with indecision. What should she tell him? What would be best for them? For their child?

The barking got louder, along with a solid rap on her front door, pulling her out of her reverie.

Who was at her door? With a dog?

Wait, she recognized that bark.

Ken was here, with Sally. She leaped off the bed, still holding the paperwork. She couldn't let him see this. Couldn't let him know, at least not yet. She needed time to decide.

The barking, and knocking, intensified.

She darted into the closet and grabbed the bin, and all the papers fell to the floor.

"Shit."

"Beth!"

He wasn't going to give up. Not with her car in the driveway. She climbed up, shoved the bin back up on the shelf, and tossed the papers on top where they couldn't be seen. Calming herself, she got down and folded the step stool, leaning it against her shoe rack.

She'd just hidden the truth from him, she thought sadly.

She walked briskly down the hall, anxious to see him, but a little scared, too. She unlocked the door and opened it slowly, her heart stuttering in her chest as she saw Ken Cavanaugh in a tight white T-shirt and jeans, the hint of a half-smile pulling at his lips, a spark in his dark eyes.

"Sally missed you," he said.

She opened the screen door, and Sally marched in, barking at Beth, then lowering her head to beg for a scratch.

"And so did I," Ken whispered, his voice rough.

She looked up at him, and that roller coaster she'd been on all day chugged to the top of a long, long drop. The free fall promised to be thrilling and wild, and she knew the ride could hurt when it hit bottom.

But she wanted to take it more than she'd ever wanted anything in her life.

She reached up to wrap her arms around his neck and pulled him in for a long, hard, soulful kiss that silenced the truth she knew she should tell him, but couldn't bear to.

Chapter Eighteen

Beth melted into Ken the way he'd imagined all the way over here. He kissed her back with the same urgency, while Sally kept barking.

All the way inside the house, she broke the kiss and gazed up at him, her eyes already dark with arousal. "Hi," she said softly.

"Hi." He stroked her hair, his hand surprisingly shaky from the kiss. "Does this mean our fight is over?"

"It wasn't a fight." She sighed into him, laying her head on his shoulder.

"But I killed my own excellent seduction."

She inched back. "What makes you so sure of that?"

He smiled and nodded at Sally, who gave up barking to lick at Beth's legs. Smart dog. "She needs you to welcome her."

"Oh, Sally." Beth let go of him to bend down, and Sally instantly dropped and rolled to offer up her massive, spotted gut for a rubdown.

"She's shameless," Ken joked.

"I'm going to want the same thing when my stomach takes up fifty percent of my body." Still rubbing Sally, Beth grinned up at him. "Will you rub my belly then?"

Emotion crushed him, pushing him down to crouch across from her. "I'll rub anything of yours I can get my hands on." With Sally flat on her back between them, Ken reached over to cup Beth's face. "I can start any time. Now, even."

She leaned in and kissed him again, and they stood. "But we need to talk," she said. "I think I have a beer in that mini-fridge if you want one."

"Water is fine," he said.

"Go sit down and I'll be right there." She gave his arms a squeeze as if the little act of kindness made her feel good, so he nodded his thanks.

Watching Sally sniff around the place, Ken did the same, checking to see that everything was dry and mold-free. He waited on the sofa while Beth got two waters and joined him, snuggling close.

"What did you do all day?" she asked.

"Thought about you. Missed you. Considered calling you. Had lunch with Law and talked about you. Checked for phone messages from you." He dropped his forehead so it touched the top of her head. "What about you?"

"Essentially the same—you."

He pushed her hair back to get a better look at her. "I'm sorry I jumped down your throat. I know you were trying to figure out if someone had been here."

"No, no." She reached up and pressed her fingers to his face. "I am the one who owes you an apology. To even think that you would…no, I'm ashamed."

They didn't speak for a moment, but stared at each other like the lovestruck kids they once were. "I wasted the first twelve hours of this free day," he said. "I should have been here taking down the rest of kitchen and starting the master bath. Can I spend the next twelve hours with you?"

Her smile was shaky, as if she still wasn't sure.

"We only have to talk," he added at her hesitation.

"I do want to talk," she said, a little slowly. "There's so much we still don't know about each other."

"All right," he said. "What do you want to talk about?"

She swallowed. "The tough stuff."

He stifled a grunt. "Maybe I'll take that beer after all."

"Let's not talk about my father," she said softly. "How about we talk about yours?"

"Okay. That's never tough. I love talking about my dad."

"You never took me to your house when we were dating," she said. "So I don't know what he was like."

"I couldn't take you there, Beth. It was small and…in Twin Palms. You lived in a mansion on the water."

"You know I didn't care about that stuff, and I still don't. So, what was your dad like?"

He closed his eyes and dropped his head back, falling into the comfortable place of his memories. "Happy," he said. "My dad was a guy who just loved life."

"He never fought with your mom?"

"They fought sometimes." He inched back to see her face. "Are you trying to determine if the apple doesn't fall far from the tree?"

"I have all the proof I need to know you're an amazing man. I want to know more about your life."

He wanted to be as open and honest with her as possible, and his childhood home hadn't always been rosy. "Actually, my parents argued their fair share, but, you know, I was a kid and ignored it most of the time. Sometimes Dad would have a few drinks and get testy."

Next to him, he could have sworn she stiffened.

"It didn't happen a lot," he added quickly. "But that's not what I remember most about him."

"What do you remember most?"

"Laughing a lot. Learning from him. Fishing with him on Sunday afternoons or working in the garage on the muscle cars he loved. The best years were when I was about twelve or thirteen." He paused for a moment, transported back to steamy summer nights working by the light of a few bare bulbs, the hood up on that Impala he loved so much, the smell of grease and the Juicy Fruit gum his dad constantly chewed. "We'd listen to rock bands at full blast, Queen and Bon Jovi, and he loved to sing. But when the music wasn't playing, he talked to me."

"What did you talk about?"

"Anything, everything. Girls, cars, sports. Mostly girls." He grinned at her. "We never talked about one thing, though. Vietnam. He was a vet, you know, but he never, ever talked about the war. But girls? Oh yeah. Until you, of course. I couldn't tell him about you because he'd have killed me for dating his boss's daughter."

"But you did tell him we were dating, didn't you? Eventually?"

He took a sip of water, his mouth surprisingly dry. "Yeah, but it didn't go well."

She sat up a little, turning to see him. "Why? What did he say? Why didn't you ever tell me?"

"Because he died that day." His voice was thick with the memory. "My sister had seen us holding hands at school, and she thought it would make a lovely breakfast topic. Oh man, he was pissed."

"He was that upset you were dating the boss's daughter?" Her voice rose, as if she were taking the whole thing personally, which he kind of understood. For a long time, he'd blamed their relationship for the fact that his last real talk with his father had been an ugly one.

"He had an issue with pride," Ken said quietly. "Not a lot of faults, a heart of gold, and he could build, fix, or make anything. But he was so ashamed of living paycheck to paycheck, of the fact that his wife had to clean motel rooms and take in sewing to make the rent. He was…embarrassed, plain and simple. He assumed you'd look down on my family."

"But I never did."

"I know, and I told him that. Which pissed him off more."

"And then…he went to work?"

"Mad as hell at me," he said. "I went to the job site after lunch, figuring he'd have cooled off by then. They were hoisting that crane to carry the generator as I walked up. I remember stopping to watch because no boy ever gets old enough to not be fascinated by a crane on a construction site and…"

He saw that hook slip…

"I didn't really know what I was looking at, you know?" He heard his voice crack, but didn't care. It hurt like hell to remember.

She squeezed his hand, but Ken barely felt it.

"The moment that I realized that thing was falling, I looked to the ground and realized my dad was right there. I opened my mouth, but it happened so fast. Five hundred fucking pounds of steel fell like it was in slow motion…" The sob broke, along with the tears he hadn't realized filled his eyes.

"Oh, Ken," she whispered.

"It crushed him." He blinked and swiped at his eyes. "I reached him first. But he already couldn't breathe. He wasn't even conscious when I reached him. There was nothing I could do to save him."

"Oh, Ken." She pulled on his hands and forced him to

look at her. "You cannot blame yourself for not knowing how to save a dying man when you were eighteen."

"I don't blame myself." He blamed Ray Endicott and some half-assed inspection, but he didn't have the heart to say that now. Not while Beth was covering him with comfort and sympathy. "But that was the moment I knew I wanted to be a medic and firefighter."

"Your dad would be so proud of you." She was so sincere, he melted into a sad smile.

"That's what my mom says."

She searched his face. "What else does she say…about what happened?"

"That Dad had himself to blame."

"Really?" she asked, sounding surprised or even hopeful. "She blames him?"

"For fighting with me on his last day on earth," he said. "For not treating every day like it could be your last."

"Are you sure that's what she meant?"

He drew back, frowning. "Yeah. Why?"

"I don't know." She took a long, slow inhale, looking away, thinking. "Blame and guilt," she finally said. "They are two very debilitating emotions."

"They are."

"They could ruin us if we let them," she said. "We could wallow around in blaming one person or ourselves for something that can't be changed and cost us everything we have."

"Well, listen to you." He put his finger on her chin and turned her face toward him. "Three *we*'s and a few *us*'s in there. I thought you ran away from those words."

She didn't answer, her own eyes as misty as his still felt. "I don't want to run away from us anymore," she whispered. "I want to be a *we*, but I'm so scared."

"Only one thing should scare you," he said, easing her body against his.

"What?"

He placed a kiss on the top of her head. "Missing the opportunity for us to have something amazing."

She looked up at him. "You really think we could?"

"I know we could." He kissed her forehead. "I know we will." He kissed her nose. "And we should start…." He kissed her lips. "Right now."

"Another excellent seduction." She whispered into his mouth.

"Did it work?"

"Like a charm." Slowly, she stood, holding her hand out in invitation. "Come to bed with me, Kenny Cavanaugh."

As Ken kissed them both back into the bedroom, Beth could feel herself letting go of all the fear and tension and secrets and guilt and blame. It fell to the floor along with the tank top he dispensed with somewhere in the hall.

Inside her room, he closed the door. "Let's not make Sally witness this," he said, pulling her into him.

He smelled like sunshine and salt water, so masculine and Ken-like that she had to press her lips on his shoulder and inhale. Still standing, he lowered his head, kissed her mouth, then dropped lower, his lips over her breasts and stomach while she threaded her fingers into his hair.

"Beth." He breathed her name onto her skin, slipping his fingers into the waistband of her flannel sleep shorts, and then began to slide them over her hips. She wore nothing underneath, which made him let out a sexy grunt as he revealed her inch by inch.

Tugging the shorts down her thighs, he knelt in front of her to suckle and lick, making her dig her fingers into his head.

At the first contact of his tongue, she stiffened in a little shock. "Oh…" He kissed her belly, then looked up with his mouth still on her flesh. "Too much."

"I'll be gentle," he promised, his voice taut, as if gentle was the last thing he wanted to be.

"It's not that. It's…intense." She stroked his head, stunned at the sparks of fire on her skin. "It's…different."

A slow smile spread as he lightly tapped the skin right under her navel. "Crazy-ass hormones exaggerate everything," he teased.

"Yeah." She sighed, pushing his head so his mouth would be back on her. "*Everything*."

Stifling a laugh, he kissed her again, then tongued her, flicking the tuft of hair and sucking lightly until her knees actually wobbled with weakness.

"I've got you," he said, standing up to lead her to the bed.

When she dropped on her back, he yanked his T-shirt over his head, making her suck in a breath at the sight of his gorgeous chest. Cuts and dips, muscles and skin, hardened nipples, and a happy trail of hair leading right where she wanted to go.

Reaching for his hips, she brought him to his knees on the bed, unsnapping his shorts and hungrily unzipping to free him.

His erection pulsed in her fingers while she stroked the length, in awe of how incredible he felt. He pushed off his shorts and stripped down, lying on top of her to give her the sweetest, slowest, warmest kiss she could remember.

His lips and tongue were so soft but demanding, his large hands holding her face like she was the most precious thing he'd ever touched. His body pressed on hers, and she spread her legs to accommodate him, wrapping them around the rock-hard muscles of his backside.

Every move made her want more, every second of skin-on-skin contact made her moan, every breath of him nearly brought her to tears.

"Ken, what is happening?"

He laughed a little, lifting up. "If I have to explain it to you, then we need to talk."

"Everything is so…intense. Can it really be because I'm pregnant?"

He stroked her cheek with one finger, and even that featherlight contact shot fire between her legs, pushing her toward a release she hadn't had time to build up to yet.

"Actually, I think it's more than the baby."

She closed her eyes, sucked in a breath, and rocked against him, eager to have him inside of her.

"It's *us*," he whispered.

The gruff, masculine way he said *us* was as sexy as the body she moved against. Every sense, even her hearing, was heightened.

Her whole body felt weak and boneless, but sparky and bright at the same time. She heard herself moan and whisper his name, but it was almost like the sensations were so powerful she couldn't be experiencing them herself.

His fingers were like brands searing her skin, but soothing her, too. When his lips touched her throat and nipples and stomach, she arched her back and moaned in pleasure.

Nothing had ever felt like this before. Fiery and fierce. Achingly good, insanely sweet. Desperate but…perfect.

She squeezed his buttocks and pushed him closer to her, pulsing and ready and dying for him.

He lifted his head. "Guess the condom ship has sailed, huh? I have an unopened box if it makes you feel better."

"You haven't been with anyone?"

"Only you that night and every night since then..." His mouth kicked up. "In my imagination."

Oh wow. Just the thought of that damn near sent her into an orgasm. "Me, too," she admitted.

"We should have been together all these weeks." He eased into her. "Like...this."

He gritted his teeth and went deeper. And deeper. Until he was all the way in.

"Like that." She sighed, then met his next thrust.

She stopped thinking, stopped fearing, stopped wondering about anything and everything. All she could feel was the power of this man, filling her, taking her, owning her...*changing* her.

All of the things she'd sworn she never wanted, but right now, they were all she wanted. Him. Us. *Them*.

He held on a long time, dragging out the pleasure and every insane, sticky, sweaty sensation until they reached the edge of control. He bowed his back, lifted his head, and slammed one more time, then lost the fight.

He groaned and let go, spilling into her. With each pulse, she could feel him surrender to the satisfaction, and that took her right to the brink of an orgasm.

She came as he finished, every cell tingling and twisting as pleasure whipped through her whole body.

He held her through her orgasm, kissing her and whispering her name, lazily thrusting as the heat deep inside rose again, twisting and burning and demanding another release.

"I can't stop," she cried, moving against him again, letting the second orgasm rock her. He clung to her, bucking to keep her satisfied and let her ride it out.

Sweat and exhaustion tingled over her body when she finally finished. He collapsed, heavy on her, and she clung to his heaving shoulders as aftershocks made her quiver.

"Kenny," she whispered.

"One more?" he asked.

"I could, so easily."

He lifted up, a spark in his eye. "You mean it?"

"Yes. No. Wait." She squeezed his shoulders. "You're amazing."

"No, *we're* amazing," he corrected, easing down to kiss her jaw and ear. "We are so good together, Beth." His breathy words tickled and made her shudder.

"I know," she admitted. *We*. How did those two little letters become so much more powerful than *me* in Beth's head?

"It's worth fighting for," he said.

It was also worth…lying for. She closed her eyes, tucking him as close to her as they could possibly get, trying not to picture that damning autopsy report not twenty feet away inside her closet.

She couldn't tell him the truth about his father. If she did, he might forgive Dad. But then Ken would blame himself. Because it was likely that John Cavanaugh's dark mood over the fact that Ken was dating Beth was what made him drink on the job that day.

"What's the matter?" He lifted his head to look at her.

"I didn't say anything." And that was the problem.

"You just…whimpered."

"Did I?" But how could she keep this from him? How could her family?

"Beth, I can tell something's wrong."

Sally's plaintive doggie moan and some desperate scratching at the door saved her from having to answer him. "Oh, get her, Ken. Don't let her cry at the door."

"And have her see us without our fur on? She's fine."

She nudged his rib. "Is that the kind of dad you're going to be? Let the kid cry in the hall for attention while we languish in bed?"

He started to get up, but froze, a flicker of emotion crossing his face. "That's what it is," he said.

"What what is?"

"That feeling." He touched her face as he slid out of her, sitting up. "The…I don't know, anticipation of languishing in bed with you, of having a kid crying, of being a family, of building that…together." His throat caught with emotion, making her eyes fill up. "I want that so bad, Beth. I want it with you and…" He placed his hand on her belly. "Her."

A wave that felt very much like what he was describing washed over her. Could they have that? Could they overcome the past hurts and the truth and family and their started-in-reverse romance to get it right?

"We could have that," he said, as if he'd read her mind. Without waiting for an answer, he got up and walked to the door, opening it so Sally could waddle in and give Ken a look of pure disgust.

"Somebody's jealous," Ken joked.

"Aww, of course she is. I would be, too, if you disappeared behind closed doors with another woman." Beth clapped lightly and patted the bed. "C'mon up, girl."

"Don't shame her. She can't jump onto the bed." He bent over and scooped up her wide belly to airlift her onto the foot of the bed.

Sally stared at Beth for a second, launching the showdown. But Beth reached out her hand to scratch Sally's neck, which did the trick. With a doggie sigh of resignation, she took a few slow steps over the bedding and pressed her considerable weight next to Beth's stomach.

"Hy, that's my spot," Ken said with an unhappy snort.

"There's room in my bed for both of you."

He joined them, letting Sally lie between them like a sack of flour.

"This is what it's going to be like with a baby," he said.

"Only less fur."

"We hope," he added, making her laugh.

It could be good. It could be perfect. Except there was the matter of that paper in her closet.

And now she had to choose between being with Ken but breaking his heart, or being alone and breaking both of their hearts. Or…she could try to keep a secret from him forever. She sighed audibly.

"I know what you're worried about, Beth."

Actually, he didn't.

"And you don't have to be."

She peered over Sally's head, wondering where he was going with this.

"Nothing's going to happen to the baby."

Except this whole relationship, as backward and unusual as it was, had its foundation on a tiny little cluster of cells forming in her not-so-competent uterus right now. If that should end…

She closed her eyes and tunneled her fingers into Sally's wiry black and tan fur and refused to think about it.

Chapter Nineteen

"Why are they called Kelly days?" Beth handed a clean scraper to Ken, after taking the half-dozen broken ceramic squares he'd ripped from the master bathroom's tub wall.

He paused in the job to work a crick out of his back, plucking at the white T-shirt that clung to sweaty muscles. Automatically, after dumping the tiles in the discard bucket, she grabbed his water bottle and gave it to him, then returned to her comfy cross-legged position against the wall.

They worked like a well-oiled machine now.

"Thanks," he said after taking a swig. "Lots of theories, but most people say they're named after a Chicago mayor who wanted firefighters to have decent working hours. Not that the shift setup is anywhere normal."

"You mean the twenty-four-hour days?" she asked, absently scratching Sally's coarse hair, already used to having the chunky dog always pressed against her leg.

"They can be hell on family life," he said, his tone gruff enough that she knew there was more to that comment. How to interpret his tone and looks was one of the many things she'd learned about him in the past few days, working next to him at her house all day and sleeping next to him at his at night, even the night when he was gone on a shift.

"But you have Sally," she said.

"And she comes with me on every shift." He gave a grin to the dog. "Don't you, Chunker?"

She laughed and patted the fat dog. "Why did you get to keep her when she was left at the station? Did you win a bet or something?"

He snorted. "Everyone at the station has dogs, but they all want Labs and retrievers and, of course, the cliché Dalmatians. Nobody wanted a fat mix of a Yorkie and a—"

"Don't say cow," she said, pressing Sally's pointy ears down. "It hurts her feelings."

He paused and turned, the scraper poised in the air as he looked at her. "You've fallen for her," he said simply.

"How can I not?"

"I'll have to find out her secret formula and drink some of it."

She smiled at him. "No secret. She's a dear dog who loves to eat."

"I love to eat."

She reached over the side of the tub and poked him. "Scrape tile."

He went back to work, the next tile popping off easily. "That's what I'm talkin' about," he murmured.

"We're due for a good section," she said, taking a drink of water.

"Like we hit on Tuesday."

She glanced at the wall behind the sink and toilet, where the tiles had popped off like candies. "Tuesday was a good day." And Tuesday night was even better.

He whacked at the next tile. "Every day this week has been good, Beth."

The way he said it made her heart stumble a little, and she couldn't argue. They *had* been good. They'd slipped easily into a natural rhythm, finishing the kitchen completely and moving in to tackle the master bath, the two most important parts of the renovation.

By mutual agreement, they let the past go—for the moment, anyway—talking about everything but his father or hers. The night he'd come over after she'd read the autopsy report, Beth had decided she cared too much about Ken to break his heart with the truth, even if it might have changed how he felt about her father. Once that decision had been made, their time together grew more blissful every hour.

"I've never had an easier demo," she mused. "I haven't lifted anything heavier than a hammer."

"That's the idea."

"I could get used to watching you in sweaty T-shirts while you do my work. It's a great way to make a living."

He laughed. "Plus, you get to interview me."

"I'm not interviewing you," she said. "I'm getting to know you. And when you talk about the guys at the station catching a run and the crazy pranks you pull, you work better, did you know that?"

"Really," he deadpanned.

"Yes, so my questions are actually a time-management system I've made up to keep you on track."

A tile popped off and dropped into the tub, cracking.

"So that's why I spent an hour this morning telling you about life on a Navy sub?"

"You finished that whole wall." She admired the stripped-down shower wall, completely cleared of hundreds of ugly white square tiles and ancient grout. "And it was fascinating," she added.

"But I'm not getting to know you," he said, coming down

off his crouched legs to sit in the tub for the next section.

"My life is dull as dirt. Besides, you're working too hard to ask questions," she said, while fighting the urge to scoot a little closer, just to, well, get closer. Ken was in her bathtub. Filthy, with grout under his nails and grime on his face and sweat dampening his neck.

And she never wanted to kiss anyone so much in her whole life.

"I can ask questions and not ruin my time."

But could she answer them and not ruin her mood? "Okay, but I'm telling you, nothing in my life is that interesting."

"I'm interested in knowing about your ex-husband."

She snorted softly and gave him a look. "Well played and sneaky."

"Why'd you marry him?"

"He was in the right place at the right time. Or wrong, I guess, depending on your perspective."

"You must have seen something in him."

She closed her eyes and conjured up an image of Justin. Not that tall, but lean and taut from long distance running. His hair was thinning, but he wore it well and he had a nice smile.

"He wasn't a bad guy," she said. "He just wasn't *the* guy."

He slid her a look, a little satisfaction and a little challenge in his eyes. Like she should know *the guy* because she was looking at him.

"Was the divorce awful?" he asked.

"It was…not fun. He'd met someone at work, but didn't cheat on me."

Ken's brows rose a little, enough to convey a little skepticism.

"He didn't," she said. "He told me as the relationship became real and he didn't want to have an affair. He wanted to have a...family. He admitted that convincing me to get my tubes tied was a mistake, but he wouldn't consider adoption. He wanted his baby, *his* seed."

"That had to hurt you."

"Tremendously," she admitted. "But now?" She gave him a wry smile and tapped her stomach. "It hurts a lot less."

For a moment, he held her gaze, nothing but hope and satisfaction in his eyes, as if he were pleased to ease her pain.

"What about your divorce?" she asked.

"It was sad," he said simply. So simply that it had far more impact than if he'd thrown down the scraper and called his ex a bitch and a shrew. "It wasn't what I wanted."

She shifted on the ground, settling in to ask a question she'd hadn't had the nerve to pose yet. "So you loved her?"

"Of course I loved her." He dug at a stubborn tile.

"Then what happened?"

He abandoned the tile and lowered the scraper. "She had big career ambitions and didn't want a family. Renee spent an inordinate amount of time being the company superstar."

Beth realized she'd never heard him use her first name. If he had to refer to the past, he'd say "my ex" or "former wife." But now she had a name: Renee.

"What company did she work for?" Beth asked.

"That big hotel chain, Southern Hospitality," he said. "She started in event planning, got promoted to sales, and wham, they had her on the fast track to management. In hotel management, every promotion means another move, which was hell on my career, but really good for hers. It's not easy to get a job in a decent fire department, let alone move up the chain of command. I'd have been a lieutenant forever, moving to another town every two years."

She frowned at him. "And that was enough to break up your marriage?" It sounded a little shallow and selfish to her, neither traits she associated with him.

"We had such different ideas of what our lives should look like," he said, a sad note in his voice. "She was a workaholic, which didn't have to ruin us, but she didn't want kids. Didn't want to be home at all." He put the scraper down and looked at her. "I bought a house without her even seeing it, because she was on the road for something like thirty-nine consecutive days, so I bought a house for us. And about a year later, she got promoted to a job in Houston and, man, I didn't want to leave that house or my station."

"So you picked them over your wife?" She couldn't stop a little horror from sneaking into her voice. The idea that he'd put a house and job ahead of a marriage didn't seem like the Ken she'd gotten to know.

"No," he said simply. "She basically told me to stay. She didn't want the, uh…" He slid into a rueful smile. "Baggage."

Beth didn't know what to say, but she reached out and touched him.

His eyes grew darker, but warm with the unspoken promise that those kinds of problems and baggage wouldn't happen to them. Could that be possible?

She so wanted to believe what she saw in his eyes that the message made her dizzy. She leaned forward, closer to him, their mouths inches from each other with the ceramic of the tub separating them.

She closed the space and gave in to the temptation to plant a light, easy kiss on his mouth. Instantly, he had a hand around her head, deepening the contact.

When the kiss ended, she kept her eyes closed. "You're not baggage," she whispered.

He eased back. "Unless you want to travel very, very light. Which you might."

Slowly, she shook her head. "My traveling light days are over. I…" She swallowed hard. "*We* have a baby on the way."

She got to her knees, and he did the same, both of them slipping into the next kiss. A now familiar warmth low in her belly forced her to lean into him, arching her back, inviting the next touch.

"Beth? You in here?"

They jerked apart at the voice, shocking both of them when they realized the man was in the hall.

"Landon?" She pushed up, shooting a look at Ken right before her stepbrother reached the bathroom door. "What are you doing here?"

"You should lock your front door, Beth. Anyone can walk right in."

She closed her eyes, standing up. "You're not the first to tell me that. Landon, this is Ken Cavanaugh. Ken, my stepbrother, Landon."

Ken pushed up, wiping his hand on his smudged khaki shorts before extending it. "Nice to meet you."

"Ken's a friend who is helping me out with the house," Beth explained.

While they shook hands, there was enough of a flicker of amusement or doubt in Landon's eyes to make her think he suspected Ken was more than *a friend*. Oh God. A chill ran over her arms. Had he heard what she just said about a baby?

"So what brings you here?" she asked quickly.

"I was down in the neighborhood and thought I'd swing by to invite you to dinner on Saturday."

She fought the urge to choke softly. A dinner invitation from the McDowells was rare, unless it was a holiday, and it would normally come as a phone call from Rebecca.

"What's the occasion?"

"Just a family dinner. Bonding and all."

Since when? She nodded, waiting for more information.

"We've got reservations at Junonia at Casa Blanca in Barefoot Bay," Landon added. "Would you join us? Rebecca and I would like it."

"Sure, thanks," she said, trying not to sound like she was skeptical of the bizarre invitation.

"But you know Rebecca," Landon said. "She likes things all traditional and balanced. RJ is bringing a date—"

"RJ is coming?" She couldn't keep the surprise out of her voice. "With Selina?"

"Yeah, he is. Shocked me by accepting the invitation, but I'm glad," Landon said. "Dad and Josie are coming, too. Maybe you can bring a date so you don't have to come alone."

She turned to Ken in time to see his jaw tense and relax in a quick, silent reaction to the idea.

"It's fine," Beth said quickly. "Family dinners are so tedious, and talking business is—"

"I'll go."

She inched back, silenced.

"I'll be there…" He swiped his stubble with a dirty hand, his gaze locked on Beth. "For you."

The last two words folded her heart in half.

"Great," Landon said. "Seven o'clock at Junonia." He backed out of the bathroom. "I can see myself out."

Beth finally looked at her stepbrother, recovering from the shock of what Ken had just agreed to do. "I'll walk with you." In the hall, Beth touched Landon's arm. "Is there a real reason for this dinner?" she asked.

Landon managed to look a little put-upon. “We can’t have a family-bonding dinner?”

She lifted a questioning brow.

“Okay, Rebecca thought it would be good for us kids to spend more time with Mom and Ray.”

They really hadn’t been a ‘us kids’ kind of family, but she gave him a warm smile. “You’re right, Landon. This is a great idea, and I appreciate the invitation.”

At the front door, she stepped outside to inhale some fresh air after having been in the bathroom almost all day.

Landon took a few steps toward his Lexus sedan, then paused, turning around. “Is it serious with him?” he asked.

She had no idea how to answer that. “Too soon to tell.”

She could have sworn his gaze dropped to her belly, but he put on a pair of sunglasses so fast that she couldn’t be certain. “Then we’ll see you Saturday.”

“See you then.” She gave him a quick wave and walked back into the house, still wondering what Rebecca was actually up to with this dinner. When she got to the bathroom door, Ken was chopping away at tiles.

“Are you sure about this?” she asked.

“Yep.” He pounded a tile and popped it off without looking up at her.

“You’re absolutely one hundred percent positive you can handle dinner with my father?”

He banged the next tile, but it didn’t budge. “Yeah.”

“What changed your mind?”

“It’s time for your dad to know the truth.”

She inched back. “The truth? About what?”

One more stab with the scraper and the ceramic flipped off the wall, dropping into the tub. “That I’m not just a guy for you.” He turned and held her in place with a long, heated look. “I’m *the* guy and the father of his grandchild.”

"He doesn't know about the baby yet, Ken."

"He will after we tell him." His eyes narrowed and she knew without a doubt that there would be no talking him out of this. "Together, on Saturday."

"Are you sure?"

"Absolutely. I want to see him and, assuming you agree, I want him to know about our baby."

"I do." She pressed her hand to her heart, expecting resentment but only feeling a flutter of happiness. "Why now?"

His gaze dropped to her stomach. "You said *we* are having a baby. *We*. If you can use that word, I can see your father. Call it a compromise."

Or a miracle.

On the way home late that afternoon, Ken swung by the station to see if there was any possibility of switching his Sunday shift. Sure, he could be there at seven a.m. Sunday, but he'd rather have the day off. He had big plans for Saturday night.

First, dinner with his arch nemesis…and the reward for surviving that? An overnight stay at Casa Blanca, but only if he could get Sunday off. He and Beth were going to celebrate getting over their greatest hurdle.

Assuming he survived that dinner.

Ken turned the corner from the bay into the main section of the station, meeting Pookie's sharp gray gaze at her desk outside Chief Banfield's office.

"Hey, Pooks. How's it going, gorgeous?"

She put down the pen she was holding, crossed her arms,

and lifted her brows in approval. “Hallelujah, the dry spell is officially over.”

He couldn’t help grinning. “You can say that again.”

She put her hand on the phone receiver. “Should I use the intercom?”

“Only if you want to die a slow death. What are the chances Captain Dobson would switch shifts with me so I can have Sunday off?”

“Dogface doesn’t switch shifts for love or money.”

“My boat for a day?”

“Oh yeah, that’d do it. Want me to call him and ask?”

He blew her a kiss on the way into his office. “I’m going to check my email and wait for the good news.”

“I was worried we’d never see you smile like that again.”

He gave her a wide, toothy smile. “No more worries. I’m happy.”

“Then so am I.”

“It’s kind of you to care about my well-being, Pooks,” he said, feeling magnanimous to the world.

“Oh, I don’t, really. But I put fifty on a baby Cavanaugh this calendar year.”

He stared at her for a second, his jaw loose. Then he relaxed into another smile. “Put another fifty in and get Dobson on the phone.”

She jumped up with a squeal. “Ken!”

“Shhh!” He pointed to the phone. “Dobson. Then in my office.”

He barely had time to scan his emails when his door closed and Pookie dropped into one of his guest chairs.

“How far along is she?”

He spun around so fast, it was a wonder he didn’t do a three-sixty. “What?”

“The calendar year ends in seven months.”

"Well, I didn't mean a baby would be born..." His voice trailed off.

"She showed up here with news that changed your life, you folded in half over a callout that involved a pregnant woman, and your Internet history includes searches for pregnancy after tubes are tied."

"You checked my search history?"

"You think it's not public on a fire department computer?"

"I could have been looking for work-related reasons."

"And I could have married Frank Sinatra if he'd have had me. When's she due?"

"December twentieth."

She fluttered her fingers in front of her mouth, stifling a squeal. "Imma be a grandma!"

"Would you stop?"

"No." She leaned over the desk, her eyes sparking with joy. "I'm so happy for you, Ken."

"Me, too." He blew out a sigh. "Now all we have to do is get to know each other, survive the family dynamic, and decide we can actually make a go of this."

"So I take it this wasn't planned."

He cocked his head with a smirk. "You saw the search. Tubes were tied."

"Are you going to marry her?"

Was he? "I don't know yet, Pooks, but if I bet like you do, I'd put my money on yes."

"Wow." She sighed and fell back on the chair. "Even after what happened to your dad?"

He jerked back. "How do you know about that?"

"You think you're the only one who can work a search engine?" she asked. "You think I don't Google any potential spouse for one of my guys or gals?" She swept her hand toward the station in general. "I need to know things."

He turned to shut down his computer and push away from the desk. "Guess you do."

"Captain," she said. "You didn't answer my question."

He straightened some papers, stood up, and rolled his chair in. "We're working on dealing with history, starting with dinner Saturday night. So give me a few days before you break my news to the free world, will ya?"

"I'm not telling anyone. How do you think I win all these bets?"

"I have no idea."

He followed her to the door, turned off the light, and they walked out together. As soon as he closed the door behind them, Pookie stood close and put her hand on his arm.

"Just so you know, I'd bet everything on you," she said. "You're my favorite for a reason."

Chapter Twenty

Sweat dribbled down Ken's back and into his eyes as he braced his body for the next heave.

"On three," he growled. "One…two…"

"It's going to catch on the plumbing." Beth leaned over the side of the tub by the drain and pointed.

Ken and Billy Hanrahan exchanged a look. "We've got this, babe," Ken said.

She narrowed her eyes at him. "I've removed bathtubs before. *Babe*."

Not pregnant, she hadn't. "We disconnected the plumbing, Beth. It won't catch."

"But please watch that pipe, because the water heater is right behind that wall and it backs into my closet, so a leak would be costly."

He nodded at the other man, who looked impressed with her knowledge of house building but also ready to have fewer orders and more brute strength to finish the job. "Cheat to your side, Irish."

"Will do, Captain."

Finally, Beth stepped back and let them hoist the ancient tub out of its sliver of space without a single pipe damaged. Gritting his teeth, he and Irish angled it so they could fit it through the bathroom door and carry it down the hall and out to the truck Irish brought to take it to the scrap metal dealer that Beth had arranged to have it.

They had to do a bit of a dance to get down the hall, but eventually they had it out to the driveway and into the truck. Beth followed them to supervise, of course, then went into the garage while he and Irish headed back to start on the cabinet and sink.

"She sure knows what she wants," Irish said under his breath when they were alone.

Ken laughed. "One of my friends refers to her as the poster child for independent women."

"Maybe I should change my bet."

"What'd you put your money on?" Ken got on his knees in front of the pipe they'd left exposed, peering into the plumbing works, digging his finger around the rusty rim.

"The whole enchilada, of course. I mean, with the baby and all."

Ken froze and drew back from the wall. "Damn it, Pookie. Who all knows?"

"I think the better question is who doesn't know."

Shit. He better tell Beth before word got back to her that he spilled the beans.

Ken put a hand on his friend's shoulder. "Keep your money where it is, Irish."

"Yeah, I am. Anybody with a brain is. Pooks is already shopping for a dress for your wedding."

"Of course she is." He flicked at some more rust, more concerned about it than amused by Pookie. "Look at how rusty this is. Wonder what kind of shape that water heater's in."

"The water heater is fine," Beth called from the hall. "I can't afford a new one."

The men shared another look, and Irish grinned. "I'm going to look at it," Ken called back, stepping into her bedroom.

"It's fine," she called. "I'll deal with it."

In the hall, he found her in front of the closet that housed the water heater. Hands on her shoulders, he nudged her to the side. "Let me look at it."

"Okay, but don't start with the fact that I need a new one. I want to clean this one up and make it work. Installing a new water heater adds another inspection and a delay." She opened the closet door and gave him access. "Here, look."

He wouldn't disagree with the fact that it was an older unit, but maybe not on its last legs.

"The rust isn't much of a problem," he said, checking the seams of the unit.

"Look under it," Irish called from the bathroom. "Ninety-nine times out of a hundred, that's where a fire starts."

"A fire?" Beth's voice rose. "You guys are just looking for trouble."

"That's what we do." Ken was already on his belly, peering under the unit. "Water heaters breathe, did you know that, Miss Fix-It? They suck in air, combust with it, and exhale it. If there's anything under the tank, like rust or dust, they breathe that in, too."

She didn't answer, tapping her foot next to his face. "I didn't know that," she admitted. "I'm not a water heater expert."

"Well, I'm a safety expert, and this thing here…" He banged a hand on the metal side.

"One of the most dangerous devices in your whole house," Irish finished, coming into the hall to join them.

"But you're good, Beth," Ken said, pushing away and up. "It looks clean. Old but clean." He grinned. "Kind of like me."

She reached up and swiped her hand over his face. “You’re anything but clean right now. So you better hurry up if you’re going to have enough time to get that tub to the scrap dealer, get home, clean up, and get back here to pick me up for my family dinner.”

“Why don’t you grab some clothes, come with me, change at my house…” He leaned closer. “And we get to dinner late?” he added in a sexy whisper.

Irish cleared his throat, looking up like he couldn’t handle the romantic exchange. “Excuse me.”

Beth stepped back. “Oh. Sorry you had to witness that, Billy,” she said.

“No, ma’am. I love the inside information when I’m betting on something. And I’m betting on the captain.”

“Wise man,” Ken said.

“But you do have a problem,” Irish continued, still squinting toward the ceiling above the water heater. “Look, Captain.” He pointed to the round duct that ran from the unit into the vent directly above the water heater.

Ken peered at it. “Single-walled,” he said. “And cheap. Do you have a step stool?”

“In my garage. No, wait. I moved it. It’s in my…I’ll get it.” She started to leave, but he snagged her.

“Let Irish get it.”

“I can carry a step stool, Kenny.”

“Kenny?” Irish snorted. “’Scuze me while I text that one in.”

Ken shot both of them a look.

“It’s in the closet in my bedroom, Billy,” Beth said.

“It’s Ken in front of my men,” he whispered to Beth when Irish headed back to her room.

“This from the man who called me ‘babe’.”

He touched her cheek, much the way she’d touched his, but not because it was dirty. Because it was gorgeous.

"You're cute when you're mad." He lifted her chin, closed the space, and put his lips on hers. "Babe."

He could feel her smile under his lips, but the sound of Irish's boots broke the moment. "I got it, but the duct in there is single-walled, too."

"What is single-walled?" she asked. "And why don't I know that?"

"Because it's something firefighters notice. Single-walled is not code, though a lot of inspectors miss it," Ken said. "When we see fires and carbon monoxide leaks, it's usually because of crappy venting." He opened the stool to stand on it, almost immediately losing his balance.

"Oh, you have to stand on the right side," she said with a laugh. "I know I need a new one. It came with the house."

Standing on the right side of the step stool, Ken tapped the vent, giving his head a very serious shake. "Irish, do you have a portable CO detector in your truck?"

"I might. Lemme look."

"Bring it to her closet." He jumped off the stool, and Beth blocked his way.

"That's not necessary."

"Are you kidding? You could have a slow carbon monoxide leak into your bedroom. I'm not letting that go."

"There's a detector in the hall."

"They aren't one hundred percent reliable, Beth. When's the last time you changed the battery?" He picked up the step stool, but she sidestepped and blocked him again.

"It passed inspection, and you don't have time to do this today. You need to take that tub to the scrap guy and be ready for dinner tonight. It's important."

He gave her a look. "So's your health. And my baby's."

Beth's shoulders sagged with resignation. "All right. But my closet is…a mess. I'll help you navigate it."

"I want to see your mess," Ken said, with a quick kiss, and got by her to go into her bedroom. He headed for the walk-in closet, which wasn't a mess at all.

"Hey, somebody give me a hand!" Irish called from the front. "Sally got out."

Ken was already up one step. "Oh man, can you get her? She'll sniff her way six houses from here in no time."

Beth hesitated, looking up to the top shelf where some storage bins sat right under the vent in question.

"I got this, Beth. Please get Sally."

"Sally!" Irish called out. "Don't go in the street!"

Beth pivoted instantly and darted down the hall, leaving Ken to wonder what the hell that was all about. Remembering to lean to the right—and making a mental note to throw this damn step stool away because it was an accident waiting to happen—he reached up to the clear plastic box that prevented him from getting to the vent.

He pulled it out, but a bunch of papers were on top and fell right into his face, forcing him to turn away as they all fluttered to the floor.

And now her closet *was* a mess. He stepped down and put the box on the ground, right on top of a paper that said…

Coronor's Autopsy Report.

He froze. Why would she have…

A shudder ran up and down his spine as the realization hit. The papers her dad gave her, the files about his father's death. The autopsy.

Don't read it. Don't read it. Don't read it.

But his hands ignored the mental warning, lifting up the plastic box that covered the paper that had fallen to the floor. His mother had never let him see the autopsy. She'd told him it would be too upsetting.

No more than the moment his father died in his arms.

Ken stared at the page, the words swimming. This was crazy. Stupid. It was going to put him in a foul mood on the very night he had to fake nice with the man who'd caused the reason this autopsy had to be performed.

Outside, he could hear Beth calling the dog. Heard Irish laugh and Sally bark. It all faded far away as he lifted the document and flipped to the next page. More ugly words, impersonal descriptions, facts that didn't—

Blood Alcohol Content: .15%

He shook his head, certain he was reading it wrong—.15 percent? That would've made him legally drunk. What? His father hadn't been drunk! He'd have known or smelled booze on him.

What the—

Sally's sharp bark right outside the closet made him look up, and right on her heels, Beth, her gaze dark, worried, and…sympathetic.

"Why didn't you tell me about this, Beth?"

"I couldn't because—"

"Because it's not true!" His voice rose to a yell, making Sally whimper and drop to her belly on the ground.

"Hey, Captain, I don't have a—"

"I don't need it!" He stepped out of the closet, shaking, actually seeing spots of red he was so mad. "Meet me in the truck, Irish. I'll be there in one minute."

At his tone, Irish inched back. "Sure. Um, bye, Beth."

"Bye, Billy. Thank you." Beth's voice was tentative and slight. She stayed rooted to her spot, staring at Ken, while they waited for Irish's footsteps to fade and the front door to close.

"I didn't tell you because you love your dad and his memory and—"

"It's not true!" he shouted again. "Don't you see, Beth?

It's a lie. Your father doctored official papers so he didn't have to go to court and take the blame. And then he planted…that." He gestured to the vile paper still on the carpet. "Forced my mother into a corner, shut her up to protect his reputation and your family, and lied about it."

The words tasted like bile in his mouth, his hatred for Ray Endicott raging in his chest like a six-alarm inferno.

"No…no. He would never do that."

"He *wouldn't*?" He choked on the word. "Are you that naïve to think your father wouldn't do whatever his millions could buy to save his company? He's a damn puppeteer, doing whatever he wants and making people bend to his will. Including you."

Her eyes widened. "I don't bend to his will anymore."

"But you will if you take up his offer to work for Endicott Development." He shoved his hand through his hair, not surprised his fingers were actually trembling with fury. "You can't do that, Beth. You can't. I won't allow it."

She sucked in a breath, eyes wide. "I can if I want to," she fired back. "If I think it's what's best for my life, my child—"

"*Our* child."

"Who *I'm* carrying."

So much for the magic *we*. Anger ripped through him as he breathed so hard his nostrils flared and neither of them spoke.

"Ken, you have to consider the possibility that what you read is true."

"I don't have to consider shit." He gave the plastic lid a light kick with his boot. "Except the fact that your old man is a liar and has the money to cover his tracks and do it so effectively that *my* father looks like the criminal."

"If it's true, then—"

"It's not," he ground out.

She met his gaze, the pain in her eyes slicing him. "What if you're wrong?"

"I don't think I am."

She stepped away, pulling the strands of caramel hair that had fallen out of a ponytail on another long and sad sigh. "We'll never get past this point, will we?" she said, her voice tight. "It's always going to come back to this. Your father. My father. Blame and guilt."

"And a pack of lies."

"Or truth. It doesn't matter," she said. "This will always be between us, ruining any chance we have."

"You have your father to blame for that."

Her eyes flashed. "*Blame* is going to strangle you and ruin your life, Ken Cavanaugh. Let it go. *Let it go*."

He tried to swallow, but it was impossible. He could barely speak. "I can't."

She lifted a shoulder. "Then let me go. Your choice."

He stood stone still, then without a word, he walked out of the closet and past her, heading down the hall. It was a small consolation that Sally followed.

But Beth didn't. He'd made his choice, and obviously, she'd made hers.

Chapter Twenty-One

The last thing Beth wanted to do was go to dinner with her family at the resort in Barefoot Bay. She wanted to roll into a ball and wallow in her misery. She wanted to jump in her car and drive to Fort Myers and talk to Ken. She wanted to turn back time, at least to the night of the reunion so she'd never—

No. No, she didn't want that.

She wanted this baby more than she'd ever wanted anything, with or without the support of a man who let his pride and his guilt and his endless blame game wreck his chance at happiness.

She still had a chance at happiness, and she'd never needed her family more.

So she took a deep breath and climbed out of her SUV in the parking lot of Casa Blanca Resort & Spa, a place she hadn't visited since that fateful night on the beach two months ago.

She had a future flash, imagining a night maybe twenty years from now. She and her daughter would share a long talk, one of many—because they'd be like the Gilmore Girls and inseparably close—and Beth would tell her the whole story of her conception in a cabana on the—

"I can't believe how nervous I am."

Beth spun around at the familiar male voice and felt a smile pull. "RJ!" She reached for her younger brother and gave him a cursory hug, eager to meet the woman next to him. "And this must be Selina."

She was shorter than Beth, with a little trepidation in her big brown eyes. "Beth?" she guessed.

"That's me." Beth reached out and gave her an impulsive hug, squeezing hard.

"I didn't think you were Rebecca," she said with a laugh.

"Not enough diamonds." Beth held her at arm's length and took a good look at the woman who would one day be her sister. Her skin was as dark and smooth as espresso and her smile genuine. "Congratulations," Beth whispered, glancing down at Selina's stomach. "How do you feel?"

"Better now."

"Were you sick?"

"She's been puking her guts out," RJ said, putting a possessive arm around her.

"Really?" Beth asked. "Because I haven't…" She caught herself. "Heard RJ say anything about that."

"The worst is over now," Selina said, lifting her brows. "Except for the 'meeting the family' part."

"And dropping the bomb," RJ added.

"You're telling everyone about the baby tonight?" Then surely she should keep her own news quiet.

"Yep. And…" He reached down and lifted Selina's hand, showing off a sparkly engagement ring. "I couldn't wait any longer for some perfect job to materialize. We're getting married here at Barefoot Bay in two months."

Beth's jaw dropped as the unexpected jagged edge of yearning dragged over her heart. "That's awesome. I'm so happy for you." She hugged them both again. "And you never know, RJ, that perfect job might materialize sooner than you think."

"I'm ready," he said, then glanced past Beth. "Landon said you were bringing that firefighter guy. Did he chicken out?" RJ asked.

"Something came up," she said vaguely, covering the sadness in her voice by sliding between them and putting an arm around both. "I'm with you two."

They all walked in, separating in the lobby so Selina could look around at the lush, Moroccan-inspired décor.

After a few minutes, they headed into Junonia and were escorted out to the expansive terrace where tables were set up overlooking Barefoot Bay.

And beyond the terrace, a row of yellow tented cabanas. Beth swallowed the lump that rose in her throat, almost unable to take her eyes off the last one.

That's where she'd bring her daughter, someday. To tell her the story of how she was conceived. Would she even know Ken? Would they have a distant relationship or a warm one?

She shook off the thought and stepped down to the level where Rebecca, Landon, Dad, and Josie were already at a long table, drinking champagne.

"There you are!" Rebecca stood, and the rest followed, and all the hugs and hellos ensued while Beth braced for Landon's questions about Ken.

But Rebecca wasted no time on that. "Where's this firefighter we've been hearing so much about?"

Beth sort of shrugged and shook her head. "He's…not able to make it, sorry."

"Oh, well, there's a chair for him. That will unbalance things."

It would unbalance them a hell of a lot more if he were

here, she thought. She sneaked a look at Dad, who had a little sympathy in his eyes. And circles underneath them.

She reached over and hugged him before sitting down across the table. "Hey, Dad."

"Hi, honey." He added a squeeze, but it wasn't terribly strong.

Josie started nattering immediately as the waiter came to fill Beth's champagne glass.

"I'll have Pellegrino water," she said.

"Beth, that's not like you," Rebecca said. "Have some champagne."

But Beth glanced back up at the waiter and whispered, "Sparkling water for me." She leaned closer to her father, searching his face again. "Did you have that doctor's appointment, Dad?"

"Yeah, he wants me to come in on Monday for another test." He sounded disgusted. "I'm *fine*."

"He's not fine," Josie said, leaning into their conversation. "He's tired, cranky, and I think he has a fever."

Dad skewered her with a dirty look. "I took a nap—that makes me tired. I couldn't go golfing—that makes me cranky." He dabbed at his glistening forehead with a handkerchief. "And it's humid out here, which makes me warm."

But Beth thought he looked pale, not flushed from humidity. The sea breeze lifted her hair and seemed to be keeping everyone else cool. She didn't argue with her father, though, turning to let the conversation drift to the other end of the table, her eye catching the empty seat next to her.

What would this have been like if Ken had come? Awkward? Uncomfortable? Or would they be holding hands under the table, silently giving each other glances of support? Not after today. Not after he called her father a liar.

Her heart squeezed at the memory. Surely by now he'd calmed down. And maybe he'd changed his mind. And maybe…she looked over Landon's shoulder toward the restaurant, imagining how she'd feel to see him walk up with that half smile she loved and a whispered apology.

Would she accept it?

"May I propose a toast?" Landon said, standing up after the waiter had poured and delivered the next round of drinks.

Landon raised his champagne glass. "To change," he said. "To new families and new businesses."

Dad cleared his throat with some effort. "Yes. Drink to that, and then I have an announcement to make about the family business."

Plenty of glasses froze midway to their destinations, including Beth's. "You made a decision?"

"I have."

"But we have news first," RJ said, shifting the attention to the other side of the table like a tennis match.

Dad nodded, giving over to RJ.

"Selina and I are getting married next month right here at Casa Blanca. We hope you'll all be there."

The reaction was strong enough to make other diners turn to their table, especially since Rebecca squealed the loudest. Beth glanced across the table to see Dad's reaction, but he was looking down, quiet.

Please don't ruin this for RJ, Beth thought.

"And there's more," Selina said, her soft voice quieting them all as they leaned in. She tapped her stomach. "It should be a very exciting Thanksgiving for RJ and me…and our baby."

Another cheer went up from Rebecca, and Josie let her jaw drop open. Dad leaned back as if the whole idea gave him heartburn.

"Sorry to interrupt your big announcement, Dad," RJ said quickly.

"No, no, this is big news. Big news, son. No need to even talk business tonight."

Beth eyed him, wondering if RJ's news would give him a change of heart. But there was too much animated discussion to draw him into a conversation about that now.

Rebecca peppered the couple with questions, regardless of the fact that she obviously knew all the answers already, and Beth sipped her water as RJ and Selina answered excitedly.

That should be Ken and me, Beth thought glumly, keeping a smile planted on her face as she listened to them talk about names and dates and morning sickness and wedding plans.

That should be us. Us. Great, now she was madly in love with the *we* and *us* idea…and now she was all alone.

"You okay?" Dad's question was quiet, and accompanied by his hand over hers.

"Yeah. You?"

He shrugged and threw a glance down the table, the lightest sheen of sweat on his upper lip. "He doesn't know it yet, but I'm going to give RJ another surprise."

Beth's eyes widened. "You are?"

He smiled, but it was shaky. "I'm going to teach him the commercial end of the business, even if it kills me."

Josie shot a look at her husband, clearly listening to both conversations at the table. "I'll kill him if it kills you."

Dad rolled his eyes but flinched a little. Knowing Beth saw it, he narrowed his eyes in a silent plea to not alert Josie.

She shifted her attention back to Selina and RJ, trying to concentrate on how happy she was for them. This was a new phase in her brother's life, and he wasn't going to blow it.

Selina seemed steady and strong and, man, were they going to have a beautiful baby.

Under the table, she slyly put her hand on her stomach, sending love to her baby. *Just like I am*, she thought. The best *we* in the world would be Mommy and Baby, the only *we* she'd ever need or have.

She felt tears threaten and blinked them back, looking at Selina, glowing in the early evening light, laughing as she leaned into RJ.

The ache for Ken was so strong it took Beth's breath away. She looked down, then back up again, and noticed someone was walking toward their table behind Selina. With the sun behind him, she could make out only his silhouette, but it was…familiar. So, so familiar.

"Oh my God," she whispered, loud enough for everyone at the table to turn and follow her gaze.

Ken approached the table, his dark eyes locked on Beth.

She couldn't breathe for a moment, feeling her hands grip the armrests of her chair.

He's here. *He's here!*

There was no doubt she'd accept that apology. She was so damn happy. She pushed herself up to greet him, and as she did, his gaze shifted from her to her father. And narrowed.

What did that expression say? Anger? Shame? Had he come to apologize…or accuse?

"You made it," she said, her breath tight in her throat.

He nodded, serious. "I want to talk to your dad."

Her heart literally slammed against her ribs, the rapid beat audible in her ears. *Talk*? Did that mean he wanted to thank him for what he'd done to protect Ken…or accuse him of doctoring an autopsy?

She swallowed, aware of every eye on her. "Um,

everyone, this is Ken Cavanaugh." She turned to the others to start what would be an awkward round of introductions, since they all, of course, knew him, but her attention stopped at Dad.

He wasn't looking up at Ken. His head was down, as if he looked at something in his lap. "Dad?"

"Ray?" Josie touched his shoulder. "Ray?" She pushed a little harder. "Ray?" Her voice rose to freak-out level, and everyone jumped up at once, exactly as Dad slumped forward, his head hitting the table with a thump.

"Oh my God, he's dead!" Josie screamed.

Chaos erupted like a volcano, with Rebecca yelling and Landon swearing, and all the patrons at the other tables standing up to see, but it all seemed to happen in slow motion. Beth felt her own cry well up in her throat as she launched toward Dad. She turned to give Ken a pleading look, and he stood stone still for one fraction of a millisecond. Then, as if he'd been shocked, he vaulted into action.

"Everyone back," he said with loud authority, coming around the table in one easy move. With one hand, he moved Beth away to get closer to Dad.

"Is he breathing? Is he alive? Oh my God, I knew—"

"Josie, hush," Rebecca said, pulling the other woman back.

"I'm a paramedic," Ken told everyone calmly, lifting Dad's head and hovering one hand over his mouth, the other supporting his neck.

"Wake him up!" Josie insisted in a shrill voice.

Ken looked up at Beth, not saying a word. He didn't have to.

"Is he breathing?" she barely whispered. "Heart beat?"

"Everyone needs to clear out!" Ken commanded, his

voice loud and totally in control. "I need space and a defibrillator." He looked at the others, his face stern, his voice unwavering. "Someone call 911. Tell them we have a possible SCA on a nonresponsive sixty-nine-year-old male. I need everyone to be quiet and stand back. And I need a defibrillator, stat!"

That second, Landon pushed the table away, making space for Ken to lay Dad down. RJ shot off with Selina, cell phone out, and Rebecca kept pulling Josie farther away. The staff moved into action as well, but Beth's attention was riveted on her father's ashen face.

As Ken laid Dad gently on the ground, easing the older man's tie off, checking him again for air and a pulse, Beth got down on her knees on the other side of his still body.

"He has a stent," she told Ken. "And heart issues."

He nodded, still checking his breath and pulse as he unbuttoned the top button of Dad's shirt. "Pacemaker?"

"No."

"On any meds?" He inserted his finger into her father's slackened mouth to check for anything blocking the airway, moving with the precision of a machine.

"Um. Yes. I can't remember what they are." She turned to ask Josie, but she was completely useless.

"Doesn't matter," Ken said. He put one hand on Dad's chest and flattened another on that and started pressing and releasing in a quick, steady rhythm.

"Is he going to die?" Beth whispered, aware of the tears pouring down her cheeks.

Ken looked up at her between the next two chest compressions, a flat expression in his eyes. "Not on my watch."

Chapter Twenty-Two

Live, damn it. Live.

Ken blocked out everything but that thought. Ray Endicott had to live. Not just for Beth and his grandbaby, but so Ken could look him in the eye and tell him he knew the whole story…and that he owed Ray a heartfelt apology.

But none of that mattered now, not one bit. Ray was dying, and quickly.

Ken mentally silenced the screaming wife and ignored the pushy onlookers and did his damnedest not to reach out to comfort the frightened daughter.

As he focused on Ray's color and counted each compression, willing a heartbeat, willing some breath, Ken stole a glance at Beth and his own heart ached.

Crouched next to him, she had her fists balled against her mouth, silent but for a soft shuddering, her gaze locked in abject terror on her dad's pallid face.

It'd been twenty-five years, but he still remembered that sickening, spiraling sensation of seeing the person who gave you life fade away before your eyes.

Push, wait, push, wait, push, wait. And breathe.

Sucking in his breath, Ken tilted Ray's head back to clear

his passageway. He waited one second, then put his mouth right over Ray's and shared a breath.

Nothing.

He started the next set of compressions, willing that damn AED to show up.

Still no heartbeat. This was not a heart attack, Ken knew. This was sudden cardiac arrest, and the chances for survival were low. Very low.

"Damn it, Ray," he ground out in a whisper. *Don't die in front of Beth. Don't die in my arms, too.*

"They have a defib!" A man's voice broke through. Landon, he realized, with several resort staff members, hustled closer. Thank *God*.

"C'mere," he ordered Beth. "This can't stop. Do five or six compressions then breathe into his mouth. Just once."

"Oh…okay." She hesitated a moment as if the order didn't compute. Or she was in shock at the situation.

"Use your weight, Beth. Push in about two inches on his sternum. Get a song in your head and follow the beat."

"A song?"

He let go and took her hands. "*Stayin' Alive* is what we use. Do this and he might." But probably not. "I'll start the AED."

She let him put her hands right over Dad's sternum and started to push. "Stayin' alive," she whispered, her face blank and almost as pale as the man's on the ground.

Instantly, Ken turned and took the AED being held out to him, ignoring the avalanche of questions, even from the staff. The only thing he heard was that an ambulance was on the way. There was a station on Mimosa Key, so they just had to get up here and through the damn resort.

He flipped the lid of the plastic box and grabbed the electro pads, turning back to Ray. "I need to get his shirt off."

"Should I stop?" she asked.

"Yes, you're good. Help me, Beth."

Together, they unbuttoned Ray's white shirt, moving in perfect unison, silent as a team.

Spreading the material, Ken was grateful Ray wasn't a hairy dude. He didn't even glance at the instructions as he applied the electrode pads. He'd done this many times in medic training and plenty in real life. One pad over the right center, one over the left rib. He slipped in the plugs, and the machine immediately lit and started the heart-rate reading.

"Everyone clear away!" he hollered. "Even you," he added to Beth. "Clear!"

The crowd backed away while the AED measured the heartbeat and flashed a warning, which meant there wasn't one.

Ray Endicott was dying…and while at one time that might have given Ken a sick satisfaction, Ken's heart hurt as much as Ray's did right now.

"It's going to shock him," Ken announced. "Clear away and do not touch his body." He backed up and counted to three, knowing when it would happen.

Ray jerked at the shock, and Josie shrieked.

Nothing. Damn it. *Come on, old man.*

Another shock rocked his body, but Ray lay lifeless on the ground. His wife wailed again, and Beth shuddered with her younger brother's arm tightly around her. Ken couldn't even look at her, he was so sure she was about to witness her father's death.

And he knew how much that hurt. He *knew*.

Another shock jerked Ray, but this time his mouth opened, and he sucked in a breath, making everyone cry out.

"He's alive!" someone screamed.

"That did it!" another person yelled.

"Praise God!"

Don't praise Him yet, Ken thought, leaning over to check him. He needed to be on cardiac life support, get some beta blockers, and pray that therapeutic hypothermia worked.

It was Ray's only chance. And it was slim.

Just then, someone called out that the medics had arrived, and Ken looked up to see the EMS crew blowing in and barking orders.

"Let us through," their captain ordered, his gaze on the victim.

Ken recognized Captain Markoff, an old friend he'd met through co-county training and fundraisers. When Markoff looked up, he reacted with the same recognition. "Cav. What's the condition?"

Bad.

"SCA," Ken said softly, not wanting to freak out Beth or anyone else who might know how serious that was. "He was out for at least a minute, maybe more."

Markoff nodded as Ken delivered additional information, speaking only as a paramedic on the scene with no skin in the game.

But he had skin in this game. Skin and soul.

Once Markoff's team took over, Ken backed away, adrenaline dumping through his veins.

As they lifted Ray onto the stretcher, Beth broke away from her family to come closer to Ken. He turned to her, fighting the urge to reach out and pull her into him, to press a kiss on her golden hair, to beg for her forgiveness.

"Thank you," she said softly. "Thank you for saving him."

Her father wasn't saved yet, but Ken didn't have the heart to tell her that now.

"I'm sure that…wasn't easy," she added, the comment slicing right through him.

"It's never easy," he said, watching an EMT tie a strap over Ray's chest, and noting that that chest rose and fell, thank God.

"I mean, with him."

He looked down at her, ready to argue, but RJ came closer, an attractive woman clinging to him with fear in her eyes.

"One of the medics said they're taking him to Naples Community."

"Good," Ken said. "They have a great cardiology department at the Heart Institute."

"Is he going to be okay?" RJ asked, fear straining his voice.

Ken swallowed…and lied. "Most likely. You'll need to get to the hospital and talk to his doctors."

"Beth, ride with us." RJ put his arm around her.

She sank deeper into her brother's side, her own adrenaline dump making her look incredibly pale.

"I'll take you to the hospital, Beth," Ken said, reaching for her.

She blinked at the suggestion and suddenly Ken realized how awkward that would be. This was her private family crisis and he was *not* family. Not even close…yet.

"Or you can go with RJ," he added. "Of course, I understand. I'll…be in touch."

"Really, man," RJ said, reaching out a hand to Ken. "You kicked ass. Thanks. We most likely owe our dad's life to you."

"No, it's okay. Just get to him." Because Ray might not even be alive when they reached the hospital.

Beth searched his face, still a little in shock, and looking as if she had a question or something to say, but RJ was already anxiously pulling her away.

"I better be with my family now," she whispered. "And thank you."

RJ guided her toward the rest of the family, his arm possessively around both women and Ken stood, watching.

He could go to the hospital but they didn't need to be dealing with anything except the effort to keep Ray alive.

Which he knew in his gut could be futile. So Ken stood in the same spot, watching the family he wasn't a part of disappear. He'd let his hatred and his blame take everything away from him, and he'd never even had a chance to tell Ray Endicott that he was sorry for that. Or, as he'd come to do, thank Ray for what he'd done for Ken's family.

And he might never get that chance.

If any good could come of the tense hours the Endicott family spent in the chilly ER waiting room, it had to be that Landon and RJ were seated next to each other, in deep conversation for a long time. After talking to Beth for a while, Selina put her head on RJ's shoulder and fell asleep.

Rebecca held Josie's hand, both of them tearful, standing in unison every time a doctor came out from behind the closed swinging doors of the ER. A few minutes after midnight, a nurse told them a doctor would be out to speak with them in about another half hour.

Beth sat alone, holding her head up, watching it all unfold, replaying the moment that she'd thought Ken had come to apologize and realized he'd come to confront her father.

And then, irony of ironies, had had to save his life.

Which he had—she hoped. But sitting there, Googling on

her phone what she heard Ken say to the other paramedic—SCA, or sudden cardiac arrest—wasn't making Beth feel much better. She certainly wasn't going to share the dismal survival statistics with her family, but the numbers were not in her father's favor.

After the nurse left, Josie stood alone and walked over to Beth, holding her hand out. "Will you get coffee with me?"

"Of course," Beth said, standing without hesitation. "Does anyone else want to come?"

"I want to go with you," Josie said. "Just you."

There was something in Josie's eyes that made Beth certain she wanted to talk about more than the current dire situation. "Okay." Beth turned to Landon and RJ. "Text me if anything happens. We'll be back in a few minutes."

In silence, Beth walked with Josie out of the ER toward another section of the hospital. They walked past a gift store that was closed, but the coffee shop next to it was open.

Taking a table, Beth offered to get coffee and croissants, but Josie shook her head. "I don't want anything except to talk to you."

Beth put her elbows on the table and stared at her stepmother. Surely this had to be about Ken, about why he came late to the dinner. About—

"Does he know?" Josie demanded.

Beth blinked, her mind jumping around at what she could mean before it settled on the obvious. "You mean does Ken know the contents of the envelope Dad gave me?"

Josie nodded. "Does he know?" This time, she asked with more force.

"He saw the autopsy report and the blood alcohol level," Beth said.

Josie closed her eyes like she'd been hit hard. "Oh."

"He thinks it's a lie."

Her eyes popped open. “Really? He doesn’t believe the autopsy report?”

“Of course not.” She swallowed hard, not sure she wanted to know the answer to the next question. “He thinks it’s fake.”

Josie choked softly. “It’s not. And I tried so hard, so damn hard, to keep the truth from those kids, from Ken and his brother and sister.”

“Why don’t you tell me exactly what happened?” Beth suggested. “At the accident, and after.”

Josie sighed in resignation. “What happened was exactly what the autopsy says. John Cavanaugh was beyond legally drunk and hadn’t attached that generator properly. He completely forgot the safety latch, then happened to be the man under it when the hook broke. If another man had been standing under it? John Cavanaugh would be in jail for manslaughter.”

“How could Ken not know he was drunk? He was right there. He held his father in his arms as he died. How could other men on the site not know?”

“John was quite skilled at hiding his drinking problem,” Josie continued. “He hid it from the supervisor, from his coworkers, his kids, even from his wife until shortly before he was killed. But Carole knew.”

“You talked to her?”

“Carole? We talk all the time.”

Beth felt a frown pull. Didn’t Carole Cavanaugh think the Endicotts were the spawn of Satan like Ken did?

“She’s my friend,” Josie said quietly. “And I made her a promise that apparently has been broken.”

“I am so lost,” Beth admitted. “How is it that she is your friend? And what promise did you make? And why?”

“I got to know Carole when she did some tailoring for me,” Josie said. “Her husband worked for EDC, and I liked giving her the business. She was sweet, and when you and Ken started dating, we had fun gossiping about it and keeping it from our husbands."

"Why?"

"John was proud, and Dad was, well, your dad."

Beth stared at her. "I had no idea."

She shrugged. "You and I weren't that close, and I didn't want you to get mad. Anyway, the accident happened. Carole was pushed to file a suit by relatives and a few lawyers who butted in, but as soon as the autopsy was completed, she backed off. Everything would have come out in the open during a lawsuit and the poor family had suffered enough. We gave her money to help her and the family."

"Why did she hide the truth?" Beth asked. "Just to protect the kids?"

Josie smiled sympathetically. "It's a shame you won't ever have kids, Beth."

She blinked at the statement, entirely unsure how to respond. "Why?"

"Because then you'd know what parents do for their children. I know I push hard for Landon, but he's my child, and nature drives me to want the best for him. Carole was no different with Ken and his siblings. They loved their dad like crazy! Especially Ken. He thought the sun rose and fell on his father and had no idea the man battled with addiction. John was a vet, did you know that?"

"Yes, I knew."

"Apparently, he saw some very bad things, and that might have been why he first started having problems with alcohol. Carole didn't talk about it until after the accident. I had no idea, honestly." She paused and leaned closer. "And neither did his kids. I made a promise to Carole that we would never ever tell anyone what happened. There seemed no reason to put Ken and his siblings through such torment."

"He went through torment," she said quietly.

"But he never blamed his father."

"No, he blamed Dad."

Josie tipped her head. "We didn't think that mattered in the long run of his life. We didn't think you two kids were serious. You were fifteen years old. And, it was actually Carole's idea to have a 'nondisclosure agreement' so she wouldn't have to talk about it and so her kids would think she'd lose the money if they did."

Beth literally held on to the table, reeling. "So why did Dad give me the papers if you both made this promise?"

"He didn't know about the promise, Beth. That was between Carole and me. How Carole handled what John's kids knew was her business as far as Dad was concerned. That's why I had to get into your house."

Beth's jaw fell open. "You…*what*?"

"I didn't get too upset about Ray giving you the papers, though he did it without consulting me, because you told him that you weren't ever going to see Ken again."

And she hadn't planned on it until the pregnancy.

"But once I saw Ken at your house," Josie said, "I knew that you two would start to get closer and closer. I was counting on the fact that you told Ray you weren't ever going to read the papers and, even if you had, I could get rid of the autopsy report so Ken would never see absolute proof. So I came up with a way I could get into your house, knowing you'd be gone, and I could take that autopsy report out of the envelope."

"Josie!" Beth was nearly breathless with disbelief. "You broke into my house? Why didn't you just tell me?"

"In case you hadn't read it yet, then I could have saved you from knowing."

"But he'd go on hating and blaming Dad."

She shrugged. "I made a promise to Carole. I'm sorry about the flood and the inconvenience, and I didn't find the papers because you showed up while I was looking. I had to run out the sliding glass door."

Beth gave a short, mirthless laugh. "So it was you." She shook her head. "For a bit, I blamed Ken."

"Don't blame him," she said. "This was all to protect Ken. Because I care about Carole, and my heart hurts for anyone who's lost a husband." Her eyes filled again. "When Landon's father died, I was gutted." She sighed and looked back down the hall from where they'd come. "I don't think I can handle it again."

Beth took Josie's folded hands in hers. "You have to stay positive. And please tell me I can explain all this to Ken."

"How much does he know?"

"He was working on something in my house and the papers fell, and he saw the autopsy. He wouldn't know that John actually caused the accident. He accused Dad of faking the report so EDC didn't get sued. Actually, I think that's why he came to dinner. To confront Dad."

"And ended up saving his life," Josie said. "At least, I hope so."

At the misery in her voice, Beth put her hand over Josie's. "All these years I've thought Dad was the one trying to control things. It was you. And for some very noble reasons."

She gave a sly smile. "Behind every controlling father is a way more controlling mother. Or stepmother," she corrected.

They shared a warm look, but Beth's phone vibrated, and they both jumped.

"The doc is out," Beth said, pulling Josie up after reading RJ's text. "Let's go."

They hustled down the hall to the ER, and when they arrived, Landon and RJ were talking to a tall, balding doctor. Beth and Rebecca flanked Josie and joined them.

"They're doing therapeutic hypothermia," Landon said.

"What does that mean?" Josie asked.

Beth knew from reading the medical sites on her phone, but she listened to the doctor explain the process of keeping the patient cold, and why, and how long it would take.

"Twenty-four hours at least in maintenance, fully sedated. No one can see him at all. Then we'll start rewarming and examine the aftereffects of his cardiac arrest. You should all go home and get some rest. You're going to need it for the next few days."

"Is he out of the woods yet?" RJ asked.

The doctor zeroed in on him, the stress lines around the man's eyes deepening. "No. But I will tell you this. The paramedics kept him alive. If he hadn't been treated as instantly as he was, and by someone who knew exactly what he was doing…" He shook his head. "He'd have died within minutes."

Josie put her head on Beth's shoulder. "Ken is a good man," she whispered. "He has my eternal gratitude."

RJ gestured behind the group. "You can tell him yourself," he said.

Beth turned in time to see Ken striding into the waiting area, looking as tired and kicked by life as she felt…and nothing ever looked better to her.

She didn't even think, but went straight to his arms and let him hold her.

Chapter Twenty-Three

Ken had waited outside the hospital for a long time, checking with some friends in ER triage about Ray's status but firmly resisting the urge to intrude on the Endicott family's privacy.

Until he couldn't resist for one more minute and went bounding into the undersized waiting room exclusively for cardiology emergencies.

And as he felt Beth fold into him, he knew he'd done the right thing.

Still in deep conversation with the doctor, the rest of the family acknowledged him, but Beth let Ken lead her a few feet away.

"How is he?" he asked, stroking her face, which looked pale and ravaged from a tough night.

She tipped her head and nuzzled into his hand for a brief moment. "Not in the clear yet, according to the doctor."

"Are they doing therapeutic hypothermia?" he asked.

"Yes, that's what the doctor is explaining now. Is that a good thing?"

"It's very good." Ken pressed her closer to his chest. "How are you doing?"

"I'm—"

RJ came over and placed a hand on Beth's shoulder. "Sorry to interrupt, but you need to hear this," RJ said. "We're making some decisions."

"Okay," she said, giving Ken's arm a squeeze. "Give me a minute."

"Of course."

RJ smiled at him. "The doc was clear about one thing, man." He shook Ken's hand and added an unexpected embrace, patting Ken's shoulder. "He wouldn't have made it if not for you. My family owes you."

"No, not at all," Ken replied. He gave a gentle nudge to Beth. "Go and I'll wait right outside in the hall."

She held his gaze for a moment, then stepped away and he walked into the hall, far enough not to eavesdrop on the family conversation.

Leaning against the wall, he closed his eyes and thought about all that had transpired that day and that night. During the events, he realized that three things had driven him since the day his father died: his desire to save lives, after feeling so helpless that day; his longing for a family so he could somehow honor his father by re-creating a relationship like they had; and his simmering hatred for the man he blamed for his father's death.

In a way, his father's death had formed him...and *de*formed him.

He'd arrived at dinner to make a public and formal apology, but he would likely never get a chance now. The odds weren't in Ray's favor, and for all he knew, they were being told that right now. Eighty percent of SCA victims died, and many of those who lived suffered life-changing brain damage.

Beth walked into the hall and reached for Ken again, sighing into another embrace.

"We're working out a schedule to stay here while he's in hypothermia," she said.

"Not you, Beth." He cupped her cheek and examined her red eyes with dark circles. "You're pregnant."

"So's Selina," she added, then she sighed and lifted her brows in question. "Why'd you come to the restaurant tonight, Ken?"

"I wanted to talk to your father."

She stared at him, waiting.

"I called my mother today," he said. "She told me everything."

Beth's eye's shuttered. "Then she's probably not mad at Josie, who committed at least one crime trying to keep her promise that you'd never find out."

He gave a soft grunt, thinking of all Josie and Ray had done, and how no one had told Ken any of that all these years. "I went to the restaurant to apologize to your dad, to your whole family, actually. And you. Especially you."

"You did a lot better than say you're sorry," she whispered. "No apology could have been more meaningful."

"You know, I thought it'd be a grand and dramatic gesture that we could follow up with the happy announcement that we're having a baby." He added a rueful smile. "Me and my big ideas."

"Oh." The word slipped out of her mouth, sad and rich with disappointment.

"Would you have liked that?" he asked.

"I'd have liked it better than what happened." She exhaled with bone-deep exhaustion. "I'm glad you came. And I'm glad you came here tonight."

Hope punched through the worry that had fogged his brain since he'd left the restaurant. "Glad enough that we can get back to where we were, Beth?"

She didn't answer for a long time, and each second that passed, his heart broke a little more. "You don't hate my father anymore," she finally said.

He snorted softly. "No. Apparently, I spent a long time hating the wrong man."

"You hate *him*, now?"

"Well, I—"

"Then we can't get back to where we were." She dropped his hands and crossed her arms in front of her.

"Why not? You just said yourself I don't hate your father anymore. I hate mine."

"Ken, don't you see?" She shook her head. "You can't love anyone when your heart is filled with hate."

He reached for her, putting his hands on her shoulders. "They don't cancel each other out, Beth. I can despise my father for the lie he lived and the way he wasted his life and the pain he left in his wake and still love you."

She slipped out of his fingertips with the same ease he could feel her heart slipping away from him. "No, you can't."

"You don't know that."

"Until you forgive him, Ken, you are carrying a burden of hate that is going to fester in your heart and eat up all the space I want for me. And for our baby."

He stared at her, each word like a fire ax against his chest. "I can love you and our baby."

She turned a little, glancing into the doorway to check on her family before looking back to him. "You have to forgive your father, and that means you have to love him every bit as much today as you did yesterday. To honor his memory and the kind of father he was, warts and addictions and mistakes and all."

"Forgive him?" He practically choked on the idea. "He

essentially killed himself, Beth. How can I think of him any other way now but drunk on the job, hiding his disease, taking chances on his own and other people's lives?" He spat out the words. "He's the polar opposite of anyone I could love. The polar opposite of the man and father I want to be."

"He's the same man he's always been to you," she said. "You know more about him, but you shouldn't love him less or hate him now."

He dropped his head into his hands, leaning on the wall. "I can't forgive him," he admitted in a cracked, broken voice. "I don't know how."

"You can, Ken. You have to. He had a disease and he made a mistake. That doesn't change how much he loved you."

"I…can't."

She rubbed his arm and said nothing as pain consumed him. He hadn't felt like this since that day on the job site.

No, this was worse. His heart was being ripped out for a second time, and his dad was dying all over again. It left him hollow, with nothing to fill that space but hate.

Except Beth wanted to replace it with love.

"A person isn't one dimension, Ken. A person can't be the sum total of one really dumb mistake he made. There was so much more to your father."

"But it's all I'll ever think about when I think of him now."

"Which is exactly why your mother and Josie worked so hard to keep the truth from you."

Slowly, he nodded and put his hands on her face. "God, Beth," he whispered. "Your father is in critical condition, and you're here helping me come to terms with mine."

"Then do come to terms with it," she said. "Forgive your father, Ken. Stop living with any hate in your heart."

He pulled her into him, letting their foreheads touch, an emotion welling up so powerfully it took his breath away.

"I need you to be strong," she said. "Because I have a bad feeling that the poster girl for independence is going to need someone to lean on for the next few days."

"And years," he whispered. "Decades, in fact." He felt her slip closer to him. "I want to be there, Beth. I want to be there for you. For this, for everything life throws at us. I'm so…I'm so…"

In love with you.

He didn't give voice to the words, looking at her, letting this one last realization press down on his chest and fill him up with a sensation he didn't remember ever feeling before. He wanted to tell her, but not here, not in a hospital waiting area at two in the morning with her whole family on the other side of—

"Well, this is not good!" Josie's voice cut through his thoughts, separating them with a quick look of surprise.

Instantly, Beth started back to the small waiting room and Ken stayed right next to her. Inside, the family was huddled around Josie, arguing in low voices.

All except Josie. Her voice rose to that pitch of complete loss of control Ken heard so often in a crisis.

"I can't go home and sleep while my husband is sedated and freezing!"

"Well, we don't need to all stay here," a woman Ken guessed was Landon's wife said, her voice also strained with exhaustion.

"Someone does!" Josie exclaimed. "What if he dies?"

"Shhh, Mom," Landon tried to calm her with a gentle tap on her shoulder. "We all need sleep. We're useless without some rest and the doctor said—"

"I'll stay."

Every eye in the family turned when Ken spoke, silent with surprise for a moment, then they all muttered responses like "no" and "you've helped us enough," but he could tell most of them loved the idea. Including Josie.

As if she'd just noticed Ken was there, she walked forward, reaching her hands to him. "Yes. You can stay here." She took Ken's hands in hers. "You're like family tonight."

He gave the slightest smile. "Maybe for more than just tonight," he said softly.

Her eyes welled up as she nodded. "Carole will be proud to hear about this."

"I talked to her today," he said, thinking again of the long conversation with his mother. "She loves you, Josie."

"And I love her." She took a long breath and looked around her family, some composure returning. "Let's all get some sleep while Ken is on duty here. Landon and Rebecca will bring me back in the morning. RJ, you'll do the afternoon. Beth—"

"I'm staying with Ken."

But even as Beth made the pronouncement, he could have sworn she swayed a little.

"No," Ken said. "You need rest, Beth. You're…" He swallowed the word and she gave him a slow smile.

"I'm pregnant," she finished for him, earning a soft gasp from a group who almost couldn't take any more shocks in one night.

"Holy guacamole, Beth." RJ put his arm around her. "You, too? How come you didn't tell us?"

She gave a soft, resigned laugh. "Waiting for the perfect moment, I guess."

"You are going home to rest, young lady," Josie ordered as they gathered around Beth, and Landon came over to shake Ken's hand.

In the small melee, Beth and Ken were separated, but they held each other's gaze.

"Thank you," she mouthed.

"I love you," he mouthed back, making her eyes go wide as she nodded silently.

That little nod was all he needed. That would get him through the night as he stood and watched the family spirit Beth away and leave him behind on duty.

There was no small irony in the fact that he was left to watch over Ray Endicott while the man fought for the chance to meet his grandchildren. No small irony at all.

And Ken was honored to have the privilege.

I love you.

Beth clung to the memory of Ken's soundless admission, rolling the words around in her heart, longing to say them back to him over and over again.

He still had wounds to heal, some fresh, some twenty-five years old. But she would be there to help him, and he would be here to…love her.

I love you.

She thought about those words all the way back to the resort, barely able to keep up a conversation with Selina and RJ, who used Beth's news to talk about something other than Dad. She insisted they drop her off at her car so she could drive it home. She didn't want to be home with no way to leave overnight in case she had to get back to the hospital in a hurry.

Landon, Rebecca, and Josie had followed to get something from Josie's car, and the whole family had one more group hug in the parking lot.

At home, she parked in the driveway and let herself in the front door, carefully locking it behind her as she'd been chided to do by so many people lately. People who cared about her. People who loved her.

I love you.

On the way back to her bedroom, she took out her phone and glanced at it, tempted to text him the same three words. Would that help him make it through the night? Or should she wait until she could finally tell him in person?

"I love you," she whispered out loud, for the joy of hearing the words spoken by her own lips.

She didn't want to be alone, not in this life, not when she could share it with Kenny "Nothing is Impossible" Cavanaugh.

She reached her bedroom and turned on a light as she practically stumbled across the room to rip off her clothes so she could take a shower. At the closet door, she stopped and stared at the papers that started this whole mess on the floor. She hadn't cleaned them up yet because the thought of touching them had hurt her heart this afternoon.

Crouching down, she flipped open the top of the bin and started storing the papers properly this time, including the autopsy report that she couldn't bear to touch. The letters between lawyers, the nondisclosure agreement. All the things required to cover up the truth.

What would they tell their child?

She stood holding the box, the question pressing down on her. Would they try to protect him or her from the past? Would they tell their baby the truth about his or her paternal grandfather? Would this child even *have* a living maternal grandfather?

They'd figure it out, together. And even that thought made her smile.

"Well, what do you know, Miss Independent?" she said as she whipped open the step stool, replaying the questions she'd just asked herself.

She had unequivocally become a *they*.

She put her foot on the first step, carefully staying to the right. "They." She said it out loud on purpose, liking the sound of it.

"We," she said, moving gingerly to the next step. "*We* is nice," she whispered. "You like that, cupcake?"

She reached the top step. "Us. Oh, I like the sound of *us*." She let go of the ladder to hold the box in two hands, lifting it high to shove it back into its slot between the other two. "They, we, us." She pushed hard, but the box wouldn't slide in place. "It sounds like a fam—"

The step stool wavered under the next push, leaning to the left, then the right, as Beth helplessly tried to regain her balance. With a shriek, she let go of the bin to grab some clothes and stop the fall, and the thick plastic fell right back on her head, stunning her as a hard corner slammed her temple.

She called out as she lost her footing, tumbling backward. The world suddenly moved in slow motion, the colors of her clothes like a flash of a rainbow in front of her eyes as she fell to the ground, the thud of her body hitting the floor a shocking force that cracked her teeth together.

It hurt. Everything hurt. Her bottom, her elbows, her head.

Her *baby*.

She put her hand on her stomach but a ping of pain shot through her temple, shocking her with intensity, making everything fade to black. Oh no, she couldn't faint. She forced her eyes open, and her mouth, trying to call out for help.

She could feel herself slipping and sinking into unconsciousness, like dropping into quicksand as a dark weight pulled her down against her will.

How long would she be on the closet floor? Who would find her? And would she ever get to say those words to Ken?

I love you.

But the world went black.

Chapter Twenty-Four

Ken texted Beth that he was on his way over as he left the hospital, his guard duty watch ending about an hour after it started. Landon had walked back into the waiting room not long after Ken poured a second cup of coffee and found ESPN on the TV in the waiting room.

Landon wanted to wait for a man who'd been a father to him and encouraged Ken to get to Beth, who looked like she was about to keel over when they'd all met back at the resort parking lot.

It was all Ken needed to hear, along with that low grade gnawing that started when he remembered he hadn't had a chance to take that CO monitor to her house, and he really didn't want her sleeping there until he confirmed it was safe.

But when he pulled into Beth's driveway, he realized she hadn't texted back.

He parked behind her Explorer and squinted at the house, deciding that at least one light was on in the hall. She could have been so tired she crashed with the lights on, poor thing.

Except how would he get in without waking her?

He hustled up to the front door only to find that, for once, she'd locked it. Great. He peered in the window and definitely saw a light on somewhere in the back, but no movement.

He stepped away from the door, puffing out a frustrated sigh. He could go pound on her bedroom window or the sliders, if the screen door to the patio wasn't locked.

But he hated to scare her like that if she'd fallen sound asleep.

Should he go home and let her rest? It was probably the smartest thing to do, but not what he wanted to do. Not at all.

He pulled out his phone again and tapped her name to call her. It rang a few times, then went to voice mail.

Now that was weird. She should jump at a ringing cell phone tonight, he thought. With her father on the edge of life and death, she would have the phone on and close to her head.

He headed toward the back where her bedroom was. He tried to peer through a window, but the shutters were closed.

Could he look through the sliders on the screened-in patio?

The screen door was locked, making him consider how much damage he wanted to do in an effort to wake her.

Or maybe she was taking a shower, he thought. That would explain the light, maybe from the hall bath. Or her closet.

He froze for a moment, his hand still on the screen door.

She could be in the closet, breathing carbon monoxide.

"Shit," he murmured, yanking a little harder at the screen door handle while he pictured her closet. But all he could see was that bin full of damning papers that had fallen and fluttered to the ground.

She probably put them back by now.

His heart popped at the thought of her…on that rickety step stool. Without taking time for one more scenario to play in his firefighter's mind, he stabbed the screen with his bare hand, tearing it away from the metal frame. He practically broke the latch unlocking it, flinging the door open and running to the sliders that lined her bedroom wall. The curtains were drawn, and the sliding glass was locked, but he smashed his face against the glass, trying to see through a crack in the drapes.

Yes, there was a faint light…like she was *in the closet.*

"Beth!" He smacked his hand on the glass more in frustration than any chance of getting in this way. He had no tools, no ax, no way to ram into the house.

Break the glass? Kick down the front door?

The hall bathroom had a door onto the patio, he remembered. Pivoting, he vaulted toward that door and tried to open it. Locked. Stepping back, he braced himself, lifted one leg, and flattened his foot against the wood exactly where it would be the weakest. It cracked but didn't open.

He called her name again, frustration and fear firing sparks up his spine. He was positive something was wrong now. No way she'd sleep through all the noise he was making trying to break into her house.

Without waiting for a response, he kicked again and again, finally splintering the wood and ramming it with his shoulder to pop the door wide open. Still calling her name, he ran into the hall, down to her bedroom, and whipped around the corner into the closet.

"Beth." He barely whispered her name, falling to his knees at the sight of her slumped body. His hands shook as he checked her pulse, like he'd never done the simple act before.

Because it had never mattered so much before.

Her heart was beating, and she was breathing. Thankfully, this wasn't the second Endicott he'd have to perform CPR on. He tapped her shoulder over and over, rocking her gently, coaxing her awake.

A purple egg rose on her left temple where she must have hit it, or something hit her. He stole a glance at the cursed storage box next to her, a sea of papers he was already too familiar with spread around her, the damn step stool on its side.

"*Mmmh.*"

When she moaned, he came closer, willing her back to consciousness. "Beth?"

"*Ohhhh.*" It was a grunt as she worked to pull herself awake.

He didn't move her, wanting her to wake and tell him if anything hurt before he decided whether or not it was safe to pick her up. She could have broken her back or—

"Baby," she murmured, lashes fluttering. "Our baby."

Or hurt the baby. On instinct, he looked down. Her dark skirt covered her thighs, but there was no sign of trauma or blood. "Beth, can you wake up? Tell me what hurts?"

She managed to open her eyes to slits. "Kenny."

"I'm here, sweetheart. Can I lift you? Does anything hurt?"

"I…fell."

"I know."

She finally opened her eyes all the way, focusing on him. "You came to me."

He lowered his head and pressed a kiss on her hair, still uncertain if he should move her. "Of course. Does your back hurt? Can you move your arms and legs? I don't want to cause more damage when I get you out of here."

"I can move." She lifted one arm, then the other. "The bin hit my head." She raised her hand to touch the bruise, but he stopped her.

"Don't touch it. I'll take care of it. Legs moving?"

She inched one leg from side to side, then the other,

looking up at him. “Nothing hurts, Ken, except my pride and my head. I shouldn’t have climbed that thing.” She reached up to touch his face. “But you came to me. Why did you leave my dad?”

“Landon came back. He really has a soft spot for your dad, and he was worried about you.” He slid his hands under her back and knees, rising slowly with her in his arms. “For good reason.”

He stood and carefully carried her out of the closet to lay her on the bed. “Let me get some ice for that bruise. Is there any in that little fridge?”

“Yeah.” She settled into the pillow. “Could this day get any worse?”

“Well, let’s see. I broke a door.”

“My hero.”

He kissed her on the forehead before leaving to get ice. “We’re lucky that bruise is all you got.” And lucky he arrived when he did. “I’m still not a hundred percent sure about that water heater,” he called as he found a small ice tray in the freezer. “But I have a monitor in the truck that I grabbed from my garage before I left for Barefoot Bay. As soon as we get ice on that, I’ll check the levels. If there’s anything, we’re going to my house.”

He waited for her to make a comment about how he’d brought a CO monitor when he’d come to Junonia, as if he *knew* he’d spend the night here. Or how she wanted to stay. Or what she was feeling.

But she didn’t say a word.

He grabbed a small towel and hustled back down the hall, glancing into the bathroom on the way. “And I’ll fix that door tomorrow.” He popped some ice into the towel. “I have the day off so we can go to Lowe’s or Home Dep—”

He stopped in the doorway at the sight of her sitting on

the bed, her skirt raised, her hand held out, a sob ripping her body in half so hard she couldn't make a word come out. He dropped the ice and towel and came right to her, sucking in a breath at the sight of blood on her exposed thigh.

"I'm bleeding," she whimpered. "I'm…losing…our baby."

Beth turned to face Ken through the rail of the hospital bed. "They don't act quite as urgent in here as they did in that cardiology department."

He wasn't surprised. An ER wouldn't treat this situation with the same frantic rush to save a life as she'd witnessed hours ago when they brought her father in. They'd taken her right away, handled all the vitals, and got her comfortable. But a miscarriage on an eight-week pregnancy wasn't something they could stop in its tracks like a sudden cardiac arrest. So an hour or two one way or the other wasn't going to matter in a place where seconds spent on another patient could save a life.

"They're bringing an ultrasound in," he assured her. "That's when we'll know."

She closed her eyes. "I already know."

He reached through the rail to put his hand on her shoulder. "You can't know anything yet. Does it feel like your bleeding is heavier?"

She shook her head. "That's not what I know."

"Then what is it?"

"I know about us."

He inched closer, barely able to hear her whisper. "What about us, Beth?"

"That we are an *us*. A *we*. A *family*." She swallowed when her voice hitched. "But without the baby…"

Without the baby, they were…

"We're not an *us* anymore," she answered for him.

"No." He sat up straighter, leaning over the rail to get in her face. "That's not true, Beth. We are still an *us*, still a *we*, still a *couple*, still *together*."

"But we're only together because of this baby, and it was always a tenuous pregnancy. Now it's over—"

The possibility squeezed the air out of his chest. "You don't know that."

She closed her eyes and turned away.

"Bethany Endicott." Ken stood, frustration stomping up his spine. "Listen to me."

She looked up at him, her eyes blue depths of pain and uncertainty.

"We're together with or without a baby." He leaned over her, placing his hands on her cheeks to underscore his point. "If we lose this baby, we'll have another one."

"My tubes are tied. I'm forty years old."

"We'll adopt one, then. And even if we don't, even if we never have kids, we'll still be a *we* and an *us*." He leaned all the way over the rail. "I love you, Beth. I love you more than I ever have, and I don't want to spend my life without you. Not one minute, not one day, not one hour, not one year. My *life*. Do you understand?"

She searched his face, some of that pain and uncertainty diminishing, but not all of it. "I love you, too. But I want this baby."

"So do I." He stroked her arm lightly. "But no matter what happens, no matter what, Beth, this baby brought us together, and we're staying that way."

Tears welled as she blinked at him and reached up and

slid her hand around his neck, pulling him closer. "I love you so much, Kenny."

He smiled, breaking the kiss to press his cheek against hers, holding on to her and the first really good thing that had happened all day. "We can weather anything, Beth," he whispered into her ear. "We won't blame anyone, we won't hate anyone. We'll hold on to each other no matter what happens, and we will be together. We will. We can do anything. Nothing is impossible with us, remember?"

She whimpered a little. "You're right. We can. We. Us. You and me and…"

He put a finger over her lips, not sure he could bear the precious name she used for the baby. Not yet. Not now.

"Excuse me." A young female tech and an orderly pulled the curtain to their bay back and wheeled in a portable ultrasound. "We're going to get this started, but your chart said your OB is Dr. Moore, right?"

"Yes," Beth said, sitting up. "She is."

"You're in luck. She's upstairs in labor and delivery right now, and she may be able to come down and talk to you."

"Oh, I'd like that," Beth said.

"Will you go check on Dr. Moore, Anthony?" the tech asked the orderly. "I'll get this set up and started for the ultra."

The young man nodded and disappeared, while the tech efficiently set up the machine, asking Beth questions in that calm, trained way of a good health care professional.

Ken wouldn't qualify as one of those at that moment, because he felt anything but calm. His palms were sweating and his pulse thumped, and he could tell Beth was going through the same stress.

Yes, they would survive this loss if they had to. But neither of them wanted to.

Even though he meant every word he'd said, he wanted to be a family so much he wanted to cry out and insist that the baby be alive and well. Instead, he held Beth's hand.

"All right, then," the tech said. "Let's open up that robe and take a look-see. Do you want your husband to stay?"

"He's not…" She caught herself and smiled, squeezing his hand. "Yes, of course. I want him here."

Her husband. *Yes, please.*

They threaded fingers and waited while the machine came to life. The tech smeared jelly on Beth's stomach, and the whole time, Beth looked up at him, almost as if she couldn't bear to look at the monitor as it flickered with life.

Life.

Please let there be life.

"Oh, Beth, what on earth are you doing in here?" A woman in her fifties, dressed in scrubs, came into the room, dark hair pulled back. "This is not how I want to be seeing my patients."

"Dr. Moore." Beth's face brightened at the sight of the woman. "I'm sorry. I took a little tumble off a step stool."

The doctor made a slight face of disapproval, then looked at Ken. "Dad?" she asked.

"Yes." He extended his hand. "Ken Cavanaugh."

The woman held his hand a second too long, her disapproval over the accident shifting to…sympathy. That wasn't good.

"I'm glad you're here, Ken."

"Me, too," he said.

"Go ahead, Melissa," Dr. Moore said. "Turn the monitor this way, please."

So they couldn't see it and have the image burned into their brains forever, Ken thought. He looked down at Beth and saw the blood drain from her cheeks at the same rate he felt it leaving his. He closed her hand in a tighter grasp and gave her a reassuring smile.

"I love you," he mouthed. "No matter what."

She didn't answer but held his gaze, pinning her eyes on him and refusing to look away, like he was her lifeline. And he always would be.

Nothing is impossible. Nothing.

Holding that thought, he turned to Dr. Moore. "So, what exactly are you looking for, Doctor?"

"We've already had one ultrasound," she replied, somewhat distracted as she studied the screen. "But it was a tad early to hear a heartbeat. You're at eight weeks now, so we should hear…" Her voice faded along with every other sound in the world.

Except the faint, steady, whoosh-*whoosh*…whoosh-*whoosh*…whoosh-*whoosh* coming through the speakers.

"We should hear *that*," Dr. Moore finished with a hint of satisfaction.

Beth sucked in a soft breath and looked at Ken. "Do you hear it?"

"Yeah. I hear it." He wanted to smile. He wanted to laugh. Wanted to jump up and down and holler, but he had to be sure.

"And then," the doctor said, still scanning the monitor with a slight frown. "We want to see…" The frown left, and her shoulders dropped with an almost imperceptible sigh. "The placenta intact."

"Is it?" Beth's question was barely a whisper, the fear in her voice tearing through Ken.

"It is." Dr. Moore's whole face lit, and she reached out to turn the screen as if she couldn't wait for the tech. "There's your baby, tucked right into its placenta where it is supposed to be."

"That cute little blob?" Ken asked, a hitch in his voice that made the tech chuckle as a palpable relief pulsed through the little room.

"Right there," Dr. Moore said, pointing to a dark shape on the screen that even a medic like Ken couldn't quite make out. "There's no tearing, nothing out of place, and there's movement. And listen to that little heart."

He did, but all he could really hear was his own pulse, rushing wildly in his head.

"I'd like to do a quick exam while I'm here to check on that bleeding," Dr. Moore said. "Beth, have you been under any unusual stress lately?"

Beth gave a humorless laugh. "This is my second visit tonight to the ER. My father had a heart attack and is upstairs in cardiology."

Dr. Moore's eyes opened wide. "Well, no wonder you're bleeding. That probably had nothing to do with the fall, which our little Endicott baby survived quite nicely."

Ken dropped his head and blew out a breath he felt like he'd been holding since he'd scooped her up and driven her to the hospital.

"Cavanaugh."

He opened his eyes and looked at Beth, not sure he heard her right.

"The baby's last name will be Cavanaugh," she said, her eyes glistening with unshed tears of happiness.

"Cupcake Cavanaugh," he whispered, making one of Beth's tears spill onto her cheek.

Dr. Moore laughed. "I've heard worse."

But Ken had never heard anything better in his whole life.

Chapter Twenty-Five

Once again, Ken stood in the same banquet hall at Casa Blanca Resort & Spa where four months earlier, he'd needed Law Monroe's glass of courage and kick in the ass to talk to Beth Endicott. Ken could use a little of both again as he eyed the man in the wheelchair across the hall and planned exactly what he would say to Ray Endicott tonight.

It had to be done alone, though. And tonight, even if that meant it had to be in this banquet hall.

He'd hoped Selina and RJ's wedding on the beach would give him an opportunity to get Ray alone outside, but an early-evening summer storm had rolled over Barefoot Bay, and the party had moved inside.

The weather hadn't dampened the festive mood of the small wedding, though. But how could it not be a happy occasion? It was Ray Endicott's first outing since his SCA and odds-beating recovery, and the older man, though in a wheelchair for a while, was in great spirits. Josie rolled him around to talk to everyone, and all the old man wanted to talk about was how his brush with death made him re-prioritize his life and company.

Endicott Development Corporation was officially divided

into three divisions now, with Beth and her two brothers each heading one. She didn't even have to finish the flip, since Ken's friend Mark Solomon and his soon-to-be wife, Emma, bought it as is and were taking over the complete renovation.

Beth had moved in with Ken, but the whole setup felt temporary and unfinished to him. Ken wanted to change that, but first he had to have a long, overdue conversation with Ray.

When the DJ announced it was time for the bride to toss her bouquet, he saw his chance. "Go out there and get that thing, Beth." Ken put his arm around her and nudged her toward the large dance floor.

She shot him a look. "Tempting, but my entire family and a good number of people—which would include pretty much everyone you've met at this wedding—know that I am four months pregnant. Not exactly 'bouquet-catching' material."

"Have you seen the bride?"

She laughed, because Selina's pregnancy was far more obvious in her cream-colored wedding gown. As one of the bridesmaids, Beth wore a loose-fitting column of gold that matched her hair and made her skin glow.

Or maybe the glow was due to her healthy, strong pregnancy with a boy—Pookie had won that bet and been quite smug about it, Ken recalled.

"I want you to catch it," he said.

She smiled up at him. "You know what that would mean, though, don't you?"

"No," he said, managing a straight face. "What would it mean?"

Narrowing her eyes, she inched away as a few other women laughed and headed to the middle of the floor. "If I catch it, you're going down, Cav."

He reached for her and pulled her back into him for a kiss. "I can't wait."

She slipped away and joined the other women as they circled around Selina and the photographer got in place. Ken glanced across the banquet hall but frowned as he lost sight of Ray. He scanned the place for Josie's black hair. She was never far from her husband.

He spotted her just as she pushed the side door open wide enough to wheel Ray out. The weather must have cleared, he thought, heading around the perimeter of the room to follow them.

Unlike the last time he was hot on the trail of an Endicott in this room, no one grabbed his arm to stop him. All the attention was on the center of the room, where some women squealed and the music built up to the big moment.

Ken leaned on the door and stepped out to the patio, which was empty but dry since it had stopped raining. The sky was clear and faintly purple as a full moon heralded a clear and beautiful night.

He looked around and spotted Josie and Ray at the far edge of the pavilion, taking in the glorious view that happened to include a row of small yellow cabanas that would always hold a place in Ken's heart.

Crossing the deck, he cleared his throat to make his presence known, and Josie gave a bright smile. "Speak of the devil, Ray, look who it is." She turned Ray's chair a little so he could see Ken.

"There you are," Ray said as Ken approached. "Are you enjoying the wedding, son?"

Son. He swallowed at the term he was still getting used to hearing. Ray had called him *son* the first time he and Beth visited after Ray was released from the hospital. He'd called Ken *son* the next time they stopped by, when Ken finally had the chance to make that apology that Ray insisted wasn't necessary. And, of course, he'd called Ken *son* when he and

Beth brought them all together to share the happy news of their healthy baby-to-be.

But this time? This would be the real test of whether or not Ray Endicott thought Ken Cavanaugh was worthy to be a *son*.

"It's a great night, sir, especially now that the rain stopped."

"Josie and I had to come out here to the scene of the crime."

For a moment, he thought they meant the cabana, and he slowed his step, but then he realized they were referring to the dining terrace at Junonia where a little over a month ago, Ken had saved Ray's life.

"That's why we were talking about you," Josie said. "I was talking to your mother again this morning and couldn't help gushing again over what you did for us. She's so proud of you, Ken."

He nodded his thanks. "And she's grateful for a friend like you, Josie." He came closer and put a light hand on Ray's shoulder. "I was wondering if I might have a chance to talk to you, sir."

"Oh, let me run inside, then." Josie stood immediately, her eyes glistening with a conspiracy, and she gave a knowing look to her husband. What had they been talking about out here? "I think they're about to do the bouquet toss, right?"

"Might have already done it," he said.

Josie grinned at him. "Then you better get to talking to my husband." She blew Ray a kiss and left them.

Ken took her seat. "Guess this isn't going to come as a big surprise," he said on a laugh.

"That you're going to ask me for my daughter's hand in marriage?"

He smiled. "That was the plan, sir. I have a whole speech ready about how much I love her, and what kind of husband I'll be, and what an honor it is to be her partner in life. You want to hear it?"

Ray leaned forward, flinching a little as his chest was most likely a bit sore still. "No," he said simply. "I know all that."

Ken looked at him. "Okay. But if you'd humor me, I still want to ask the question, sir."

"I think this time, I should do the asking," Ray said.

Ken frowned. "Excuse me?"

The older man inhaled slowly, then let out a ragged breath. "I would like to ask you, Kenneth Cavanaugh, if you would do me the honor of allowing me to be your father."

Ken blinked in surprise.

"They are big shoes to fill," Ray said. "I happen to know that for a fact."

"They were…" Big shoes? Ken swallowed anything he could say, since he was still unable to think about his father without a low-grade unhappiness that he was still trying to overcome. "One of a kind," he finished somberly.

Ray reached his hand out to Ken's. "I remember Johnny Cavanaugh quite well, and when I think of him, I don't think about his troubles or struggles."

Ken simply stared at Ray, locked on eyes the same color as Beth's but with a lot more years and experience around the crinkled edges.

"I remember a man who could fix anything, a man who didn't give up when a job was challenging, and a man who always took the high road. He didn't badmouth anyone. He didn't point fingers or make enemies. Everyone loved him. Everyone. God knows they can't say that about me."

The words hovered over Ken's heart, making his chest

ache in a way he'd never expected when he walked out here.

"He was generous, your father," Ray continued. "He'd give you the shirt off his back and never complained. Never. Can't put a price on that in my business." Ray leaned a little closer, the hint of tears in his eyes. "John Cavanaugh was a very good man. Competent, kind, and he loved you kids like crazy. He'd beg for overtime to cover Christmas, but gave up hours if you or your brother had a baseball game to play."

It was true. Dad never missed a sporting event, Ken thought, and they always had presents under the tree.

"He put his family first, and that's a lesson I could have learned from him," Ray said.

Ken closed his eyes as the truth of that hit, tempered by the other truth they both knew.

"You think your dad had…issues. A disease. Maybe he did, but we all have issues, son." Ray pressed his hand on Ken's. "I try to control the family I'm supposed to love. I scoff at the very people God put in my life to inspire. We all have flaws and baggage and things we hide. But the older a man gets, the more it's clear what really matters."

"That's true, sir."

"So, instead of you asking me for Beth's hand…" Ray put his wrinkled hand on top of Ken's. "I'm asking if you would let me be your father."

Ken opened his mouth to respond, but nothing came out. But he was swamped by an unexpected jolt of emotion that made him close his eyes for a second before he spoke.

"You know," Ken finally said with a half smile. "I could really, really use a father." He turned his hand over to hold Ray's. "Thanks…Dad."

Ray gave a slow, satisfied grin as the door to the banquet room opened and Beth stepped out, as bright and beautiful as the shiny gold dress she wore. She lifted a cheery bouquet with gold and white streamers fluttering in the breeze.

"Captain Cav," she called playfully. "Guess what I have."

He leaned a little closer to Ray. "She has my heart, that's what. Forever."

"Then go pop the question, son. I'm going to dance at *that* wedding."

"So what was that all about?" Beth asked after they handed Dad back over to Josie and lingered outside, watching her wheel him back into the wedding.

"You know, man talk."

She gave a dry laugh. "You and my father having a man talk."

"As I like to tell you, Bethany Endicott, nothing is impossible. Now come with me." He put his arm around her and turned her toward the beach. "I have a few questions to ask you."

Her heart fluttered. A few? "Where are we going?"

"Right there." He pointed to the yellow tent. "Cupcake's cabana."

That made her laugh. "He's going to kill us if we call him Cupcake."

"They already do at the station. Kid's going to have to learn to be tough with that nickname."

"If I had known it was a boy, I would have called him Sledgehammer or something suitably masculine."

"You want to take off your shoes?" Ken asked as they reached the edge of the deck.

"I assume that's a rhetorical question. I want to take them off and throw them into the bay." She happily kicked off heels that had been slicing into her toes for hours. "Ahhh." She sighed as her feet touched the cool, damp sand. "This feels like déjà vu."

"Yeah," he agreed, barefoot now as well. "Best night of my life." He wrapped his arm around her and added a squeeze. "So far."

"There are a lot of good ones ahead," she agreed, then tapped her growing stomach. "Sleepless ones, too."

"We can handle it," he said, guiding her into the empty cabana, then turning to close them in by sliding the drapes across.

"Uh, you can't really be serious with my brothers and dad twenty feet away."

He laughed. "That's not why I want privacy."

She perched on the edge of the chaise, taking a calming breath and a moment to admire the way his white dress shirt fit his broad shoulders. He'd loosened his tie since the dancing started, and he was every bit as hot and sexy as the night he came and found her right here three months ago.

"What *were* you and my dad talking about?" she asked.

"My father."

"Oh." She sighed a little. "I thought you two had that conversation already."

"Not like this." He reached for her hand to pull her up.

"Don't you want to lie down with me?"

"No, I want you to stand right here."

She did, eyeing him. "Why?"

"So that when I get down on one knee, I can be looking up at you."

She inhaled a quick breath. "Oh…one knee."

"You prefer two?"

She laughed, shaking her head. "One's good." She knew it was happening. They'd been talking about the future, and with every conversation, a life together became more crystal clear and right. But still…this *moment.* She pressed her palms together, realizing her fingers were trembling. "I would never doubt your sincerity on one knee or two."

"Okay, then." He took her hands in his. "This is it."

Her breath caught at the words. *This is it.* "You've said that to me before." Long ago, in the rain.

"But this is…better," he said. "We're older and wiser. But not too old for a down-on-one-knee proposal, are we?"

"Not if you can still get up."

He closed his eyes and let out a slow exhale, lifting her hands closer to his heart. "Since the day I met you, Bethany Endicott, twenty-five years ago, I fantasized about this moment."

She bit her lip, tears welling. "Me, too," she admitted.

"I have always wanted you to be my wife. I spent more than half of my life thinking I missed the best woman in the world and had no one but myself to blame for that loss." He tightened his grip on her hands. "But since I don't blame anyone for anything anymore, I'm okay with what happened in those twenty-five years, because that's what made us who we are. And, I really love who you are."

She tried to swallow, but it was getting more difficult every second. "And I love who you are, Kenny Cavanaugh."

Very slowly, still holding her hands, he lowered himself to one knee and looked up at her. "Beth, I want to marry you and be the best husband, father, friend, and soul mate you can imagine." He reached into his pocket and pulled out a small black box, flipping it open, and even in the dim light, she could see the diamond spark.

"Will you complete my life and be my wife?"

"You already completed mine," she whispered. "So my answer is yes. A thousand, million times yes."

He put the ring on her finger, then stood and pulled her close for a long, sweet kiss that lasted until they gave in and slowly eased each other onto the chaise.

"You know what this is?" she asked, tapping the leather cushions under them.

"The place where we baked a cupcake?"

"And..." She touched his face and smiled. "It's the place where you and I officially became a *we*."

. . . Sneak Peek . . .

Barefoot at Midnight

Barefoot Bay Timeless #3

roxanne st. claire

Chapter One

W*hen it's time to take a chance, move fast. Think too hard, and you'll wimp out.*

The words of Lawson Monroe's late great friend and mentor echoed louder than the controlled chaos of the Naples Ritz-Carlton main kitchen serving four top-notch restaurants in the middle of a dinner rush. Louder than the orders being barked at other sous chefs by the arrogant, incompetent, and clueless moron in charge. Louder, even, than the warning bells that reminded Law of just how hard he'd worked to get to this point.

"You got a problem with that, Monroe?"

Law glared across the stainless steel pass. "I have a better idea, Chef."

"You always have a better idea," Executive Chef Delbert Tracey-Dobbs leaned closer, his beady brown eyes like pinpoints of hate. "But I'm the one in charge."

Proving that life went way beyond unfair and possibly into the zip code of pointless. At least this argument was. Still, Law had principles. And that sauce? It crushed his principles and his palate. "I think we should—"

"I don't care what sous chefs think, Monroe. Don't care what *we* should do. I'll tell you what *you're* going to do and then, guess what? You'll do it. Today, tomorrow, and for the rest of your days in this kitchen which, if I have anything to say about it, will be few."

"One can hope," Law muttered.

"Excuse me?" Chef slammed his hands on the pass, shaking a few waiting dishes and toppling a tower of thinly sliced tuna that another sous chef had spent ten minutes building. Here it comes, Law thought. A reminder of how many people wanted his job.

"I have a hundred resumes on my desk for a sous chef position," Chef barked, right on cue. "I could have you replaced before midnight."

Some of the clatter around him died down as a few people nearby slowed their choreographed movements on the line to listen to the showdown, most of them probably expecting it since Chef Del arrived six months ago and decided he wanted Sous Chef Law Monroe out of his kitchen.

Law looked down at the whimsical fennel grapefruit salad screaming for cognac sauce. But the sauce was crap and Law refused to use it.

"Add the cognac and get the order up," Chef said between grit teeth.

Law didn't make the flat, lifeless sauce, but this was his dish and he was the one who'd writhe in shame when a discerning customer sent it back. Or when a heady-with-Internet-power diner tossed a shitty review up on Trip Advisor, adding to the string they'd been getting since the new executive chef had arrived.

Law could outlast him, couldn't he? Law could keep his smart mouth shut and cook. Just until he figured out who owned the restaurant where he was *supposed* to be now…the place Jake Peterson had allegedly left Law in his will.

Except that will had yet to turn up anywhere and the Toasted Pelican was currently owned and managed by…a nameless, faceless company.

"The sauce, Monroe. Now!"

Jake never steered Law wrong. In fact, until the day he died, Jake was nothing but a fountain of wisdom and he knew what that man would tell him to do in this situation.

Make your statements with actions, not words.

Very slowly, Law lifted his hand and fingered the top button of his chef's coat. Del's eyes sparked.

"You wouldn't," the other man said.

Law flicked the button open.

"In the middle of a rush on a Saturday night?" Del's voice rose in disbelief and now everyone in the kitchen stilled to watch the drama unfold.

The next button slid right through the hole with no effort at all.

"You'll never work for a Ritz-Carlton again."

He didn't want to work *for* anyone but himself. So that threat was music to his ears. In fact, it played the perfect melody to flip that third button without taking his gaze off his boss's reddened face.

"You'll never work in this city again."

Fine. Naples, Florida was full of old fart millionaires and their trophy wives. The last button was the easiest.

"You're finished, Monroe! Get the hell out of here! Go back to the twelve-step program you came from."

Law slipped the jacket off and folded it neatly next to the fennel and grapefruit. "With pleasure, Chef."

With every eye in the kitchen on him and most of their mouths gaping, Law strode down the line with his head held high and his muscles and ink on full display under a tight undershirt.

Without a word, he grabbed his backpack from his locker and headed out the back door to the employees' parking lot, where a blast of hot August air smacked him in the face, despite the proximity to the beach.

He sucked in a mouthful of it, getting a whiff of the Dumpster where that sauce belonged.

Trying to not think too hard about the fact that he'd just quit the job he spent ten years working to get, he slid a leg over the side of his bike, jammed the key in the ignition and flattened his thumb on the starter button.

Okay, Jake. Took that risk and took it fast, all action, no words. Now what?

He drowned out any mental answer with a rev of the engine and roared out of the lot loud enough to piss off the Ritz management. He didn't hate them and he didn't hate the restaurant. He hated being under anyone or anything, and the very definition of the word *sous* in his title meant "under" in French.

Well, now he wasn't under anything, including a helmet. With the wind in his hair he'd cut short for summer, he blew out on to the main road. He didn't have a "home"—or wouldn't after tonight. After Jake died, Law had moved out of the house they'd rented after combing every inch of his friend's belongings for that will he'd promised to write. Since he hadn't found it, Law's life was put on hold, so he opted for a cut in pay at his job at the Ritz and took one of the tiny efficiency apartments they offered to the staff, deep in the bowels of the resort.

So he'd have to move out of there tomorrow, making him officially homeless *and* jobless.

At least he was sober.

He waited for the kick of desire, the little tweak from a demon that lived in his belly and rose up on occasions like this to whisper "Jack and Coke, baby. That'll numb all this misery."

And that usually sent him straight over the causeway to Mimosa Key. There, he'd have slipped into the back door of the Toasted Pelican. Only a former drunk would appreciate the irony that his soft, safe place to fall was a bar and a glass of non-alcoholic beer.

Jake would be there, offering O'Doul's and advice, cleaning up after the last customer had left.

Except Jake wasn't there anymore. Instead the locks had been changed and the employees worked for a "shell" company that had mysteriously taken over. And Law had bruises from the brick walls he'd hit trying to figure out who or what had stolen the business Jake had promised to him.

He took the tight turn onto the causeway, settling into the seat as he accelerated up the long bridge over the Gulf, headed to the tiny island where he'd grown up and still thought of as home. If only it could be home again. He thought it *would* be. Jake had sworn it would be...but nothing concrete had emerged to show his friend had kept that promise.

Consumed by grief for the loss of his closest friend and the man who'd changed—no, *saved*—his life, Law didn't care about Jake Peterson's missing last will and testament at first. He'd gone into the Toasted Pelican a few days after the memorial and cleaned out the closet Jake used as an office, taking every shred of paper and files he could find. When he still didn't find the will, he'd made an appointment with an attorney only to learn that the bar had been taken over by a private company in Miami that claimed to have ties to Jake Peterson.

Ties? What kind of ties? Jake had no heirs, no family, no ties to anyone or anything. He had his regular customers, his friends, the strays he occasionally collected, and a handful of locals who joked about how bad the drinks were and shitty the food was—when Law wasn't cooking, that was.

Who would even want that rickety old bar and restaurant built in the 1940's? Besides Law, of course.

But no one could identify the owner. One by one, a few of the staff had been contacted by some guy named Sam in Miami. The manager was entrusted with cash, and paychecks came in, and the business stayed open. But no one knew who owned it.

Someone had to know. And on a Saturday night? Maybe that someone was loose-lipped at the bar.

Parking in the back, Law shut off the bike and climbed off, noting that the lot was sparsely filled. Business had been crappy for months, and now it was completely in the shitter. Good. Surely whoever picked it up didn't want this financial drain. If only he could find out who that was, he'd make an offer. Law had some money saved. Not much, but he'd get a loan if he had to.

Cause a former alcoholic who walked out of a five-star restaurant kitchen in the middle of a dinner rush was such a good risk. Screw 'em. He *was* a good risk. Jake had thought so.

Hadn't he?

He yanked open the door and sucked in a whiff of two-day-old oil from the fryer and stale beer. God, he had such plans for this place. The kitchen was serviceable and the layout would work. He needed to update it, clean it, and launch that gastro pub menu he'd been working on since before Jake died. Everything would change, except the name. The Toasted Pelican was forever.

He glanced into the open door of the kitchen when he passed, noting the youth of the crew of only two guys on the grill. Pushing open the back door, he checked out the stairs that led upstairs to a small apartment that Jake had used as a storage area.

Something was…different.

Frowning, he noticed that the stain on the stairs had been stripped off and long boards of hardwood were laying on the landing. What the hell? They were renovating up there?

Fire and fury shot through him. Some stranger was renovating his property. Well, Jake's…but it was supposed to be his.

More determined to get hard facts than ever before, he cruised through the dining area, which consisted of a dozen not very busy tables, and into the bar, where the real action was.

Only there wasn't much of that, either. He glanced around the dimly lit area, counting few booths full and mostly empty seats at the bar. This place could not be running in the black. So who had the cash to lay hardwood upstairs…and *why*?

He slid onto a stool and looked around for the bartender. It would be one of the two guys who started working after Jake died, young guys, not locals, who claimed to have no idea who signed their paycheck. He couldn't see around the tower of bottles and mirrors in the center of the round bar—that would be the first thing he'd get rid of. The booze rack blocked views of across the bar, a stupid design for a circular bar. He twisted all the way to look back at the booths, wondering if one of them had to handle the floor, too.

"I thought you didn't drink, Lawless."

At the woman's question, he pivoted around to the bartender and came face to face with…oh, baby what a face. "Libby Chesterfield, you gorgeous piece of womanhood."

She didn't smile, didn't move actually, except for the slightest tilt of her head and a shutter of heavily made up pale blue eyes fringed with what had to be fake lashes. Blonde hair—long, silky, sinful blond hair—spilled over bare shoulders. One perfectly arched brow twitched and full lips pouted ever so slightly to remind a man that she owned a mouth that was made for one thing and one thing only. Kissing. Well, maybe two things.

"*Piece of womanhood*?" She repeated the words as if the very taste of them was vile in her mouth. "That's the best you've got?"

She put her hands on her hips, drawing his gaze over a form-fitting red tank top and cut-off jean shorts, and about five foot six inches of *luscious*. Every stinkin' curve was pure perfection, especially the ones that rightfully earned her the name "Chesty Chesterfield" in high school.

She'd always been smokin' hot. In high school, she'd been a boner maker, and all she'd done in the years since then was get better.

"Lib, you're forty-five years old and you still make mouths water, heads turn, and cocks rise up to praise you. How do you manage to stay so exquisite all these years?"

She leaned over the bar enough to blind him with a glimpse of cleavage. "And you, too, Law, are a miracle of nature. Forty-five years old and you still think, act, and talk like an eighth grader. How did you manage to stay so incredibly immature all these years?"

"Forty-six now," he corrected. "You missed my birthday."

"Aww, what a shame. I could have blown…out the candles."

"My candle can be lit and blown anytime, gorgeous."

She leaned over the bar, pursed her lips, and puffed air in his face. "There. You're blown…*off*. What are you drinking?"

Why was she bartending would be a better question.

"O'Doul's," he said, automatically ordering the non-alc

beer. "So, uh, when did you start gracing the poor schmucks at the Pelican with all that hotness?"

She lifted a shoulder. "Both bartenders are gone and…" She turned to the fridge. "I'm helping out." With her back to him as she got a glass, he used the opportunity to feast his eyes on the flip side of Libby, which was as sexy as the front in those denim shorts that hugged a heart-shaped ass and skimmed tight, toned thighs. *Damn.*

"Why would you help out here?" he asked.

"Just for something to do."

Bartending at a dive? He'd chatted her up a little at the reunion a few months ago—well, attempted to get her in bed, an effort that had failed miserably. But he knew Libby drove a nice car, wore quality clothes, and the rumor mill said she'd taken her last husband to the cleaners in divorce court. Why the hell would she tend bar?

"I've been in and out of this place on a regular basis for most of my life, and I've seen you in here exactly once, about a month ago." He remembered it well, though. Well, he remembered the sprayed-on black pants that could make a grown man weep. "You were on your way to some girlie exercise class," he recalled.

She snorted softly as she yanked the tap. "It's called yoga and I'd suggest you try it, but it's really a practice for people seeking balance and wisdom." She took a look at his body, her gaze lingering on the biceps on full display under the tight short sleeves of his T-shirt. "Obviously, you'd rather throw iron around a gym and grunt."

"I like iron and grunting."

She put the drink down with the tiniest spark of appreciation in eyes that weren't quite blue or gray but a haunting mix of both. "I admit, it suits you."

"Was that a compliment?"

"Unlikely." She looked away when a couple took the last two seats at the bar. "Nurse that one for a while, Law. I have to work."

"You really work here?" Since when?

But she'd slipped down to the other side, a much friendlier smile for the new patrons than the sassy one he got. He heard the woman order a margarita and could have sworn Libby inched back with a little trepidation at the order.

And while she made it, he figured out in a few scant seconds of observation that Libby Chesterfield didn't know squat about mixing a drink or navigating her way behind the bar. So *what* was she doing here?

Law sat up straighter and looked around. Something was definitely up at the TP. It was damn near empty. The staff was thin at best. Some things had been taken off the wall. And Libby was bartending.

Okay, then. The first tendril of hope he'd felt all day—hell, in the year since Jake died—curled through his gut. If change was in the air at the Pelican and Libby was behind the bar, she *had* to know who owned this place.

And he would use every tool in his arsenal to get it out of her.

Books Set in Barefoot Bay

The Barefoot Bay Billionaires

Secrets on the Sand

Seduction on the Sand

Scandal on the Sand

The Barefoot Bay Brides

Barefoot in White

Barefoot in Lace

Barefoot in Pearls

Barefoot Bay Undercover

Barefoot Bound (prequel)

Barefoot with a Bodyguard

Barefoot with a Stranger

Barefoot with a Bad Boy (Gabe's book!)

Barefoot Bay Timeless

Barefoot at Sunset

Barefoot at Moonrise

Barefoot at Midnight

The Original Barefoot Bay Quartet

Barefoot in the Sand

Barefoot in the Rain

Barefoot in the Sun

Barefoot by the Sea

About The Author

Published since 2003, **Roxanne St. Claire** is a New York Times and USA Today bestselling author of more than forty romance and suspense novels. She has written several popular series, including Barefoot Bay, the Guardian Angelinos, and the Bullet Catchers.

In addition to being an eight-time nominee and one-time winner of the prestigious RITA™ Award for the best in romance writing, Roxanne's novels have won the National Readers' Choice Award for best romantic suspense four times, as well as the Maggie, the Daphne du Maurier Award, the HOLT Medallion, Booksellers Best, Book Buyers Best, the Award of Excellence, and many others.

She lives in Florida with her husband, and still attempts to run the lives of her teenage daughter and 20-something son. She loves dogs, books, chocolate, and wine, but not always in that order.

www.roxannestclaire.com
www.twitter.com/roxannestclaire
www.facebook.com/roxannestclaire